THE CHAPERONE

THE CHAPERONE

SOPHIA HOLLOWAY

Allison & Busby Limited
11 Wardour Mews
London W1F 8AN
allisonandbusby.com

First published in Great Britain by Allison & Busby in 2023.

A CIP catalogue record for this book is available from
the British Library.

First Edition

ISBN 978-0-7490-3090-2

Typeset in 11/16 pt Adobe Garamond Pro by
Allison & Busby Ltd.

FSC
www.fsc.org
MIX
Paper | Supporting
responsible forestry
FSC® C171272

By choosing this product, you help take care of the world's forests.
Learn more: www.fsc.org.

Printed and bound by
CPI Group (UK) Ltd, Croydon, CR0 4YY

For K M L B

CHAPTER ONE

'NO, MAMA, SURELY YOU DO NOT MEAN IT.'

'I am sorry, my dear, but I really see no alternative.' Lady Chelmarsh looked at her eldest child, not without sympathy. 'If I am to bring out your cousin Susan at the same time as Harriet, then I will need assistance, especially if Frances has need of me as her time draws near. You are old enough and sensible enough to guide the girls for a couple of weeks and your sister will need—'

'Am I advanced in years, Mama?'

'Maturity, Sophronia, would be the word I would use. Your maturity will make it perfectly acceptable for me to do so.'

Sophy Hadlow pulled a face. She had absolutely no wish to spend another Season in London. She was a young woman who laboured under several disadvantages, not the least of which, in her own opinion, was having a name which made her wince. Thankfully, only her mother ever called her Sophronia at home, and she was perfectly happy as Sophy, though less so as 'Soppy', which name her younger brother Jasper, Viscount Elvington, used when he wanted to annoy her. However, hearing her name announced in ringing tones at society functions as 'Lady Sophronia Hadlow' always made her shrink. Perhaps her mama had felt a premonition at her birth that shrinking might be useful, for her other major problem was her height. Sophy stood nearly five foot ten in her stockinged feet, and stood out like a sore thumb at parties among the other debutantes. Lady Chelmarsh had known even before attempting to launch her first-born into society that it would not be easy. Whilst Sophy was still in the schoolroom she had shaken her head over her chances, and at one stage even suggested to her lord that they put Sophronia on a strict diet. He had vetoed this idea on the sound grounds that whilst it might make the poor girl hungry and emaciated it would not decrease her height. A tall man himself, the Earl of Chelmarsh could not fully appreciate the problem.

Lady Chelmarsh had given up, but always tried to get Sophy to bend her knees when standing with other young ladies. This made her very self-conscious about her looks, and gave her a strained back. Her mama never ceased telling her how difficult she made things for herself, as if her stature was her own fault. Added to her height, which was mostly accounted for by long legs, Sophy was possessed not of a maypole figure, but one rather more generously endowed in the bosom than would be expected of so slim a lady. The fashion of gowns accentuated both her height and bosom, and her mama despaired, predicting failure, which duly ensued. Lacking confidence and made constantly aware of her 'oddity', Sophy crept miserably through her first Season, and then a second and third when her younger sister Frances was brought out.

Frances was a more average height, a little on the tall side, perhaps, but only by the smallest of margins. She basked in maternal approval and formed a very suitable connection within the year. Young Lady Tattersett had then proceeded to fulfil wifely expectations within eighteen months of marriage and was due to be confined for the first time in early May.

Sophy had determinedly avoided a pointless return to London since her sister's triumph, and had not thought it necessary that she should attend for the come-out of her youngest sister, Harriet, six years her junior. The death of Lady Chelmarsh's sister, however, meant that her ladyship faced guiding two inexperienced damsels, and felt the need for reinforcements.

'What about Aunt Augusta? She would be far more help than I could be, Mama.'

'Your Aunt Augusta has declined.' Lady Chelmarsh coloured, not wishing to reveal the tone of her sister-in-law's refusal, nor her reason.

Sophy was about to ask why, but noted the look upon

her mother's face, and thought the better of it. Aunt Augusta, Lady Warsash, was a very strict and proper individual, and from what Sophy could remember of her cousin Susan when last she had seen her, the two would not get on well. Susan bore every sign of being an ill-disciplined romp of a girl, and it was only from a strong sense of sisterly duty that Lady Chelmarsh had agreed to bring her out, since Susan's older, and far more staid, brother, the current Lord Tyneham, was still single.

'Would it not be possible to delay Harriet's coming-out for a year, and Susan's also? Frances is unlikely to produce another infant within twelve months of the first, surely.'

'No, I will not have Harriet dawdling about at home. She is far too pretty a girl, and already young Minsterley, and half the neighbourhood, are hanging about our gates.'

This was an exaggeration. Harriet was very popular with the young men with whom she had grown up, and who now noticed that she was no longer a fubsy schoolroom miss, but a fledgling beauty, although none were to be found lingering by the lodge in the hope of a mere sight of her.

'Besides, Susan will be nineteen before the Season is half over. If she is to be launched into Society at all this is her chance.'

'At all, Mama?'

'I meant,' Lady Chelmarsh corrected herself, rather hurriedly, 'that if she is to make a good match, she cannot afford to be *twenty*.' She said the number as if it were three score years and ten.

'I am three and twenty, Mama,' murmured Sophy.

'Yes, my dear, but . . . some girls are not destined for marriage. One never quite gives up hope but . . . And do not think I do not appreciate you, for I do. I was only saying to your father the other day what a consolation it is to know that we have you on hand to keep us young, when we get older.'

Sophy did not find this very cheering. Being a prop to one's ageing parents did not strike her as an ambition in life. Not that she could lay claim to having any ambitions of her own. Once, perhaps, she had dreamt of being swept off her feet by a tall, and she always counted that as important, handsome man who would worship the ground upon which she trod, and whisk her away to a neatly proportioned country seat where the chimneys did not smoke, and they could live in blissful union for the rest of their lives. Her first Season had shown her how unlikely an eventuality that was. Her mother clearly thought her a lost cause in the marriage market, but then she always had been most pessimistic about her chances.

Lady Chelmarsh's thoughts had moved on to matters of the moment, and she asked Sophy if she had seen her tatting, which was really an instruction for her daughter to go in search of it.

Lady Harriet Hadlow was too old for the schoolroom. She told herself this, even as she sat in it, daydreaming about a spectacularly successful debut in the adult world. Since the departure of the governess, this had become a quiet refuge from the bustle that surrounded the preparations for a London Season. It was all terribly exciting, of course, but gave little time for imagining, and Lady Harriet was a natural dreamer. Mama had already said that they would take up residence in Hill Street early enough to visit the most fashionable modistes for most of her dresses, and she had brought several recent copies of *La Belle Assemblée* to provide her with inspiration. The fashion plates depicted gowns more suited to dashing young matrons than modest debutantes, but there were several in which she could see herself stunning the most apparently hard-hearted, but secretly romantic, eligible gentlemen, who would combine title, riches, handsome features and a capacity for love.

She heard footsteps in the passageway, and her sister popped her head around the door.

'I thought you would be here, Harry. Has Mama told you that I am being dragged to London too?'

'Oh yes,' declared that damsel, blithely revealing that Lady Chelmarsh had informed other members of the family before telling Sophy herself. 'Mama said you would dislike it, but that must be a hum, because how could you prefer staying here with Papa and his stud books, or whatever you call them for cows? There will be nobody interesting left in the vicinity, and you would be reduced to mending flounces and inviting as dinner guests old Sir Humphrey Mawdsley, who sneezes snuff over one, or Lady Wadderton, with her ear trumpet.'

It had to be said, Lady Harriet did not paint a

picture of pleasure and excitement.

'But Lady Wadderton tells such funny stories. That one about the effete *vicomte* and the roses . . .' Sophy's lips twitched.

'Oh yes, that one, or the one about the carriage that bolted. Those are the two stories she always tells. Alternatively, there is the one about how she saw her cousin 'in flagrante' with her aunt's coachman, in an arbour at Ranelagh Gardens. I only heard that one the once, when Mama had started inviting me to join her when she had visitors to take tea, at this time last year. Mama spilt milk over her green Berlin silk.' Harriet sounded quite matter-of fact. 'I did ask Miss Welling what "in flagrante" meant, when I returned here, but she boxed my ears,' she added, pensively.

'Yes, well, anyway, I would prefer the boring mediocrity of life at home to gadding about to parties where I will stand against the wall and be expected to chaperone Susan.'

'Oh, it will be such fun having Susan with us. She is so lively and exuberant.'

'Harry, our cousin Susan is wild. She does not know the meaning of the word decorum.' On the other hand, Sophy thought it quite likely that she would have had no need to ask a governess what 'in flagrante' meant. 'If you wish to fulfil Mama's expectations, and to be admired by gentlemen who might make you an offer, you will not ape her manners. Aunt Clarissa indulged her far too much from an early age, and she never had

13

the benefit of a governess who remained as a steady influence, as Miss Welling did with us.'

'I remember when we met the year before last, just before Aunt Clarissa died, Susan said she had "survived" eight different governesses.'

'She probably meant literally. Trying to educate her would easily have driven any governess possessing nerves to an early grave. It must have been quite traumatic.'

'She did say that she got rid of her first one by putting a frog in her soup and a dead mouse in her bed.' Harriet giggled, and Sophy gave her a look so repressive that she said it rivalled Mama's.

'I am being serious, Harry. I have this dread of Susan landing in all sorts of scrapes, and the danger is that her behaviour will reflect on us, on you, and damage your chances.' Sophy took her youngest sister's hand. 'You will be like Frances, Harry, and make a very good match.'

'Sophy,' Harriet avoided looking her eldest sister in the eye, 'does Frances love Lord Tattersett?'

'What sort of a question is that?'

'An honest one. When we visited her before Christmas, and she said she was increasing, she looked more worried than radiant.'

'It is her first time, Harry, and I expect she is nervous, and at that time she was still feeling sickly. That is why Mama is going to her in April, to help her prepare. She was certainly exceedingly fond of Tattersett when they married, and her letters to me have never indicated that her feelings have changed at all.'

14

'I do not want to marry a man I do not love. Would Mama make me do so?' Harriet looked at Sophy, a little uncertainly.

'No. I am sure she would not, Harry, at least not a man whom you could not love. I have seen a great many young ladies marry men of whom they were merely very fond, and when they have got to know them better, after marriage, they have learnt to love them. I think the idea that love hits one as a *coup de foudre* is a myth perpetuated in those lurid romances which Miss Welling forbade you to read, and which you borrowed from Eliza Sapperton and hid under your bed.'

'You knew? And did not tell?'

'I knew. And I am not a sneak. I trusted that you would read them, but be a sensible girl and see them for what they were, nonsensical fairy tales with no relation to reality.'

'Oh, of course not. I mean, there are no such things as headless monks, and young ladies are not chained in dungeons full of bats.' Harriet frowned. 'At least, not in England. But some of the heroes were very brave and dashing.'

'There is not much call for gentlemen to be brave and dashing at Almack's or in Hyde Park. One has to content oneself with polite and thoughtful.'

'But would it not be wonderful to be rescued by a hero, Sophy?'

'No, because in order to do so, one would have to be in peril, which would undoubtedly be most unpleasant.'

'I fear you are not a romantic, Sophy.'

'Which is also a good thing, since if I were I would be a very disappointed one.'

She saw Harriet's face fall, and smiled.

'I am sorry, Harry, do I depress you? It is not my intention. You will have a very enjoyable time in London, except that you will learn what it is to have feet that ache from dancing, and if you do not turn heads you may call me . . .'

'Sophronia.'

'Hmm.'

It was later that afternoon when she knocked upon the study door, and was invited to enter by her sire. Lord Chelmarsh was reading correspondence, and looked up with a smile.

'Sophy, my dear.' He saw her expression. 'You wish to unburden yourself, I see.'

'Am I that transparent, Papa?' She smiled, wryly.

'To me, yes.'

Sophy was deeply attached to her father, and looked up to him, not only in respect but literally. She had, she supposed, always found it reassuring that she had one member of her family who remained taller than she was.

'London, Papa.' She sighed. 'I really do not want to go.'

'Your mama feels the need for your support, Sophy.'

His daughter did not enquire about him giving support. Lord Chelmarsh rarely went up to Town, preferring to spend his time in improving his estates. His correspondents and friends were men of similar interests whom he would not find in London except under duress. He immersed himself in cattle breeding and his lady wife was sometimes heard to complain that he held his prize bulls in greater esteem than his children. This was not true, quite.

'I am not sure that I will not simply be there merely to keep Susan out of mischief.'

'Of course that is why you will be there. Your cousin is . . . wilful and innocent, which is a dangerous combination in a girl her age.'

'You say that, Papa,' Sophy laughed, 'as if it were a trait to be bred out, as you do with poor milkers.'

'Might be easier for everyone if it could be, my dear.'

He invited her to sit, and studied her face. He could not see why she had never 'taken'. Her hair was somewhere between brown and gold, her complexion healthy and unblemished, and her features good, with a straight nose, naturally arching brows, and remarkably fine, blue green eyes. Her mouth might be considered fractionally too large for perfection, but it was a mouth used to smiling at the world, except when in London.

'London will surely not be so bad, Sophy. You assuredly will not find a husband here.'

'You know as well as I do that I do not go for that reason. I know Mama despairs of getting me off your hands. She is now talking of me as a prop for your declining years.'

'I can think of few things less appealing than to become a prop. Marriage would save you from that. I would like to see you mistress of your own establishment, setting up your nursery, but that does not mean I would see you wed to anyone less than a man for whom you cared deeply, and most certainly I do not seek "getting you off my hands".' There was an edge of mild reproof in his voice.

'I am sorry, Papa, but . . . if you only knew how much I detest being on show. I hope you realise it is all your fault too.'

'Mine?'

'Yes, sir, since it is from you I inherit my excessive inches, and you were mightily remiss in permitting Mama to name me after her godmother, which I know was in some expectation of largesse which never materialised.'

'The first was beyond my control, and de facto, the second also. It is very difficult to impose a name upon a child, when the mother is in the euphoria of relief at having survived, and simultaneously cast down by the perceived failure of not being delivered of a son.'

'Yet she did not give Frances a cumbersome name, and it was only after her that Jasper arrived.' Sophy ignored the idea that her not being a boy was a failure on her mother's part.

'Very true. I have to admit that I did put my foot down at her first choice.'

'Which was?'

'Euphemia. Sounds like "euphemism" to me. Ghastly name.'

'And Sophronia is not?'

'It is easily shortened to Sophy, which I happen to like.'

'As do I, Papa,' she laid her hand on his, 'but in public I am always announced as Sophronia. If only you had been a mere viscount, I could have been simply "Miss Hadlow" and been comfortable.'

'But by that reasoning, the fault lies with your grandfather for not living beyond his seventieth year, for until then I was a viscount, and at birth you were "Miss Hadlow".'

'Being right and reasonable is not fair, Papa. I am neither, but it is how I feel.'

'And do you "feel" better for having had the opportunity to vent your complaints?'

'Yes, Papa, for you do at least listen.' She sighed.

'I listen, but I do not change things when it comes to matters better understood by your mama. To London you will still go, but try to do so with a more positive outlook. If you are fortunate, Mama will be so taken up with launching Harriet and Susan into Polite Society that she may not notice if you chance upon a suitable beau of your own choosing. You are a good girl, Sophy, and if the world was fair, which it is not, you would undoubtedly find one. Your mother's efforts were perhaps too self-conscious. See what happens when you leave the matter to fate.'

'My fate, Papa, will be to be Mama's scapegoat when my unrestrainable cousin proves to be . . . unrestrainable.'

CHAPTER TWO

THE HONOURABLE SUSAN TYNEHAM SAT WITH HER hands folded in her lap, deceptively demure. Her brother, some eight years her senior, sat opposite her, his face stony. There had been an altercation when they had set off upon their journey, and it had concluded with each side still holding the same views as at the outset. Lord Tyneham, a slightly stocky but not ill-favoured young man, had withdrawn into dignified silence. Susan had decided that to look daggers at him would be a waste, and frowning would incline her brow to wrinkles, so she taunted him by looking as angelic as he knew she was not.

There was little to mark them as brother and sister, and if the old gossip was true, their relationship did not extend to having the same paternity. Lady Tyneham had been a beauty in her youth, and in the eyes of the world had married well, for Tyneham was an exceptionally wealthy man, although only a baron. Upon his marriage he had lavished that wealth upon his bride; his wealth but not his affection, and affection was what she craved above all things. Lady Tyneham had dutifully presented him with an heir within the year, after which their mutual incompatibility had been denied by neither party.

Whilst this meant that his lordship resumed much the same life he had as a single man, paying for his pleasures with a succession of attractive but demanding and expensive barques of frailty, his lady had become a lonely figure among the young matrons on the social circuit. It was some years afterwards that she came into the orbit of a charming but casual lover, with whom, despite the advice of older and wiser heads who warned her of his reputation, she had enjoyed a passionate and barely concealed alliance. He had treated her as the centre of his universe for one whole Season, but at its end, however, he had dropped her as if they had never been upon more than terms of nodding acquaintanceship. She withdrew to Tyneham Court, broken-hearted and carrying a child whom everyone believed was not her lord's. Since the fruit of this illicit union was only a girl, Tyneham was content to appear 'generous' and keep both his spouse and the child, whom he saw as a constant reminder to his erring wife of the penalties of infidelity. To the world he announced his paternity, and dared them to say otherwise. They did not say, but they whispered, and

Lady Tyneham did not return to London again, even after her husband died, some thirteen years later.

It might have been assumed that she would have resented the little girl, but with her son sent away to school, and a husband who largely ignored her, but who kept her almost exclusively in the country, she focussed her love on the only person left to her. Susan was indulged. Susan was never reprimanded. Susan became the 'household god' whom none dared gainsay. She seemed to have inherited more than suspiciously dark locks, which gave the lie to the sandy-haired baron's protestations. Her character, unrestrained, was wayward, selfish and bold to the point of being heedless. Upon the death of Lady Tyneham, some eighteen months previously, her elder brother had been put in the difficult position of guardian, and had taken the line of least effort, leaving his sister in the care of the last, and most resilient, of her governesses. Pretending she was just a child helped, but in the locality of Tyneham Court, Miss Tyneham was regarded as dangerous.

Now Aunt Chelmarsh was going to bring Susan out, and hopefully find her a husband who could assume the burden of responsibility for her. Tyneham would be so very glad to wash his hands of his troublesome sister. She was a beauty, and he would ensure that she came with a sizeable dowry, so it ought not to be too hard to find a man who would overlook her faults, thought Lord Tyneham, gazing dispassionately at her, as long as he did not know her too well.

They arrived in Hill Street a little after four. When the liveried groom assisted Miss Tyneham from the carriage, she threw him a look which would haunt his dreams for weeks, and made his insides go weak, and she swept into the house with a smile lurking in her eyes. Men were so easy.

Lady Chelmarsh greeted her nephew with mild pleasure, and her niece with barely concealed trepidation. Susan made her curtsey prettily enough, but as she raised her eyes to her aunt's face, Lady Chelmarsh could see the spark of rebellion in them. She reached automatically for her vinaigrette.

'Susan dear, how much you have grown,' she murmured, weakly.

'Indeed, Aunt, I am most certainly not a child any more.' Susan's words, delivered in her low, and irrepressibly sensuous voice, made her aunt clutch the little silver box more tightly.

'I leave it up to you, ma'am, to rig my sister out in suitable style. Just let me know the figures involved, and I will let you have a draft upon my bank.' Lord Tyneham ignored his sister's implication.

'Yes, er, of course, Tyneham. Are you staying up in Town?'

Sophy entered, trying her best to look pleased at Susan's arrival, and made her curtsey to her older cousin.

'I shall remain in London some time, yes.' He

addressed Lady Chelmarsh, but his eyes were on Sophy. 'Your servant, cousin.'

'I hope you are in good health, Augustus.'

'Thank you, yes. I had a bad chill at New Year, but thankfully it did not settle upon the lungs. Doctor Chislet advocated plenty of goose grease for the chest and I have to say it worked, though I was initially sceptical. One cannot be too careful with chills.'

He answered her prosaically, and she controlled the urge to smile. She had merely asked out of politeness, not expecting details of his most recent ailment. Susan looked at her brother with ill-concealed disdain.

'Being ill is just boring. Most of the time one may avoid illness simply by refusing to admit its existence. I do not count wounds, of course. They are romantic.'

'Foolish girl. Romantic indeed, what idiocy.' Tyneham snorted. 'You have never seen a wound.'

'If I did, I would not swoon. You went as white as paper merely over a nosebleed.'

'I was very fortunate not to break my nose, and Doctor Chislet said that it is possible to exsanguinate through a nosebleed.'

'Pah! He says anything to please you because he enjoys the way you call for him at the first hint of a sore throat.'

Sophy was at a loss. This was clearly a spat between siblings, but that it should be conducted in front of their aunt, whom they did not even know very well, struck her as unpleasant, and Susan was clearly the one goading.

'Some people are very susceptible to a putrid sore throat. My own Aunt Dorothea died of one.' Lady Chelmarsh tried to pour oil upon the waters.

'I thought that was the diphtheria,' remarked Sophy, without thinking, and received a look of reproach.

'How much more putrid could a throat get?' countered Lady Chelmarsh.

This was unanswerable. It did, however, cause a break in the hostilities between brother and sister, and Sophy, keen to make amends for her unhelpful comment, drew the conversation into something less contentious.

'It is fortuitous, Susan, that you arrive the day before we have an appointment with Mme Clément for Harriet's new gowns. I am sure you will come away with your head full of the most ravishing designs.'

'Oh yes. The trouble is that all the nicest dresses are for those who are married, or at least not in their debut season. All those gowns recommended for their "simplicity and charm" tend to be so very dull and lacking in dash. Who would wish to wear white and pearl pink when there is bronze green and magenta. It is not so bad for you, cousin, since you count as quite old enough to be among the matrons.'

Whether this was merely a thoughtless remark, or one designed as barbed, Sophy still coloured. Susan seemed to comprehend that she had caused offence and made an attempt to negotiate her way out of the awkward situation. All she did was dig a deeper hole.

'I am sorry, that did not sound kind. It is only that

you have been out for so long . . .'

'You would look very nice in white, Susan, with your lovely dark hair.' Lady Chelmarsh declared quickly, and rather loudly. She was getting desperate.

'Do you think so, Aunt? I wondered if it might not make me look sallow.' Susan, diverted onto her favourite topic, herself, immediately forgot Sophy.

Her cousin was able to regain her composure, therefore, until she realised that she was being regarded most earnestly by Lord Tyneham.

'I apologise, unreservedly, for my sister's outrageous remark,' he murmured. 'That she should dare to say . . . unforgivable.' He was looking up at her, and his expression reminded her quite forcibly of the estate gamekeeper's loyal spaniel. 'She cannot appreciate that not all men look for silly girls as their helpmeet through life.'

She was unsure how to reply. In fact, she would prefer not to reply at all. Her mother noted the spaniel look. Lady Chelmarsh did not think much of Tyneham as a man, but he had wealth, and at Sophronia's age, perhaps he might prove the only chance she would get. It would be well to watch, and if necessary, cultivate him. The biggest problem looked like being that he and his sister would be at odds within minutes if in the same room.

Sophy was saved by the arrival of Harriet, who was patently eager to show her cousin her room and discuss the current plans for their being launched into society. Lady Chelmarsh would normally have repressed such an unladylike display of enthusiasm, but in the current circumstances was simply glad to get Susan to remove from the drawing room.

'And I too, Mama, have tasks to which I ought to give my attention,' declared Sophy, keen to make her escape.

'Yes, indeed, my dear. I am sure Tyneham understands.' Lady Chelmarsh saw the look of entreaty in her daughter's face, but was not going to keep her nephew at arm's length. As Sophy made her apologies to her cousin and withdrew, she was heard to invite him to dine with them on the morrow, for they had no engagement this early in the Season. Sophy sighed.

Madame Clément was perfectly happy to extend the appointment of the Hadlow ladies to include the beautiful Miss Tyneham, especially when it was made clear that expense was not an issue. Harriet was delighted simply to be the centre of attention and have gowns designed specifically for her, having, in the schoolroom, been quite used to wearing those adapted from clothes her older sisters had outgrown. Lady Chelmarsh had seen no reason why this piece of domestic economy should not be employed whilst Harriet was learning French grammar and dabbling with watercolours. Now she was to be launched into the Ton it was a different matter, a matter of pride, even, that Lady Harriet Hadlow should not be dismissed as 'just another chit' on the marriage market. If Sophronia had been a disaster, Frances had been a success, and Lady Chelmarsh was determined to build upon that. Presenting her youngest daughter in flattering but modest apparel, making her, and not her gowns, the focus of attention, was her prime concern, and Mme Clément fully comprehended her customer's requirements.

Fortunately for the dressmaker, Harriet lacked her sisters' inches but had a pleasing figure, and suited dresses in a variety of styles, though she admitted the Russian bodice was not as flattering,

While Harriet was the centre of attention, Susan, naturally, became bored, and took to inspecting some of the ensembles upon display. It was a natural progression to calling a minion and demanding to be permitted to try on a very dashing spencer in red velvet and decorated in the military style with gold braid and buttons. The minion was caught between knowing it was not designed for so youthful a lady, and the mulish look on Miss Tyneham's face, which indicated she would make a nasty scene if refused.

Thus it was that Lady Chelmarsh's discussion about the suitability of a spangled half dress was interrupted by Miss Tyneham parading up and down in the spencer and announcing that it would be just the thing to wear to the military review in Hyde Park that her aunt had mentioned as one of the treats of the next two months.

'Er, yes, my dear, but it is hardly . . .'

Susan's body language and expression made Lady Chelmarsh wish she had brought her smelling salts.

'With a very boringly simple white walking dress beneath, ma'am, it would not look too dashing, and the colour suits me so very well.'

It had to be admitted that it did. Mme Clément, seeing both the chance of pleasing her client and making a sale, proffered her professional advice.

'Mademoiselle does indeed suit the colour, but worn with anything but a gown, ah, of the simplest but most carefully fitted, and in white, would make Mademoiselle look a little . . . old.'

This made Susan glance in the long mirror. The concept of looking 'old' was one she had not considered. 'Sophisticated' was a look to which she aspired, 'old' was not.

'Do you truly think so?'

'Why yes, Mademoiselle.' Madame managed to sound surprised. 'When one has the advantages of youth and beauty also, what need has one to make others look at the gown and not oneself?' She gave a quick sidelong glance at Lady Chelmarsh, who was nodding approvingly, and saw her path clear. 'You will not mind me saying this, Mademoiselle. Some young ladies must disguise their imperfections with detail. You have no such problem. Advertise your perfections with gowns of good cut but simple fabrics, and let lesser demoiselles hide their faults.'

This made perfect sense to Susan, and, after all, the dressmaker must see very many young clients. What in her aunt she would have dismissed, she lapped up from Mme Clément, not realising that an exquisitely cut gown on simple lines might cost as much as one more opulent in trimming. She was in London to be admired, and break hearts. She would do so better this way.

'Why yes, that is very true.'

Lady Chelmarsh could have embraced the proprietress, but contented herself with announcing that Madame would create her niece's wardrobe for the Season, and that Susan might have the spencer, as a gift from her aunt.

Sophy, watching this scene unfold before her, smiled at the adroitness of Madame Clément, and caught the lady's eye. Everyone had quite successfully forgotten Sophy, which troubled her not at all.

'But *miladi,* are you not looking for a gown to make an impression upon the beaux this Season?'

'Me? Oh no. I have sufficient to—'

'Actually, my love, I do think you ought to refresh your wardrobe.' Lady Chelmarsh was in such a good humour at getting past the hurdle of purchasing appropriate toilettes for her niece that a little added expense upon her eldest daughter seemed reasonable, and if Tyneham was interested in her, it might even be considered an investment. 'Perhaps a new pelisse for when you promenade with your sister and cousin, and a ball dress or two.'

Sophy, knowing that Madame Clément was not cheap, would have demurred, but her mama seemed so keen she simply let the pair of them have their way, and had to admit that having new clothes was rather nice. She consoled herself with the thought that her father would not object to a moderate amount spent upon her to cover the Season.

* * *

Other than the fact that Susan chattered all the way back to Hill Street about how many other debutantes would be cast into the shade by her appearance on the social scene, and made Harriet convinced that she would be one of them, the expedition could be termed a great success.

'For I do not disguise from you, Sophronia, that I positively quaked at the thought of trying to get Susan not to behave petulantly if I did not permit her to select gowns entirely inappropriate to her years. I almost felt that I had to purchase some extra gowns for you in gratitude to Madame Clément, for the way she handled the girl.'

'So glad I was able to be useful,' murmured Sophy.

'And you saw that she was perfectly meek about the choices we made for her.' Her mother ignored the comment.

What Sophy had seen was adroit handling by an experienced saleswoman, but she refrained from comment.

Lord Tyneham presented himself punctually for dinner, and was delighted to have been placed between his aunt and Sophy at the table. He set about impressing her with his knowledge on a variety of subjects. He sounded, she thought, like an encyclopaedia. He then surprised her by actually asking her opinion.

'Do you think that young ladies ought to be taught Italian as a language? I can see that being taught to sing in it is useful, but if one went to Italy, it would only be seemly for the husband to engage in conversation with the locals.'

'I think that . . .'

What she thought was, it then appeared, unimportant, because he launched into a reminiscence of his sole trip abroad, which had been to Holland because he had an interest in Delft pottery.

'Oh no, not your boring vases and jugs again.' Susan sounded disgusted. 'They are all just blue and white.'

'Their very uniformity of colour is one of the attractions,' declared her brother, repressively. 'It gives the displays order, and one may appreciate the forms.'

'They are just pots. Blue and white pots. Even Uncle Chelmarsh's interest in cows is more interesting. They do move, and they are not all the same colour.'

'I do not think Papa would like blue and white cows,' whispered Harriet, to her sister.

'I have a very fine cow creamer in blue and white.' Lord Tyneham had clearly overheard, and his mind inclined to make very literal connections. 'There are some collectors who prefer the tulip—'

'Are we going to purchase hats tomorrow, ma'am?' Susan cut across her brother.

'I . . .' Lady Chelmarsh was so surprised at the interjection that she blinked, and answered rather than admonish her niece for her rudeness. 'I thought that we would do so, yes.'

'Oh good. Just remind me not to look at any with

blue ribands. I have quite gone off the colour, and dislike it with white. So very obvious a contrast, and I would hate to look the least like a cow creamer.' Susan gave a deceptively innocent smile, but threw her brother a swift, challenging look.

He coloured, but refrained from taking the bait, which she merely saw as a sign of cowardice, and stuck her nose in the air, convinced of her victory.

Harriet, whose relations with her brother, her nearest in age, were good, frowned. As brother and sister, it was natural to banter in private, but they would never do so before company, even in jest, and this was not in jest at all. Susan seemed to want to needle her brother at every opportunity. Harriet secretly admired her cousin's boldness, or at least the self-confidence it showed, but this shocked her.

Sophy, seeing the look on her sister's face, was pleased. It would be far better if Harriet took no cues from their ill-disciplined cousin. She also rewarded Tyneham for his reticence, by enquiring about the porcelain from the Orient which had inspired the European potters, knowing full well it would enable him to lecture her at length. After five minutes, she regretted this generous act. Her parent, meanwhile, was occupying Susan with a description of the fashions when she had made her own come-out, a generation previously. This was sufficiently entertaining for that young lady to forget brother baiting, and to ask youthful questions and relax in a way which Lady Chelmarsh chose to see as a sign that having her under her roof might not be as bad as she had anticipated. She remarked as such as she stood outside her bedroom door upon retiring, and was wishing Sophy goodnight.

'Perhaps,' suggested Lady Chelmarsh, hopefully, 'Susan has outgrown her childish volatility.'

'On the evidence of what we witnessed yesterday and today, Mama, I fear that is wishful thinking.'

CHAPTER THREE

LADY CHELMARSH DID NOT HAVE LONG TO LINGER IN her happy self-deception. She was not a woman much given to nervous spasms, but Susan could have induced them in the hardiest of dames. Her mere presence in the house in Hill Street seemed to set it by the ears and create an atmosphere of tension. Bembridge, the butler, who had been in the family service man and boy for forty years, struggled for four days and then went to his mistress and requested a few minutes of her time upon a serious matter.

'I am so very sorry to have to bring this to your ladyship's attention, but the situation is such . . .' He coloured, and looked extremely uncomfortable.

Lady Chelmarsh felt her heart sink. Her household was not one where disturbance occurred, but there been one very obvious change in it.

'My niece?'

'Yes, my lady, I fear Miss Tyneham has been . . . unmindful of the distance between those above and below stairs. The staff here, I say without puffing myself up, ma'am, are well trained, discreet, and trustworthy. I would not engage, or rather retain on your ladyship's behalf, any who were not. However, I feel I ought to ask permission to call a meeting of the staff, the male staff that is, and issue firm directions upon the way in which they react to the young lady. I, er, have reason to believe that several young men were turned off at Tyneham Court following "incidents", my lady. I would not wish such an unfortunate occurrence here.'

'I see.'

He hoped, most devoutly, that she did not. He had already had stern words with two of the footmen, whom he had overheard arguing over which of them 'young miss' preferred, and had to give his protégé, Norris, whom he was grooming to take the position of butler when he should retire, some fatherly advice and a strictly medicinal glass of Lord Chelmarsh's second best sherry.

'I am sure Miss Tyneham means nothing by it, my lady, but . . . She is a very attractive young lady, and it fair turns the heads of the young men when she . . . it is very difficult when . . . she plays her tricks off upon the staff.'

'Her tricks, Bembridge?'

'She, well, she . . . flirts. Your ladyship will understand it makes things very awkward for the footmen, being young and impressionable, when she speaks to them just so, and gives them looks which, from young women of their own station, they would see as indicative of, er, interest.'

'Oh dear,' murmured Lady Chelmarsh, starting to pleat a lace-edged handkerchief.

'It will be all innocence, no doubt, ma'am,' lied Bembridge, who privately thought Miss Tyneham a risk to the entire male gender, and would rather a tiger had been introduced into the household, 'but I feel I ought to remind the staff that her behaviour must not be taken at face value.'

'I see,' repeated Lady Chelmarsh. 'Indeed, I fear you are right to speak with the men. I am sorry, Bembridge, that the staff are put in this . . . difficulty. At least it is only for this one Season.'

Bembridge did not think he could survive a second, but made an appropriate response.

Lady Chelmarsh was still working her handkerchief through her fingers when Sophy came in to ask if there was anything her mama needed at Grafton House, whither Sophy was bound to hunt for lace edging for a petticoat.

'I need peace and quiet, dear, and you cannot purchase me that.'

'But surely, Mama, one does not come to London for peace and quiet?'

'Oh no, I meant to be free of worry about . . . I have just had a very upsetting interview with Bembridge. Susan has been "playing off her tricks".'

'Not on dear old Bembridge, surely?'

'Not on him, at least he did not say so, but on the other men. It is terribly distressing.'

'I saw her this morning, looking sideways at the new under-footman. She uses them as practice, I think. I believe she likes to feel the adulation. She is not likely to try and run off with a servant.'

'Do not even say such a thing. It gives me palpitations.'

'I am sorry, Mama. I have told Susan her behaviour is wrong, and unfair, but she shrugs and says it means nothing, and men should not be so easily duped.'

'Where will it end? Oh, Sophronia, how can one find a suitable parti for a girl like Susan?'

'I hate to say it, Mama, but the best thing for her would be a man for whom she feels a partiality but who does not respond to her "tricks". Perhaps, you know, she needs to fall for a rake.'

'No, oh no. She could not. It would be unthinkable. What people would say . . .'

'Unpalatable it may be, Mama, but it does not make it less true.' Sophy paused. 'Shall I take her with me shopping, and Harriet also?'

'Yes. No. Yes. Oh, Sophy I wish your father were here.'

'You do not really, Mama, for he would look miserable, and declare you know best in all such matters anyway.'

With which Sophy left her mother to her musings and went to find her sister and her wayward cousin.

* * *

Harriet was in Susan's room, sat upon the bed and watching her cousin instructing the maid how best to dress her hair, and finding fault with every pin. Sophy arrived just as Susan exclaimed that it would look better if she did it herself. The maid was flustered, and thus even more hesitant.

'Let me, cousin.' Sophy stepped forward, dismissed the maid with a smile and thanks, and calmly placed the last few pins with deft fingers. 'You should not berate the maid simply because you are out of patience, Susan.'

'I was not. She was slow, and clumsy.' Susan pouted. 'I am bored.'

'Well, you need not be so. I am going to Grafton House for lace, and thought you and Harry might accompany me. You were thinking of some hair ribands only yesterday, Harry, and it is a delightful place to spend one's pin money.'

Harriet was instantly enthusiastic, and Susan became so when she realised that they were walking the short distance to New Bond Street, which might mean the opportunity to see gentlemen, if not upon the Strut at such an early hour of the day, then about their business.

It was but a few minutes' walk from the house in Hill Street to the ladylike delights of the linen-drapers at Grafton House. They passed through Berkeley Square, and, after gazing into a few enticing windows in Bruton Street, turned right into the lower end of New Bond Street. Whilst the elegant modistes might be visited by young unmarried ladies only with the support of parental wealth,

Grafton House was an emporium within whose portals one might spend one's shillings upon furbelows, and, if one was reduced to such levels, materials with which to make one's own gowns, or take to a lesser dressmaker. It was not the most fashionable of shops, but was popular. Sophy, having discovered it during her first Season when she wanted to replace some buttons on a pelisse, knew it to be the perfect source of trimming for the petticoat she had nearly finished at home, and had brought up to Town to occupy any quiet time with restful hemming. She was not a notable needlewoman, and had neither the need nor inclination to make her own dresses, but petticoats were a different matter, and provided employment on rainy afternoons in the country.

There was an added advantage to taking her sister and cousin to Grafton House; it was not a place where Susan might be distracted by gentlemen. In this Sophy was correct, but she forgot that Susan was as likely to flutter her eyelashes at a breathless draper's assistant as at a duke.

They arrived before the shop was too crowded, and whilst Sophy pondered over the advantages of a narrow ecru lace that was unlikely to tear over the more opulent wider examples, she let the younger ladies, with the protection of the maidservant, wander among the fabrics, braids and ribbons. Having selected and requested the appropriate yardage for her project, Sophy's eye was caught by some very fine lawn, from which she might make both a tucker and some handkerchiefs to embroider for female relatives, and it was only then that she went to seek out her sister.

Harriet was trying to decide between a broad satin ribbon in cerulean blue, and one in a soft green. Susan was contemplating the purchase of silk stockings, not least because handling one she had successfully caught the eye of a young man whose Adam's apple was bobbing up and down and pulse was racing as she held the item in her hand and gave him a look that turned his mind, firmly focused upon commerce, to jelly, just as she intended that it would.

'I am bound to wear holes in the heels when we are at balls and parties every night, for I fully intend to dance every dance, so I think investing in another couple of pairs would be a very good idea, do not you, cousin?' She smiled up at Sophy.

'Yes, but that presupposes that your dance card will be full.'

'Oh, it will be full, I can assure you.' Susan's self-confidence was boundless, and Sophy realised that nothing she could say would dent it. Then Susan added the comment that cut. 'You just watch, and listen to the mamas as they wish their daughters were as fortunate.'

'Thank you, I might even manage a dance myself, you know.'

'Oh yes, . . . of course,' faltered Susan, under a rather steely stare. 'I . . . I shall take two pairs of the stockings, though. Has Harriet decided about her ribands yet?'

Harriet had not, and eventually took a length of both colours. Having paid for their purchases, they were placed in the basket held by the maidservant, but Susan, to Sophy's surprise, chose to carry the wrapped parcel of stockings herself. Had she known her cousin rather better, she would have been suspicious.

They retraced their steps, lingering over shop windows, and making hypothetical purchases which would, in reality, have been wildly profligate. They were gazing into the window of a jewellers near the corner of Bruton Street, and Harriet was waxing lyrical over a necklet of graduated topaz stones.

Susan, catching sight in the window reflection of a personable gentleman passing behind them, contrived to let her package of stockings slip to the ground, and exclaimed in feigned surprise.

The gentleman bent to pick up the package which had slipped so artlessly from Miss Tyneham's grasp, a smile flickering at the corner of his mouth. Sophy, herself under no illusions as to what had happened, had the distinct impression that he also knew exactly what Susan had done.

'Your parcel, ma'am.' He handed back the package, dangling it by the string from one long, gloved finger. He was dressed elegantly, without ostentation, and was, of course, good-looking, with hair as dark as Susan's own. She would never have dropped the packet had he been middle-aged and corpulent.

'Oh, sir, how kind. So silly of me to let it slip through my fingers,' Susan answered breathily, and presented a small kid-encased hand.

42

The gentleman took the bait, as she had hoped, and before handing over the parcel took the hand in a reverent grasp and bent low over it. Susan threw her cousins a look of triumph. Sophy squirmed inwardly, and as the gentleman stood straight again, caught the understanding gleam in his eye. Susan might think herself clever, but the stranger knew the game she was playing, and was responding in kind. Sophy was not sure whether this sprang from understanding, for Susan was patently inexperienced, or roguishness.

'I . . . I do not know whom to thank, sir,' ventured Susan, peeping coyly at him from under her long lashes.

'No, you do not, do you? How vexatious. However, I am sure that we will be introduced in a more proper setting.' The smile held a trace of the lupine, and his eyes danced.

Susan was both entranced and antagonised simultaneously, and could think of no instant response.

'Your servant, ladies.' The gentleman bowed, primarily to Sophy, since she was clearly the most senior, and turned away, striding purposefully towards Piccadilly.

'Well, how you had the sheer effrontery to do that, Susan, I do not know,' Sophy reprimanded her cousin.

'Pho! It was just a little tease. A little fun for both parties, if you prefer. Why should I be ashamed?'

'You had as well tied your garter in public.' Sophy could barely contain her anger.

'Now that, Cousin Sophy, I have never yet done, but it is a temptation, I assure you. I think I might have purchased something suitable for garters in Grafton House.' Susan mocked her cousin. She felt so very pleased with herself. After all, she had attracted the attention of a very smart-looking gentleman, and she had absolutely no doubt that when he did espy her at a party, he would ensure an introduction.

'Susan, you cannot even suggest such a thing,' whispered Harriet, quite shocked.

'Buying garters?' Susan's lips twitched.

'No. I mean . . . you know . . . tying them in public.' Harriet's whisper dropped even further, and she blushed scarlet.

'I just did. Though I admit if one really did have recourse to anything quite as obvious, then one would be unworthy of one's femininity.'

'Why?' Harriet did not understand.

'Because men are simpletons, that is why. To catch them that way is just too easy. What skill has a fisherman, if the fish leap into his net as he stands there?'

'You really do not have a very good opinion of the male of the species, do you, Susan?' Sophy tried to think charitably. Surely her cousin had had little cause to do so.

'I have certainly never met one yet worthy of shedding a tear over. They are selfish, and set themselves up as so clever and powerful, but if you are clever, then it is you who have the power. My mama was weak. She let my papa tread upon her, keep her cooped up at Tyneham, while he did as he pleased. It shall not be so with me. I shall have men at my feet, and it is I who shall do the treading.'

There was a fierce defiance in her tone, and Sophy, for all that her cousin's behaviour was appalling, could understand how, with such an example before her, and no sound guidance, Susan might have decided upon her potentially ruinous course.

'The fault I have with your view, cousin,' she responded, not unkindly, 'is that you have met so very few gentlemen in your life that you might find yourself "treading upon" the worthy as well as the unworthy among the gender. Or are you saying that in falling at your feet they will show themselves unworthy? That does not reflect very well upon you, you know.'

Susan had no immediate answer to this.

'But you do want to be married, surely?' Harriet found her cousin inexplicable.

'Yes. Of course. Would I want to remain in my brother's house, especially when he finds some very boring woman to become his wife? No. That does not mean I want to be married to a man who will tell me what I may and may not do. I want to be married to a man who will accept whatever I do, because I am me, and he adores me.' She lifted her chin, challenging the world.

'But you see, Susan, there are limits, even for a man who might adore you.'

'If so, he will not be adoring me enough.'

It seemed so black and white to Susan. Having lived with disappointment and reality as her companions over the last few years, Sophy saw the shades of grey, and the word 'compromise'. There was a part of her which sympathised with Susan, but then she recalled the way she used her wiles upon those whose social position made it impossible to respond, the shop assistant, the footmen. Susan had become so used to teasing men, she did not make any distinctions, and that way lay danger. She had also learnt to do the opposite of what she saw as boring convention just to see what would result. Well, in London that would risk ruin, for herself and, by association, Harriet.

'I fear, Susan, that you aim too high, and in the process may ruin all. You really have to be careful in Town. You cannot set the Ton by its ears and escape censure. The way to a good match is conformity, at least to the basic rules of Society, and that means behaving with modesty and decorum. I have several more years' experience and—'

'Are unmarried. Are you sure you are the person to advise me, Cousin Sophy?' Susan did not take well to advice.

Sophy glared at her. In private she might well have boxed her ears, but this was impossible in Berkeley Square, as Susan well knew. The remainder of the walk home passed in silence, and Sophy almost stalked into the house. She did thank the maid, and take her parcels up the stairs, and would have continued to her bedchamber where she might vent her frustrated anger in private, but her mother emerged from her writing room and intercepted her.

'Ah Sophronia, was your expedition successful?'

'Yes, Mama, it was.' Sophy thought it best not to

mention Susan's behaviour. 'I found just the right lace and at a very reasonable price.'

'And there was a very kind gentleman who picked up my parcel when I dropped it,' added Susan, passing them, and smiling innocently.

Lady Chelmarsh gave her eldest daughter a look that combined panic and enquiry.

'There was a gentleman, but he did not introduce himself, merely handed back the package.'

'But he did suggest we would be introduced on a more formal occasion,' added Susan, blithely, from halfway up the next flight of stairs.

This could not be said to have cheered her aunt. She took Sophy's arm and drew her back into the small chamber.

'Tell me the worst, Sophronia.'

'It is not so very bad, ma'am. Susan dropped her parcel, and yes, it was intentional, but the gentleman who picked it up seemed . . .' Sophy paused, recollecting his expression, and found herself smiling, 'well aware of her ploy and amused by it, merely amused. I am sure he put it down to her youth.'

'I can only hope that he never discovers her identity.'

He did so within the week.

CHAPTER FOUR

L ONDON WAS A LITTLE THIN OF COMPANY SO EARLY in the Season, though many mamas with daughters to present were availing themselves of the opportunity to dress their offspring for their launch into Society. It meant that Lady Chelmarsh was able to pay morning calls upon several old friends in the same situation as herself, and thus introduce Harriet and Susan to their peers, and, in Susan's view, rivals. Sophy wished she could become invisible, since upon every occasion, the lady of the house would look at her and then at Lady Chelmarsh, sigh sympathetically, as though to say 'what chance did you ever have there. At least my daughters are all married', and then address some 'kindly' comment to her face before ignoring her in a pointed manner for the rest of the visit in a way that showed her presence was an embarrassment to all. Harriet, keen to make friends, did not see the slights. Susan saw, and it made her even more determined to be a success, upon her own terms. These did not include being 'nice' to people whom she despised, and both Lady Chelmarsh and Sophy spoke to her about the necessity of being respectful.

'I have said nothing impolite,' averred Susan, on the defensive.

'No, but when you show contempt in every feature, you might as well do so,' riposted Sophy, when they returned from a trying half hour with Lady Fazeley and her whey-faced daughter. 'You looked at our hostess as if she were a fool.'

'Well, is she not? Sitting there telling us how her Amelia would charm everyone with her singing and pretty manners, when no man will take a second glance at a girl who is so plain and commonplace. Being friends with her would not even serve to accentuate my own advantages, since almost any girl would look better beside her.'

'That, Susan, is a very unkind and selfish way of looking at things.' Lady Chelmarsh was horrified. Clearly one wanted one's own offspring to shine in the firmament, but for a girl to look upon the other debutantes only in terms of how they might advance her own chances was hard-hearted in the extreme. 'This is not only an opportunity to find a suitable husband. Yes, I am honest enough to say that it is the prime objective, but the friends one makes among the other young ladies will also be important in later years. It means one has friends wherever one goes.'

'I have not seen Sophy going to see friends.'

'That is because London is still a little thin of company and several of her closest friends are not in Town this year, in the expectation of confinement.'

It was not quite untrue. Sophy had not made many friends in her debut year, and none without whose frequent correspondence she might feel bereft, but it was true that they had all married and looked towards husbands and children rather than spinsters who could have no insight into their concerns.

Susan gave her cousin a look of pity. She was not fooled.

'If you set up the backs of the mamas, Susan, you will find that the invitations are fewer, and your opportunity to dazzle the gentlemen curtailed.' Sophy decided that appealing to her cousin's better nature was pointless, since if she had one it was buried very deeply. She therefore worked upon her self-interest. 'You may think them as foolish as you please in the privacy of your own chamber, but if you value your chances, you will be circumspect in public. Remember also that many of these same ladies are the mothers of the men you would aspire to impress. They may think you beautiful, but if their parents and sisters have you marked down as an unpleasant, rude young woman, few will seek to know you better.'

Reluctantly, Susan saw the sense of this, and promised that she would 'try'.

* * *

Susan might seek to look nonchalant and poised, but the contemplation of her very first London party was enough to make her as excited as Harriet. Lady Chelmarsh was not planning their own party until the Season had more life to it, and could guarantee a squeeze, but had secured invitations from one of her old friends, Lady Orpington, to her rout. Whilst the girls were advised to lie for an hour upon their beds in the afternoon to ensure that they were ready for the fray, it proved impossible for either to do so. Instead, they pestered Sophy about the most trivial details of their hair and jewellery. She recalled her own first party, though in her case it had been more in trepidation than excitement, and with her mama's admonitions upon how to try and lessen her obvious height disadvantage ringing in her ears. She could not blame two pretty girls being giggly and nervous.

'Mama has said just pearls, but do you think I might add the bracelet Godmama sent me for my birthday? She said it was for my first Season and it is pearls and diamond chips.'

'I cannot see why not, but Mama is the person to ask, Harry, not me.'

'But you do not think she would object?'

'No, I do not think she would.' Sophy kept a straight face at her sister's earnest expression. 'Which gown have you and Mama decided upon?'

This gave Harriet the opportunity to launch into how they came to their decision and what particular factors influenced them. It was so very innocent, and

Sophy let her run on for some time.

'. . . and Mama said that though it will not be a crush, we might meet Lady Jersey, who is one of Lady Orpington's closest friends, and of course she is a Patroness and . . . Almack's, Sophy . . . Will that not be wonderful?'

Almack's, thought her eldest sister, was indeed wonderful if one were popular, and not the sort of girl whom hostesses had to thrust upon partners who would be too gentlemanly to refuse. She herself was not a bad dancer, in that she knew the steps and was light upon her feet, but few men enjoyed dancing with a woman to whom they had to look upward every time the dance brought them together, which limited the number of potential partners considerably. She recalled, even now, the horror of being presented with a partner, just after she had been granted permission to waltz, whose height meant that he spent the dance addressing what few pleasantries he could bring to mind to her bosom. There had been sniggers from some quarters.

'Wonderful, indeed, Harry, but remember that it is a place where one commonly has to sit out some sets.'

'Oh yes, I would not even imagine standing up for every dance.'

'I would.' Susan had seen the door ajar, heard the voices. 'Wallflowers do not win suitors. Surely one should aspire to returning home exhausted, with sore feet, and a dance card without any gaps?'

'Ah, but one does not get to know a man simply upon

the dance floor. There are some very fine gentlemen who do not generally dance, and it does not mean they are old, or crippled. Would that not limit your number of admirers?'

Susan thought about this.

'I had not considered the matter. I suppose you are right, but it would have to be a very special reason if a man did not choose to ask for his name to go upon my card. I am certainly not interested in men too old to dance, even if one was a duke.'

'How good to hear that you are not mercenary, Susan,' commented Sophy, wryly, and received a dagger's look.

'If you wish to be beastly . . .' Susan turned away.

Sophy felt guilty, a weakness Susan resolutely refused to acknowledge, and sighed.

'No, I do not. I am sorry, cousin. Did you come in to speak to me or to Harriet?'

'Actually, it was you. You have so much more experience. I was wondering how to decline an invitation to dance without letting the gentleman know that one would not dance with him were he the last man standing in the room.'

'If the hostess has introduced him to you as a partner, you smile sweetly and offer your hand, Susan, because to refuse insults her also, and it is her party. Be clear upon that. Even if the gentleman is not to your taste.'

Susan looked mulish, but sighed, and nodded her head.

'If he approaches you himself and is an undesirable

partner because you have seen he is a clumsy dancer, then claiming to be overheated and in need of refreshment is perfectly acceptable, as long as you converse with him if he procures you a glass, or escorts you to the refreshments.'

'But what if you are trying to catch the attention of someone far better? How provoking if you were waylaid by somebody unimportant.'

'That, Susan, is called courtesy. You are not meant to be so very single-minded that you only dance with men high on your list of "suitable partners". If gentlemen applied the same rules, very many young ladies would sit out the evenings, and, incidentally, many matches would not be made, for it is not only the prettiest girls who make good matches. Some who are not "diamonds of the first water" do so because of their sweetness of nature, their humour and goodwill. Looks alone will not get you a husband.'

'But they are such a good start.'

This was unanswerable.

Considering the date, Lady Orpington's rout was very well attended. She had judged it better to have as many as were already up in Town come through her door, and linger, than to hold her first social event in the height of the Season, when it might be low on the list of priorities, and have guests drift in late and leave early, having other and more important commitments. Lady Chelmarsh judged the arrival of her party carefully, neither so early that they might find themselves 'rattling about the rooms', nor so late that any gentlemen would have already picked out likely partners for any dancing, and ensuring introductions.

Precedence meant that Sophy followed immediately behind her mother, with her sister and cousin to the rear, as they ascended the main staircase and were presented to the hostess. The sonorous voice still had the power to make Sophy shrink as 'the Lady Sophronia Hadlow, the Lady Harriet Hadlow, and Miss Tyneham' were announced.

Lady Orpington, assured of the success of her party, was in a very good humour, complimented the young ladies upon their gowns, and promised that there would be plentiful partners for such delightful debutantes. This effectively discounted Sophy, but then, she was not expecting to be picked out. Rather, she hoped to spend a pleasant evening chatting with acquaintances whom she had not seen for a considerable time, when not keeping a watchful eye upon her sister and cousin, and enjoying the music. Harriet looked charming, but clearly unsure of herself. It was not unappealing. Susan, by contrast, glanced about the room as if she owned it, and her manner shouted 'look at me'. It was not that she crossed the borders of propriety in any way, just that she expected to be admired, and simply awaited gentlemen vying for her attention. It was so at odds with the youthfulness of her form that Sophy did not know whether to be amused or horrified. She most certainly had to control the urge to laugh when it was Harriet who was first solicited to dance. Susan might tell herself that the young man was too callow for her taste, but when he diffidently requested an introduction, and then led Harriet into the quadrille, Sophy saw Susan stiffen.

Lady Chelmarsh was caught between pride and a dread that her niece would thereafter set out to count how many dances she stood up for during the evening, and treat Harriet as another rival. This was increased when, much to her surprise, Sophy was invited to join the next set forming up. Susan did compress her lips for a moment, and asked who the gentleman might be, but upon hearing he was but a baronet she relaxed.

'Sir Esmond Fawley? Oh, well he looks terribly serious and boring, and not important at all. He should be the ideal partner for Sophy.'

The gentleman thus dismissed, was at the same moment discussing her with his partner.

'I see that Lady Chelmarsh is not only bringing out your sister but another young lady.'

'My cousin, Lord Tyneham's sister.'

'Tyneham? Who would have thought a fellow such as Tyneham would have a sister so full of . . . vivacity. She is clearly not much like him.' His eyes strayed for a moment to where Susan was trying to look unconcerned, and fanning herself, idly.

'Did you ask me to dance to find out about her, Sir Esmond?' Sophy raised an eyebrow, but smiled.

'Not in the least, Lady Sophronia,' he responded,

promptly. 'I happen to recall that you were a very fine dancer, and would not be tongue-tied, as I fear so many of the young ladies will be tonight.'

'Now you put me to the blush, sir, for I sound as if fishing for compliments, and I was not.'

'Then I apologise, instantly. I take it that you would not wish me to say that I have been disappointed, and must have been thinking of a different lady?'

'I would not believe that, for how well I know that I linger in the memory as "that very tall girl who could at least dance".'

'I prefer "that excellent dancer who was not abysmally short".'

Sophy laughed.

Susan, watching them, frowned. The serious, and unimportant, Sir Esmond seemed to be entertaining her cousin quite amazingly. When he led her from the floor at the conclusion of the dance, Susan spared him a second glance. He was tall and broad-shouldered, and looked the sort of man Susan would have thought more at home upon the hunting field than the dance floor, although he had shown himself nimble enough. He was certainly not a callow youth, and, had he not been merely a baronet, Susan told herself he might have been worth putting herself out to ensnare.

Sir Esmond caught her evaluating him, and read her like a book. His lips twitched, very slightly. It was most unusual to find a 'predator' among the debutantes. It would be interesting to watch her machinations. As he had said to Sophy, so many girls in their first Season took time to find their feet, and were thus rather bland. Miss Tyneham would not be bland.

Lady Chelmarsh had withdrawn to an alcove with a friend she had not seen for some years. Sophy, rather buoyed by having had the fun of dancing, did not see the gentleman who had picked up Susan's parcel in Bond Street until he was making his bow.

'I trust that Fawley has not trodden upon your toes with his big feet, ma'am.' The gentleman grinned at Sir Esmond. 'You have the advantage, Fawley. Do introduce us.'

'I had assumed you would know Lady Sophronia, but . . . May I present Lord Rothley to you, ma'am. He is a terrible fellow as you will no doubt find out but—'

'And I am being traduced by a man I call a friend!' Lord Rothley countered, looking theatrical. He swept a bow. 'Your servant, Lady Sophronia . . .' He paused, awaiting the full introduction.

'The Lady Sophronia Hadlow, also her sister . . . My apologies, for I did not catch your name, ma'am,' Sir Esmond looked at Harriet, who blushed, curtsied, and gave her name. 'And Miss Tyneham.'

'Lady Sophronia. Lady Harriet. Miss Tyneham, I trust you have not dropped your fan, or indeed your reticule, this evening?' Lord Rothley's eyes danced, and the tone was faintly mocking.

'Oh no, my lord.' Susan looked at him quite squarely. 'My grip is quite tenacious when I wish it to be.'

Sophy shuddered.

'Not too tenacious, I hope, or else it would be difficult to part in the moves of the dances. Might I ask for the next dance, ma'am?'

For a moment, just a moment, Susan considered refusing him because of his mockery, but the desire not to remain a mere onlooker was too strong.

'You may ask, my lord. It so happens that I am not engaged for this particular dance and so I am able to accede to your request.'

She offered her hand, like a queen dispensing a favour. Sir Esmond, watching the pair as they took their places, murmured to Sophy, 'Not the shy, retiring maiden, your cousin, ma'am.'

'No, those are not the adjectives commonly used in association with her name, Sir Esmond.' She looked at her cousin, and the man with whom she was dancing. 'I wonder why I was not acquainted with Lord Rothley?'

'He . . . er . . . spent some time abroad after his mother died a few years ago. Must be that.' His eyes followed hers. Susan was attempting flirtation, one could see that without hearing a word. Lord Rothley looked amused, his dark head bending to hers as the steps of the dance brought them together. They made a fine couple. Sir Esmond also noted Lady Harriet looking a little wistful.

'Having had the delight of dancing with the senior sister, might I complete the pleasure of the evening by requesting the next dance with you, Lady Harriet?'

'With me, sir?'

'Yes, if you would be so generous.'

Sophy, knowing what he had said about debutantes, recognised that he was being kind, and gave him a brief, grateful smile. Harriet blushed, and nodded. At the conclusion of the dance, Susan returned, looking triumphant. Not only had she danced with a more highly ranking, and dashing-looking gentleman, she knew that in doing so she had shown herself off far more than by merely standing about. She was confident that she would receive further requests to dance, and indeed, almost immediately, Lady Orpington came up to her with a gentleman whom she presented as a desirable partner. That this gentleman was the scion of a very wealthy house made him all the more acceptable to Susan.

'You appear, my lord, to have been eclipsed almost instantly, by greater wealth and title,' commented Sophy to Lord Rothley, wondering if he might take it as a slight.

'Lowering, isn't it? However, ma'am, perhaps you would provide the balm to my ego by dancing with me.'

'You asked my cousin to dance because she is beautiful, but you ask me to dance to bolster your self-esteem, my lord. I see just where I stand.'

'I wonder if you do, Lady Sophronia.' That dangerous twinkle remained. Sophy found it captivating and thus disquieting.

'I shall only dance with you upon a very strict condition, sir.'

'And what is that?'

'That you promise not to address me as "Lady Sophronia" again.'

'It is your name.'

'And I loathe it. Sophronia was the name my mother thrust upon me in the hope that a godmother might prove generous to one of her own name – a misplaced hope, I add. I am now advanced enough in years to be able to request that acquaintances use Sophy, instead. I should have mentioned it to Sir Esmond.'

'The name is henceforth banished from my lips. Now, shall we dance, ma'am?'

Lord Rothley was not quite as tall as Sir Esmond, barely taller than Sophy herself, and built upon slightly lighter lines, being more sinewy than muscular, but he both danced well and could maintain an entertaining conversation whilst he did so. Sophy expected him to mention her cousin, but he restricted himself to asking about how she was finding London.

'For you did not come up last Season, did you?'

'No, we remained at home.'

'Do you dislike the Metropolis?'

'Not at all. I like the shops, the variety of entertainments . . .'

'But?'

'I did not say "but", sir.'

'It was a silent "but", ma'am.'

'It is easy for a gentleman . . .' The dance parted them for a minute.

'What is?'

'Returning Season after Season, my lord. It is different if one is female, and . . . unmarried.'

'Are you too nice in your requirements, Lady Sophy?'

'It is not my requirements, sir, as I am sure you are well aware. I beg you will not poke fun at me for it.'

'Forgive me, but I assure you that I do not.' He sounded genuine enough, she thought.

'Let us be honest, Lord Rothley. I am too tall to "take", and I have not my cousin's . . . bravura.'

'Bravura . . . mmm, one might term it that.'

'She has not had . . . discipline. I think perhaps, beneath everything, she is quite lonely, or rather too used to being without friends, and she has not learnt to curb her . . . enthusiasms.'

'Very cousinly words. You mean she is a handful.' He smiled again, and Sophy wished he would not, because it made her want to smile back, whatever he had said. 'You may say she is beautiful, and I do not deny her looks, but, privately, ma'am, I have to say you are the better dancer. But do not tell your cousin that.'

Lady Chelmarsh returned. She smiled at the sight of all three of her charges upon the dance floor, until she recognised Sophy's partner. When the dance concluded and he escorted her from the floor, she received him graciously, but without any enthusiasm, and he did not linger.

'How comes it that you were dancing with Rothley, Sophronia?'

'He requested a dance, Mama. Both Harriet and

62

Susan had partners for the dance, so I did not think I was being derelict in my duty.' Sophy thought that her mother was being rather harsh if she expected her to refrain from dancing in such a circumstance.

'Well, at least he did not dance with Susan,' murmured Lady Chelmarsh, inexplicably.

'Oh, but he did, before he danced with me. Sir Esmond Fawley introduced us, but you see it turns out he was the gentleman who picked up Susan's parcel in Bond Street the other day.'

Her ladyship's face went white beneath her powder.

'Oh my God!' she whispered.

CHAPTER FIVE

Lady Chelmarsh was somewhat restored by a glass of ratafia, but refused to elaborate upon why she regarded Lord Rothley with such disfavour. She simply told Sophy that it was not a suitable matter for discussion, and changed the subject as the younger girls returned with their partners. These two gentlemen at least found favour with her, and then offered their escort to supper. Lady Chelmarsh was perfectly content to enjoy the repast in the company of her eldest daughter, and nearly jumped when Lord Tyneham's voice hailed her, and offered them both, with ponderous gallantry, his arm.

'I . . . I did not know you would be here, Tyneham.'

Sophy wondered why her mother sounded nervous.

'I was at school with the Orpingtons' son, Ludovic.

Indeed, I spent several weeks at their home one summer when we were boys.'

'Oh.' Lady Chelmarsh had little recollection of Augustus Tyneham as a child.

'I see Bollington is taking Susan into supper. Excellent. Not that one expects much from a first party of course.'

Sophy was slightly shocked that Tyneham was quite as mercenary as his sister. Lady Chelmarsh made an indeterminate noise in her throat.

'I do not generally dance, cousin, but in your case I would happily make an exception, after supper, for one of the country dances, perhaps.' Tyneham smiled at her in a way which made her itch to tell him she would rather dance with one of the link boys from outside the house.

He made it sound, thought Sophy, that this was by nature of a kind gesture to one who might otherwise sit out the entire evening. However true that might be upon occasion, tonight she had already danced, very pleasurably, with two gentlemen, and to end it by dancing with her cousin would be, somehow, depressing. She answered in as non-committal a way as possible, and was delighted to be swept away by a lady whom she had not seen for some years as soon as supper was over. It was only when they were in the carriage home, that Sophy addressed the 'problem' of Lord Rothley again. Susan and Harriet were tired but jubilant, each feeling that the evening had been a huge success, and having secured partners after supper, which enabled both to claim suitably tired feet. Lady Chelmarsh was very quiet, and upon their arrival in Hill Street, went straight to her room, claiming a headache. Sophy made her preparations for bed in a thoughtful mood, dismissed the sleepy maid with thanks, and lay beneath the covers prey to many questions and no answers. It was while still contemplating these that she fell asleep, and dreamt of slavering wolves with twinkling eyes.

She resolved to press her mama upon the subject of Lord Rothley after breakfast, but found that Lady Chelmarsh was not only taking that repast in bed, but had issued instructions that she was not to be disturbed because she had slept badly. Harriet and Susan were unlikely to appear until noon at the earliest, and so Sophy, most unusually, had time to herself, without chaperoning duties. It was a clear morning, and although it was unfashionably early to do so, she sought to blow away the clouds of dreams from her head with a brisk walk in the Park. She selected a serviceable rather than ostentatious pelisse, and called upon the services of a footman rather than a maid, who would be inclined to dawdle. Under this doughty escort she was soon enjoying the fresh air of Hyde Park. She watched the morning riders, those interested in exercise rather than merely 'being seen' in the afternoon, with envy, and decided that she ought to hire mounts for herself and Harriet for the duration of their sojourn in London. She was not sure how well Susan rode, or indeed if she did at all, though she expected that she did, and as recklessly as she did everything else. So given up

66

was she to thoughts of selecting horses that she did not at first hear herself hailed by a rider trotting up to walk beside her.

Sir Esmond Fawley looked down at her from his big bay.

'I see you are not a lie-abed, Lady Sophronia,' he commented in his slightly lazy voice.

'No, indeed, Sir Esmond. I wish I had thought to provide myself with a mount, but thus far we have been so occupied with other things . . .'

He dismounted, and took his horse's reins over its head so that he might walk beside her and not peer down onto the top of her bonnet.

'Might I offer my services, ma'am, if you would prefer a gentleman as escort? Not that I think you need me to advise you, but . . . It is a very male environment, and you might feel more comfortable.'

She smiled, touched by his thoughtfulness.

'Why, Sir Esmond, that would be most kind of you. I know just the sort of mount my sister would choose, but it is possible that my cousin might also accompany us. I say this in case you wish to rescind the offer.'

'You think me cowardly, ma'am?' He raised an eyebrow, and smiled, though there was seriousness beneath it.

'Not at all, sir, but wisdom would dictate that if you sought a quiet life, you would not choose my cousin as company.'

'Alas, not a coward, but in my dotage, to need "the

quiet life". Behold me crestfallen, Lady Sophronia, and may I assure you that I have not yet attained the decrepitude of thirty.' He laughed, but she thought perhaps she had touched him upon the raw.

'I do not think you advanced in years at all, Sir Esmond, but I do think you a man of sense, and to such my cousin might prove . . . trying.'

'I am considered an even-tempered sort of fellow, I believe. I shall not be reduced to strangling your cousin, you know.'

'The thought had occurred to me upon several occasions, however.' Sophy chuckled, and he thought how natural she was, how at ease. 'If, despite this knowledge, your offer stands, I accept with gratitude. You have but to tell me when it might be convenient to venture upon the expedition.'

'I am at your disposal, Lady Sophronia.'

'Then might I also ask another favour?'

'Of course.'

'Do not address me as Sophronia. Other than my mama, my family and close acquaintance call me Sophy, which I infinitely prefer.'

'I am honoured to be admitted to their ranks, Lady Sophy.' He bowed. 'And are you engaged tomorrow afternoon?'

'I do not believe so, sir. Are you attending the Leominster's soirée this evening? I might be able to confirm then.'

'I am engaged with friends this evening. However,

you might send a note to my address.' He gave it, and she repeated it back to him. 'Then I await your missive, ma'am. Now, I ought to leave you to your perambulations and give this chap some decent exercise.' He patted his horse's nose.

Sophy extended her hand.

'Thank you, Sir Esmond.'

'Not at all, ma'am. It is a pleasure to be of use.'

He bowed slightly over her hand, gathered his reins and mounted, to trot off with the virtuous feeling that he had indeed been useful.

Sophy returned to Hill Street in good humour, and had even forgotten her perplexity over Lord Rothley with the anticipation of selecting horseflesh, even if it was simply to hire. She arrived to the sound of her cousin's laughter, and found her with Harriet, admiring a bouquet of creamy roses, which had been delivered with an accompanying note from Lord Bollington.

'See, cousin, I have made a conquest already, upon a little flattery and a single dance.' Susan was obviously jubilant.

'Who are they from, may I enquire?' asked Sophy, calmly.

'Why, from Bollington. The heir to a marquessate, and at little more than a snap of the fingers,' crowed Susan, leaning to take in the scent of the flowers.

'Whilst I hate to burst this particular bubble, Susan, a bunch of roses is . . . a bunch of roses, not an offer for your hand. I might also add that treating your "conquests" as though shooting pheasant is not appealing.' Sophy sounded repressive, and Susan pulled a face.

'Just because you cannot "bag" a man, there is no need to sound like some stuffy aunt.'

Sophy kept her temper, just. She gazed down at her cousin with a stare so chill that Susan actually squirmed.

'That, Susan, shows both your extreme youth and your total lack of manners. You will retire to your room until we take tea at four.'

'You are not my aunt.'

'No, but in her absence, I stand in her stead. Or would you prefer that I inform her of your behaviour?'

Susan scowled, tossed her head and sniffed.

'I have a headache.'

With which she withdrew, leaving Sophy seething.

'They are nice flowers,' offered Harriet, placatingly, 'and you cannot blame her for feeling elated at receiving them.'

'They are, and if she had expressed one word which showed that Viscount Bollington had made an impression upon her feelings, I would have been delighted for her. But you heard her, Harry, she crowed at the success because he was a "conquest" made easily. I try to be charitable, for she has had little experience of thinking of anyone but herself, but I think her heart so buried it will take a lot for her to discover it beneath the vanity, and she may yet do so too late.' She sighed, her happiness deflated. 'Oh, and I am engaged with Sir Esmond Fawley to pick ourselves hacks for the duration of our visit. I had meant to ask Susan if she wished to accompany me, for I know that you simply want a neat animal with good manners and no vices, but all this with the flowers put it from my head. I shall ask her at tea, and then send a note to Sir Esmond.'

'How came you to make this arrangement, Sophy?'

'Oh, he was out riding in Hyde Park when I went for a walk to clear my head. Do not worry, I had Samuel in attendance. I do not forget the proprieties.'

'I liked Sir Esmond,' remarked Harriet, looking sidelong at her sister. 'His voice is slow but his wits are not.'

'Yes, he is quick, and the drawl is not exaggerated.' Sophy laughed. 'It is nice to know that there is at least one gentleman, besides Tyneham, who will be happy to stand up with me.'

'You forget Lord Rothley, Sophy.'

'Hmmm, I do not know for certain that Lord Rothley is a gentleman.'

It could not be said that when Sophy did manage to catch her mother alone, Lady Chelmarsh gave her daughter any reason to condemn Lord Rothley as a scoundrel. By the same token, and in a very non-specific way, she remained keen that the girls did not put themselves 'in his way'. Sophy was writing the list of those to whom she should send out invitations to the Chelmarsh party, and asked whether she should omit him.

'Oh dear, that is so very awkward. His poor mother was such a nice woman, too, and had so much to put up with. I would vastly prefer not to do so, but that in itself might lead to talk. I wish he were elsewhere, and most certainly that you had not been introduced. I mean, there are plenty of gentlemen with whom none of you have yet stood up. Plenty.'

Sophy felt as if this were somehow laid at her door.

'But Mama, I could not have known he was not bon Ton. He was a guest at Lady Orpington's and I am sure that—'

'I do not blame you, Sophronia, not at all. You could not have known . . . And he is received everywhere. His Ton is not in question but there are reasons . . .' Lady Chelmarsh did not look her first-born in the eye, but focussed upon a Dresden shepherdess in a particularly coy pose, adorning the mantelshelf.

'Mama, I am not a girl in her first Season. Do you not think I might be told the truth of the situation. I shall neither swoon nor—'

'No, Sophronia, there are some things which I really feel I may not discuss with you. Suffice to say that it is terribly important that you, and especially Susan, are not seen in his company. The damage it might do . . .'

'Are you saying we must not even acknowledge him?' Sophy was confused, for he had not seemed at all unpopular with either the other gentlemen present, or indeed the ladies, at Lady Orpington's. She had seen hopeful mothers introduce him to their daughters, and if

72

he was so desperate a man, why should they do so?

'No, you must not make it that obvious. It would be almost as bad . . .' Lady Chelmarsh did not elaborate as to why. 'I simply do not want you to encourage him.'

'Do we refuse to dance with him?'

'I . . . It would be better if you did not, but of course it might be awkward . . . Oh dear, it is so complicated.' Lady Chelmarsh wrung her hands. 'And so we are back to the question of whether we should invite him to our party. Would it look too obvious if we did not? Oh dear.'

'Please, Mama, do not agitate yourself. Susan is, I am sure, aiming far higher than a viscount, and will not make an exhibition of herself over Lord Rothley. She received roses from Bollington this morning and is massively buoyed up by it.'

Lady Chelmarsh shook her head at that, but took some comfort.

'And Rothley will inherit but an earldom. I never thought to be relieved by Susan's mercenary mind.'

'Will he? I did not know.' Sophy was not particularly interested in his lineage. 'I never came across him in London before, but Sir Esmond Fawley said that he had been abroad, following the death of his mother. Oh, is that, I wonder, where his reputation fell by the wayside?'

Her mama ignored the question, and took up instead the name of Sir Esmond Fawley.

'Now there is a gentleman. Reserved, of course, not one to let his feelings become engaged, but always polite.'

'I am so glad that you do at least approve of one of

my dancing partners, then, Mama, especially as I am going, probably with Susan, to select hacks under his aegis tomorrow.'

'Goodness. You did not mention this last night, Sophronia.'

'The arrangement was made this morning, Mama.'

Sophy told her mother of the encounter in Hyde Park. Lady Chelmarsh listened, and privately thought that, to her total surprise, Lord Tyneham might have a rival in the offing. It was more than she could ever have hoped for her woefully tall daughter.

Ironically, both gentlemen under discussion in Hill Street were later to be found at Limmer's as members of a party enjoying a convivial and female-free evening where the gentlemen might enjoy a good English dinner, and discuss horseflesh and the animals to watch as the flat racing season developed. The party was relaxed, with much laughter over the tale of Mr Hubert Apperley's 'system', which involved betting on horses according to the letters of the alphabet, so that at his first meeting of the season he placed them upon animals beginning with the letter A, and at the next only those beginning with B. As Lord Rothley remarked, he might find very few bets to place when he reached the letter X. Several of the gentlemen about the table tried to come up with possible names for horses beginning with X, but only managed Xerxes and Xenophobe.

'As well to stick a pin in the race card,' declared Mr

Tyrley, debating whether to take more apple pudding, or essay the peaches in brandy.

'If it did not count as tampering, I should say he would do better simply sticking a pin in the horse direct,' responded Sir Esmond Fawley, 'As I recall, Apperley's "system" last year was based upon selecting horses with a white stocking on the off hind. You will note that his losses outweighed his winnings, as usual.'

'What system would you advise, then, Fawley?' Lord Rothley twisted the stem of his wine glass between thumb and fingers, and gazed into the dark liquid as if it were Delphic.

'Me? Simple. I never bet upon any horse I have not seen run before, and I do not trust "certainties from a knowing source".'

'You n-never b-bet upon m-m-maidens?' enquired Lord Marsden, with some difficulty.

'Never, Marsden. Why is it do you think I am still unmarried?' There was much ribald laughter. 'They are so damned predictably unpredictable.'

'And not up to your weight?' Lord Pinkney, passing their table, could not resist.

'Oh, I would not say that, Pinkney. I am renowned for my good seat and light hands.'

The riposte was made lightly, but the gleam in Sir Esmond's eye was not entirely friendly. Sir Esmond placed the occasional bet, and liked to attend the most prestigious race meetings of the year. Pinkney was a gamester to the core, and waged sums on everything from cockfights to cards with a devil-may-care attitude in all things, which marked him as 'dangerous'. That he frequently lived in dun territory was no secret, but it seemed that just at the present his pockets were not to let.

'Laid a monkey on Just As I Said at twenty to one, and it romped home by five lengths,' whispered Mr Tyrley to Lord Marsden, 'when you would have thought Synopsis would have been unbeatable.'

They shook their heads at the mysteries of fate.

'Then his creditors will be presenting their bills again shortly, no doubt,' drawled Sir Esmond.

'I rather doubt that Pinkney will, er, "waste" any more of his winnings than completely necessary upon debts of any sort.' Lord Rothley added. There then followed a lively debate on what counted as 'pressing'.

It was some time in the early hours when Sir Esmond Fawley left to seek his bed, and Lord Rothley offered his companionship part way, since they resided in adjacent streets. Neither gentleman was entirely sober, but was feeling pleasantly friendly towards the world at large, and could walk without weaving or staggering to any noticeable degree. In this slightly uninhibited mood, Lord Rothley took Sir Esmond's arm as they turned south from Berkeley Square, and voiced the thought then uppermost in his head.

'Talking of fillies . . .'

'Were we?'

'Mmmm, at some point, yes. Talking of them . . .

Wondered if any of this Season's maidens had caught your eye, dear fellow.'

'Saw Carshalton's filly, Three Wishes, at—'

'No, not four legs . . . two . . . Never saw a horse at Almack's.' This was irrefutable. 'Just wondered. Not often you take to the floor and yet . . . Danced with both Chelmarsh's daughters t'other night.'

'Not sure why I did, but I am escorting Lady Soapy to hire horses tomorr . . . today.'

'Lady Soapy!' Lord Rothley choked.

'Soapy?'

'You just called her "Lady Soapy".'

'Did I? Mistake. Slip of the tongue, you know. Tell you what, Rothley, that second bottle of claret was a bad move. Not even that good.'

'Funny the way these things occur to one after the event. Pity they don't beforehand. Save a lot of bother. Ooh look, this is where I live. Would invite you in for a nightcap, but to be frank, think I might just fall asleep. Goodnight, Fawley. Happy horse hunting.'

Lord Rothley raised a hand in friendly valediction and the two gentlemen parted, Lord Rothley to dream of dancing horses, Lady Sophronia Hadlow, and a bar of soap.

CHAPTER SIX

S IR ESMOND FAWLEY EVINCED NO SIGN OF THE previous evening's inebriation when he was admitted to the Chelmarsh residence the following day at half past eleven. With little expectation of ladies being prompt, he was most surprised to find the Lady Sophronia Hadlow and Miss Tyneham pulling on their gloves and ready for an almost immediate departure.

'Yes, you had thought you would be kicking your heels for a good quarter hour, Sir Esmond, I have no doubt, but one of my least feminine traits is a habit of keeping to time. Ought I to apologise?' Sophy curtsied as she spoke, and he returned the compliment with a bow that took in Susan, who was intrigued by her cousin's ability to be so natural with a member of the opposite sex, and not 'do' anything. Sir Esmond was smiling, interested, and

Sophy had not batted one eyelash, moved one muscle to create that response. Susan did not understand it at all. The voice of calculation told her that she was still looking at a woman who had not found a husband in several Seasons, but she could see, could sense, amity. Calculation snorted and dismissed 'amity'. What use was amity if it did not bring a man to heel and leave him begging for acknowledgement.

'Susan?' Sophy spoke her name a second time. 'You were wool gathering.'

'I am sorry.' Susan coloured. 'I was . . . trying to remember something.'

'Just try to remember you are not a member of Astley's circus and choose a horse that will behave itself. Now, let us be on our way.'

Sophy was not knowledgeable about the availability of horses for hiring in Mayfair, but Sir Esmond, with years of experience in Town, had selected, among the most convenient stables, the two where one was not likely to encounter ewe necks, wall eyes or general slugs. They were accompanied by Deeping, Lady Chelmarsh's head groom, both as a nod to the proprieties and for practical purposes. Sophy secretly thought him a man very unlikely to be persuaded by Susan's 'charms', and she could not guarantee, absolutely, that Sir Esmond would not waver if her cousin put on the full performance.

The proprietor of the stables was only too pleased to show off his animals with the prospect of their being retained for the Season. Whilst his initial comments were addressed to Sir Esmond, he swiftly recognised that the tall lady was the one most important to the decision making. Her first thought was to select a mount for Harriet, who enjoyed riding but not doing anything daring. Harriet liked to hack but not to hunt. Mr Cannings listened to the requirements and had three horses trotted out for inspection. The first made Jeremiah Deeping suck his teeth and sniff, being, in that worthy's muttered opinion, so staid it would take her ladyship an hour to get it to move, and it overreached. The second appealed to Sophy, having an intelligent eye, and an interest in the yard about it, but Deeping regretted that whoever had ridden it recently had ruined its mouth. Thankfully the third, a neat little gelding with a contented demeanour, was passed as just right. For herself, Sophy required something taller, and with a little more spirit. There were few mounts used to a side-saddle that fitted the bill. Fortunately, the one that Mr Cannings suggested, a bay mare that came out upon her toes, being, as Mr Cannings admitted, not hired out as frequently and merely exercised by one of his lads, received the Deeping nod.

Sir Esmond might have been bored, but he found watching the efficiency of Lady Sophy and the almost unconscious way that Miss Tyneham managed to attract the attention of three stable lads, a man returning a cob, and Mr Cannings himself, better than a box at the play. Lady Sophy was sensible, and he rather admired her coolness. He also thought she had wit as well as wits.

Miss Tyneham was, on the face of it – and a very pretty but brazen face it was – the sort of girl from whom any sane man should actually run away, being a nightmare in muslin. He had a shrewd idea that she did not truly understand exactly what she stirred in the opposite sex, at least he sincerely hoped that was the case. There were, of course, ladies among the ranks of the upper ten thousand who were, at heart, if they possessed such things, simply better dressed and perfumed strumpets. Miss Tyneham gave that impression and yet her age and the very aggressive way in which she showed off her dubious tricks reminded him of a child dressing up and pretending. He wondered why she felt the need to do so. From what Lady Sophy had said, he gathered she had had no curbs upon her, and was thoroughly spoilt. That explained some things, but not all. He watched her preen. She believed she had these men eating out of her hand, and did not feel flattered; it was more that she felt victorious. It was most curious. She also could not see that what she was really arousing was not a desire to do anything she might command. That, he considered, meant she was potentially putting herself in danger. She turned at that moment, saw him regarding her in wry amusement and consideration, and her head went up. Her look commanded: admire me. He shook his head, and his smile broadened. Miss Tyneham glared at him.

'Have you anything specific in mind, Susan?' Sophy enquired of her cousin, and caught the flash of Susan's angry eyes at Sir Esmond.

'I want a beast with some fire beneath me,' declared Susan, tossing her head.

Mr Cannings swallowed rather hard and felt the day had become rather warm in an instant.

'I doubt they stable dragons in London,' murmured Sir Esmond, provocatively.

Miss Tyneham made a sound akin to a high-pitched growl, but did not look at him.

'I do not want some plodder. I can ride, not just sit on a horse that puts one foot in front of the other. Show me something exciting.'

Mr Cannings was caught. The tall lady's expression told him he should obey sense and ignore the young lady, but she was . . . magnificent. The assertive confidence, the flashing eyes and heightened colour, combined to hold him in thrall. Of course, he did not have the sort of mettlesome mount she clearly envisaged, since hiring out an animal that would be unmanageable to anyone less than an excellent horseman or woman, and risking retribution if anyone suffered injury, would put him out of business. He called for the liveliest mount he owned, and one which was sometimes ridden by older and more substantially dimensioned ladies used to hunting, and hoped that the young lady would not be too disparaging.

The former was a moody beast, inclined to kick out at the stable lads when out of humour, but today clearly at peace with the world. The lady curled her lip. The other was a handsome animal, with an arrogance to the carriage of its head, but too big and strong for a young lady of her

82

stature. Susan eyed it speculatively, and saw potential. She would attract attention upon a horse like that, and if it was not going to show off her skills in controlling wildness, it would mark her out as being upon an impressively built beast that other young ladies would be afraid to ride. A slow smile dawned upon her face.

'Your ladyship would not be advised to take him,' declared Deeping, grimly. 'You are too light for him, and controlling such . . .' He shook his head.

'I did not request your opinion. Trot him up and down for me.' She was imperious.

The stable lad obeyed instantly.

'I asked Deeping to come with us because of his experience, cousin. You would do well to listen.' Sophy heard herself, and resented that she was forced to sound like a censorious aunt.

'But my brother will be paying for the hiring of the horse, and if you will not arrange for it to be kept in my uncle's stables, I shall come here.'

'Really, Miss Tyneham, the horse is simply too large.' Sir Esmond added his vote against.

Miss Tyneham did not appear to hear him.

Sophy had not considered that she had no veto, but this was the case. She was tempted to tell her cousin that it was her decision but if she broke her neck, it was her own silly fault, but that would sound petty. Instead, she spoke to Deeping.

'Thank you, Deeping. I accept your assessment, but if Miss Tyneham ignores advice, it is upon her own head.

I assume that there is no problem accommodating three horses in our stables?'

'None, my lady. There are but two pairs of carriage horses at present.'

'And Mr Cannings, if we feed and lodge the animals, I take it there will be a reduction in the charge?'

Mr Cannings, still slightly overwhelmed by Miss Tyneham, nodded.

'Good, then I am happy to sign an undertaking to lease them upon a monthly basis. You may send them round this afternoon.' Sophy was keen to leave what she found to be an embarrassing situation. 'Thank you for your assistance, Mr Cannings.'

She glanced at Sir Esmond. He did not look shocked, outraged or disgusted. If anything, he looked mildly entertained. Sophy resented being reduced to 'entertainment', though she could scarcely blame the gentleman.

'You may rely upon my discretion, ma'am,' he murmured as he offered his arm to her, seeing her face and thinking she feared her cousin's behaviour might become known.

'Oh, I do not doubt it, sir, but regret that I should be reliant upon it. She makes me feel old you know, even older than my years.'

He laughed, and Susan, who had been watching 'her' horse led back to its box, frowned.

'Your years, ma'am? You make it sound as if you numbered those of Methuselah.'

'Not that many, it is true, but enough to mark me as "no longer youthful", and trying to hold my cousin in check makes me feel the equivalent of my own mama. I shall start needing regular restorative naps!'

'You are looking in a distorting mirror, ma'am, I assure you.' He dropped his voice. 'You are confusing years and maturity. I think your cousin very young in that, younger than her number of birthdays may declare.'

Sophy looked at Sir Esmond with respect.

'How . . . perspicacious of you.'

'Not really. You know, I think perhaps she makes me feel old too.' The smile became very nearly a grin.

Sophy's lips twitched, and it was a lady in far better humour who invited him into the house in Hill Street to take a glass of wine and a light nuncheon in thanks for his putting himself at their disposal. He wavered, but Lady Chelmarsh added her entreaties, looking rather too keen that he remain, in her daughter's opinion.

'And why should I not be pleased, Sophronia, dear?' she asked when he departed. 'To be sure he is a very nice man, and tall too. He does not seem to mind you being unnatural.'

Sophy choked.

'Unnaturally tall, I meant,' explained her mother, hastily.

'Mama, he has stood up for one dance with me and been gentlemanly enough to offer assistance this morning.'

'"From little acorns", my dear, and as I recall we

never got as far as even an acorn before.'

'Thank you for that encouraging thought, Mama.'

'But it is encouraging, Sophronia. There is Sir Esmond, being agreeable, and then there is Tyneham, and—'

'I would not marry my cousin Tyneham were he the last man on earth,' declared Sophy, belligerently.

'Sadly, Sophronia, for your chances of marriage it is possible he may as well be.'

Sophy went up to her room to change for the afternoon in a chastened frame of mind.

She did not encounter either of the gentlemen Lady Chelmarsh had lined up as putative suitors at Lady Madditson's party that evening, but did find herself next to the 'dangerous' Lord Rothley. She actually jumped when he spoke to her.

'I am sorry, did I take you by surprise, ma'am?'

'Yes, my lord, you did. You have an unnerving ability to appear as if conjured out of the floor.'

'Should I fold my arms in a genie-like pose and offer you three wishes, perhaps?' He smiled, and, whether Mama was looking or not, Sophy smiled back. It was simply impossible not to do so. 'Or would you like me to engage a herald to announce my approach?'

'You are roasting me, sir.'

'Gently, ma'am, and over the lowest of heats, I assure you.'

'Now you are treating me as a . . . a joint of meat. That is hardly flattering.'

'I did not initiate the culinary analogy, Lady Sophy. You did.'

This was terrible. There was the wolfish twinkle again, and oh, how nice it was to—goodness, was she flirting?

'Only very politely,' he confirmed, gravely.

'Oh, my goodness!' Her hand went to her cheek, and she coloured. 'I didn't just say that out lou—'

'Do you speak your thoughts often? If so, I promise not to reveal this trait to others, but I will pay extra attention to whatever you say in the future. Not that I was ignoring you thus far, of course.' The wolfish look was replaced by something more kindly. 'Shall I procure you a glass of champagne, or the fruit cup, if you prefer? I have discommoded you. Forgive me.'

He was dangerous. Sophy recognised it now, for when he made his supplication like that, she could forgive him almost anything. She glanced to where Lady Chelmarsh was engrossed in conversation with an elderly and rotund gentleman. Taking refreshments with Lord Rothley had not been specifically banned, and it did mean Mama need not see that she and he had been in conversation. It was duplicitous but would upset that lady the less.

'Thank you, champagne would be very nice.'

He bowed, and threaded his way towards a servant bearing a salver of glasses. Sophy watched him as he all but disappeared from view, his dark head nodding as he acknowledged acquaintances as he completed his 'quest'. Whilst not as tall as Sir Esmond, his presence was not so much to do with his physicality as an indefinable quality to him. He returned with two glasses.

'Here is your restorative champagne, ma'am. You need not look concerned, for I am sure none but I heard or saw anything.'

In this he was only partially correct.

It was at this point that Susan bustled up, giving Lord Rothley her widest-eyed attention, and disregarding her cousin.

'My lord, I declare, what could you have said to put my unflappable cousin to the blush? She is long past maidenly confusion.'

'You ought to have brought me hot milk, not champagne,' murmured Sophy. 'And where did I leave my ear trumpet?'

Lord Rothley's lips twitched. Susan responded as if she had made the sally.

'It is unkind of you to unsettle her. I think the least you can do is leave her in peace and partner me for the next dance. Sir Julius Wragby was my last partner, and he was not nearly so good a dancer as you are, my lord.'

Sophy, knowing the strength of her mother's objection to Lord Rothley, felt both guilty and in a predicament. She could not suddenly be aloof and cold with him after the last few minutes. The only answer that came to her mind was not what she would wish, but her only solution.

'But cousin, Lord Rothley has just solicited my aged

hand for the next dance, presumably before I am reduced to so geriatric a state that anything beyond creeping slowly across the floor is beyond me. Please hold my champagne for me.'

Lord Rothley did not, by so much as a muscle, indicate surprise at the lie. Susan looked thwarted, but not vanquished, and took the glass automatically.

'Then, sir, I hope my cousin does not tread upon your toes so much that you cannot lead me out for the following dance. I know it is rather forward of me to ask you, but you are so obliging I am sure you will take pity upon me.' She gave him a look which was an odd mixture of butter would not melt in her mouth and clumsy adolescent coquetry. He was not sure why he gave in to it, but there was something about Miss Tyneham that drew him to her.

'Pity was never such pleasure, Miss Tyneham. I would be delighted if you would honour me with the next available dance. Now, Lady Sophy, if you lean upon my arm, we might make it to the floor before the set finishes forming up, do you not think?'

He smiled at her and offered his arm. He said nothing until facing away from Miss Tyneham.

'So, are you going to tell me why you cut your cousin out? I would swear you had no inclination for dancing until the irrepressible little madam treated us to a performance.' His lips twitched.

'I had as well ask you, sir, why you let her have her way?' Sophy could not give him a logical answer.

'To tell you the truth, I am not entirely sure. There is something bizarrely attractive about such repellent behaviour, perhaps.'

'So you do not intend to become one of her acolytes, Lord Rothley?'

'Me? No. Was that your fear? Are you dancing with me to "protect" your cousin? That makes me wonder how I have been portrayed to you, ma'am? As a wolf that preys upon little lambs, even bold ones?' A frown crossed his features.

Sophy was glad the dance parted them before she had to answer. It gave her a chance to formulate a response.

'I have not heard such a calumny, my lord.'

'There is that large, silent "but" again, ma'am.'

'I . . . I was trying to prevent her foisting herself upon you.'

'By "foisting" yourself in her stead? That does not ring quite true.'

'She can be very trying.' Sophy did not look him in the eye.

'Oh, I have little doubt of that, but, you know, I do not think I look the sort of man that could not handle a minx like Miss Tyneham. Do I?'

'No.' She could not add to the lies.

'Which leads us back to my first question, not that I think you wish to answer it. I wish I knew why.'

She looked at him then, and the perplexity on his face seemed so very genuine, as though he really did regret that she did not trust him enough to tell the truth.

'I am glad to dance with you, you know. Your cousin makes it a pantomime; you make it as natural as breathing.' He smiled.

She blushed at words and tone combined.

'Yet you accepted the pantomime.'

'Yes. You might thank me too, for if I had refused, how long would you have had her complaints ringing in your ears that you had "stolen" her partner?'

'I am developing a thick skin when it comes to my cousin.'

'In all other situations I hope it remains as it is now.'

The blush deepened.

'My lord, I am unused to compliments. You should retain them for such as appreciate them.'

'You think me insincere. I can see I will have much to do to persuade you otherwise.'

'I beg you will not put yourself to the trouble, my lord.'

The comment came out sharply, for the thought that he might seek her company the more would fly in the face of her mother's instructions. He looked hurt.

'That has given me my *congé*, has it not. My apologies, ma'am.'

They parted, moved through other couples and came together once more for the end of the dance. She looked not so much angered, he thought, as beleaguered. He did not understand. When he led her to where Susan stood, eager to thrust the champagne glass back into her cousin's hand, her thanks were mechanical. Dancing with the vivacious Miss Tyneham, whose every signal was perfectly clear, was a lot easier, if less fulfilling, and he had to admit the girl could be very winning when she tried.

'Sophronia! Did you not attend to my words?' hissed Lady Chelmarsh, coming up and laying a hand on her daughter's arm. 'Not only did I just catch you dancing with That Man, but now you pass him on to your cousin, when I specifically asked you to avoid him.'

'I danced with him, Mama, in an attempt to keep him from dancing with Susan, but short of creating a very embarrassing scene there was nothing more I could do.' She sounded terse. Her head was beginning to ache and the evening one of gold turning to dross. 'I am sorry, Mama, if I appear disobedient. My head is starting to throb. Might I have your leave to call our carriage and go home? There is no need for you to drag Harriet or Susan away from the entertainment.'

Lady Chelmarsh, who had been drawing up further angry comments, relented. Sophronia rarely complained of a headache.

'Oh, my dear, try lavender water upon your pillow. Is it very bad? I would come, but Harriet has secured the next three dances to my certain knowledge, and Lady Boscombe has promised me the juiciest of *on dits* about Cornelia Sempringham. By all means retire. Just send the carriage back again to await us.'

Thus it was that when Lord Rothley brought a flushed and proud Miss Tyneham off the floor, it was to find her aunt where her cousin had been, and to the intelligence that Lady Sophronia Hadlow had gone home, unwell. He expressed the very genuine wish that her indisposition might be transitory, and withdrew, with the worrying thought that he had been instrumental in her sudden decline.

CHAPTER SEVEN

Sophy's headache meant that sleep eluded her for some time. The combination of the throbbing at her temples and the disquieting thoughts within her mind did not facilitate rest in any way. She lay in the darkness, prey to guilt, confusion, and a weird, elated feeling which concerned her more than the rest.

She had not been entirely honest with her mama. She had danced with Lord Rothley to prevent him doing so with Susan, and failed, but before that . . . Politeness meant that she would have had to exchange civilities with him when he spoke to her, but it had seemed so very natural to respond as she had, to flirt with him. She did not consider herself flirtatious, so it must have been him encouraging her to be so. He had that lupine smile and the appreciative look in his grey eyes. She chastised herself, for she had noted the colour of his eyes, imprinted them upon her mind's eye. She was being a fool. Mama would not want her charges to keep at arm's length from the heir to an earldom for no good reason. She had not heard that he was living under a mountain of debt, and so the only logical cause must be that he was the sort of man who made a woman the object of his gallantry to the point where she was besotted, took advantage, and then turned his back upon her. He had the attributes of such a man; the wolfish smile, the ability to make one feel the centre of his attention, and girlishly excited.

So she was not just duplicitous, she was a fool, for she was beginning to slide down the slope towards her heart beating the faster just because she knew him to be in the same room, wanting his eyes to meet hers, wanting him to engage in the light-hearted but quick-witted badinage that had thrilled her at the party. He did not act as if everything had to be explained, but accepted that she could keep pace with him. An image of her cousin Tyneham intruded. There was a man who would treat every woman as though a child. She banished him. Mama might say he could be her last chance of marriage, but spinsterhood was preferable to facing such a man at breakfast, or . . . She shuddered. Mama also had hopes of Sir Esmond, upon the very flimsiest of evidence. He did not treat her as a child, and she liked him, thus far. He was companionable, friendly, and showed signs of having surprisingly acute understanding. Looking at it calmly, which was not altogether easy at two o'clock in the morning and with a sick headache, an offer from Sir Esmond would not be unwelcome, except for the fact that it was not his image that appeared in her dreams.

Undoubtedly she was the idiot, then, to even consider that she would reject companionship, friendship, comfort, and the potential for love for the sake of, and her brain echoed her mother's tone, 'That Man'.

When sleep eventually claimed her it was not restful, but it did mean that Sophy, normally enjoying the day by half past nine, slept until eleven, and came downstairs looking, in her mama's depressing but accurate words, 'a trifle hag-ridden'.

'I do hope you are not going down with something contagious, Sophronia, just when the Season is about to start properly. Of course, Harriet had the mumps and measles when young, and the chickenpox, blessedly, never left but the one mark upon her, and that where no public gaze may see it. What a pity you had to leave early last night. Harriet created quite an impression upon Emily Cowper, not but that I was relying upon Sally Fane, Lady Jersey rather, to procure us admission to Almack's. Fortunately, Susan was on her best behaviour at that point and not in view either. Bollington was introducing her to his mother, which is a terribly good sign, as long as Lady Wetherden does not watch her too closely hereafter.'

Sophy noted that any concern for her eldest daughter's

health had now been superseded in her mama's mind by the 'business' of the Season, getting Harriet and Susan suitably attached. Since neither Harriet nor Susan were likely to surface before noon, Lady Chelmarsh felt that she could speak quite freely about 'progress' thus far, without either damsel interrupting.

'For it would do neither any good to mention things to them at this stage. Of course, it is different with you, Sophronia. I need not fear that what I might say would go to your head. You are a sensible girl, and fully aware of the situation in which you find yourself.'

Ah, thought Sophy, if her mama did but know the situation. How could one possibly explain even the most tentative attraction to the very man in all London against whom one had been warned?

The afternoon brought a call from one of Lady Chelmarsh's old friends, which Susan described, not inaccurately, as the sort guaranteed to bring on a fit of the dismals, since all she did was enumerate their mutual acquaintances who were wasting away from diseases unspecified, or had already cast the rest of their family into blacks. As if that were not enough, they then received a visit from Lord Tyneham. Susan stiffened immediately.

'I hear Bollington introduced Susan to his mother last night. That is very good, very good indeed.' He rubbed his hands together.

'We did not see you there, Tyneham.' Lady Chelmarsh regarded the hand rubbing with disfavour.

'Oh no, a friend of mine mentioned it when we bumped into each other today. I thought you would like to know I have made it known, discreetly, of course, that she comes with good Settlements. Not that Bollington is short of the readies, but it is helpful.'

Susan was almost grinding her teeth, and Sophy could understand why. Being referred to as 'she' as if an animal for sale would annoy the most even-tempered of young ladies. Lady Chelmarsh looked even more displeased.

'You have done what, Tyneham?'

He looked suddenly less assured.

'I . . . Er, I simply made sure that it would circulate that my sister does not come dowerless.'

'I think that could safely be assumed anyway, Tyneham.'

'But my father did not—'

'Since everyone knows your estates are in good order, they will know that your sister is not some church mouse.' Lady Chelmarsh interrupted, with a note of finality and a glare at her nephew. If Susan, still seething, had not noticed it, Sophy had. There was an undercurrent, but she did not know of what. 'However, to bandy such things about in your club, where no doubt you made the information public, shows a sad lack of sense on your part, Tyneham. There will be those who will wonder why you stated the obvious, and those whom one would not wish to encourage, who will prick up their ears at the scent of a potential heiress, since you make so much of it. It was an act of stupidity,

Tyneham, the worst that you could have done.'

Lord Tyneham looked uncomfortable. He disliked censure, especially from an aunt. He set about a rather convoluted self-exculpatory speech to which nobody attended.

'Might I just say,' announced Susan, cutting across the end of this monologue, 'that whilst you are clearly prepared to do almost anything to get me off your hands, the feeling is mutual, and I would even entertain the most unsuitable of men if he was guaranteed to ensure my escape from your aegis.'

'Marry to disoblige me, madam, and you will get not one penny beyond the little our mother left to you.'

'Almost, brother, you persuade me to do just that,' she spat back at him.

'Susan, please. This is unseemly heat for my drawing room.' Lady Chelmarsh attempted to regain control of the situation. 'And I find these outbursts of sibling animosity unedifying, Tyneham. You will kindly remember where you are.'

Her nephew squirmed, but her niece tossed her head.

'I apologise, ma'am, but for the location, not my sentiments. I am not a commodity to be sold for the most advantageous price, nor a burden to be placed upon another's shoulders.'

Her brother half stifled his snort of disagreement with this view. Lady Chelmarsh looked at Sophy, her expression one of entreaty to do something, say something, that would part the arguing pair. The only choice was to initiate a completely different line of conversation, however odd it might sound.

'Have you a mount stabled in London, cousin? We have but yesterday obtained horses so that we may take exercise in the Park at the social hour.' Privately, Sophy would be happy to exercise at a less social hour also, but had no intention of letting her cousin know this.

'I have had my curricle brought up, but not my hack. You should have asked my advice. I would have been happy to have assisted you.'

'Oh, we had the assistance of Sir Esmond Fawley, so we did not need yours,' murmured Susan, smiling very sweetly.

Lord Tyneham ignored this comment.

'Will you be riding later this afternoon?' He addressed Sophy.

'It is likely, for we would like to try our new mounts.'

'Then I may encounter you. I sometimes drive for an hour then.'

Sophy hoped fervently that they would not, but was to be disappointed.

Since the weather was clement, and she wished to see how her charges looked upon horseback, Lady Chelmarsh decided to order her barouche so that she might take a turn about the Park at the fashionable hour. This could not be said to have been greeted with unalloyed delight by the three young ladies, who considered walking, or at best trotting, behind the equipage most unexciting.

Her ladyship was on the point of leaving the house when a letter was delivered, franked by her son-in-law. She dithered, opened it, and looked worried. The girls were already outside and mounted, so she came out and approached Sophy, looking up at her daughter.

'I have just received a letter from Tattersett. I really think I am going to have to go to Frances immediately, Sophronia.'

'Has something happened, Mama?'

'No, not exactly, but . . . take your ride. I shall have to make plans, of course. It is at the most awkward moment, and I had hoped to remain in Town another month but . . . I shall have things ordered in my mind by your return.'

Sophy would have dismounted and abandoned riding, but her mama assured her it would be better if she could think 'without interruption', and so reluctantly, the trio set off as the barouche was driven back to the stables.

'Poor Frances. I do hope nothing awful has happened,' murmured Harriet, rather pale.

'I think if anything too dreadful had occurred, Mama would have said and been less composed. Perhaps Frances is just in need of maternal support rather more than anticipated. We must not jump to terrible conclusions, Harry.' Sophy reached and squeezed her sister's gloved hand.

Susan, without any emotional involvement in the situation, was more concerned with London practicalities.

'What about our Presentation? Will we have to cancel our own party?'

'I am sure that Mama will arrange everything. Whether it is possible for me to present you I do not know, but if not, I am sure she would be able to call upon a friend such as Lady Orpington to do so in her absence. As for our own party, I am perfectly happy to act as hostess. After all, I have been at Mama's right hand throughout the preparations. Now, let us be calm and enjoy our ride as much as is possible, and at least present a facade of normality.'

They crossed into Hyde Park, where the evidence of spring was showing in every unfurling leaf. Sophy's mare was a little on her toes, and inclined to break from the trot at which Sophy held her. Sophy wanted her to know who was in control from the outset. Harriet's mount was amenable and contented enough to merely look about him and enjoy the air. She had christened him Bramble, for no better reason than, she said, it sounded gentle. Susan sniffed.

'But brambles have nasty thorns, and tear holes in one's hem.'

'I did not mean he is like a bramble. Besides, bramble jelly was always one of my favourites with nursery tea. What are you calling your horse?'

'Huge,' suggested Sophy, not entirely joking.

Harriet giggled.

'Oooh, I could call him Hugo. He was the villain in this lurid romance I read last year.'

'I sincerely hope he does not prove to be a villain today.' Sophy eyed the animal with a sense of foreboding. It was not that he looked vicious, but if he took it into his head to do as he wished, she did not see Susan having much chance of holding him back. 'Let us hope he is not afraid of children or small dogs or—'

'Cavalry officers.' Susan sighed.

'Well, I . . . oh. Oh no. Susan, for goodness' sake, do not—'

She was wasting her breath. Susan urged Hugo into a loping canter that emphasised his size and showed off her petite frame. She had been quite right that the combination was arresting. The two scarlet-coated officers who had been trotting towards them did a sharp 'eyes left' as she passed them, with the hem of her habit blowing sufficiently to give a glimpse of an elegantly booted ankle, and wheeled about. Sophy, despairing, kicked the mare on, so that at least Susan would not be in company with the unknown gentlemen alone, and called upon Harriet to keep up. Bramble clearly thought rushing was asking a lot of him, but reluctantly increased his pace.

Susan, hearing the hooves behind her, brought Hugo back to a sedate trot, and smiled to herself. The two officers came up beside her.

'I say, ma'am, you do look the most complete hand upon such an animal. How do you manage him?'

'One just has to be assertive, gentlemen.' She gave them a look which, as the one later remarked to the other, did queer things to a man's insides. It was a very promising start, but from this point she lost control of the situation. Her cousins caught up, Sophy looking ice cool and commanding.

'Good afternoon, gentlemen. I do not think we have been introduced.' Her tone implied that she was not particularly keen that they should remain long enough to perform introductions. They coloured.

Whatever they were going to say was halted by the party being hailed by another rider. Sophy turned, and tried not to let her pulse quicken. Lord Rothley, mounted upon a tidy steel grey, raised his hat to her.

'I am so sorry to be late,' he announced, quite taking her breath away with the barefaced lie. His glance took in the two young officers. 'Your servant, Kesgrave. How is your brother George?'

'Er, very well, thank you, Rothley.' The Honourable Rowland Kesgrave tried not to look juvenile, but since his elder brother had been at school with Rothley, this was not easy.

'Perhaps you would be so kind as to introduce these officers, my lord,' requested Sophy, smoothly.

'Of course, ma'am. Anything to be of use to you.' There was interrogation in his eyes. 'May I present Lieutenant Kesgrave, younger brother of Lord Kesgrave, and . . .' He raised an eyebrow at the other young man, who stammered his response.

'L-L-Lieutenant M-M-Madeley, sir.'

'Ah, Lieutenant Madeley, both of the Life Guards.

Gentlemen, may I present th[...]
fraction of a second, 'the Lady [...]
Lady Harriet Hadlow, and Miss Tyne[...]

Sophy could tell he was laughing at h[...]
him in a situation to use her much hated name.

'So, tell us, my lord, what it was that delayed yo[...]
Sophy felt the least she could do in revenge for his
mockery was to put him upon the spot.

'Del—oh the most mundane of things, ma'am.
I . . . er . . . completely forgot to equip myself with a
handkerchief, and had to turn back. I very much fear
I might have the first signs of a slight cold,' he sniffed,
rather theatrically, 'and would not wish to contaminate
others with it.'

'You would have been better to have taken to your
bed and have your man rub your chest with goose fat,
my lord.' Sophy kept a very straight face.

'You are joking?' Lord Rothley's look of utter horror
almost broke her.

'Not even roasting you over the lowest of heats, my
lord.' Her eyes held his.

His eyes narrowed at that.

'Touché, ma'am,' he murmured.

'It is quite true, my lord.' Susan was keen to involve
herself in the conversation. 'My brother swears by the
application of goose grease to the chest.'

'I think I would be more likely to swear if anyone
attempted to rub it upon any part of my anatomy.'

Harriet giggled.

and b-b-brandy

from her lip. Lord

suspicion.

have kept our . . .

even my h alth is worth risking,' he

blushed. He looked to the

were by now a little on the

ur horses look as though they
were exp   better ex   cise.'

The young   ers knew when they were being
dismissed. Lord Rothley smiled, not unkindly, and asked
that his best wishes be passed to Lord Kesgrave. Susan
cast him a look of reproach as they made their excuses
and rode on.

'Nice enough youths, but sadly, tongues wag at young
ladies who are under the escort of blades in scarlet coats.'
He was looking at Susan, but then turned to Sophy. 'I
thought perhaps you would be better without them.'

'Hence the lie.'

'The er, *ruse de guerre*, Lady Sophy, *ruse de guerre*.'

'The problem I see is that you took it upon yourself
to decide what we should or should not be seen doing,
sir. Indeed, is it better that we are seen with you?' Sophy
looked quizzically at him.

He was not quite certain that she was in jest.

'I believe so, ma'am, for there are three of you and I
am but making light conversation.'

'And the officers were not?' Susan was not appeased.

'No, they looked very much as if they were too struck by your charms to do more than make cakes of themselves, Miss Tyneham.'

'And you will not, my lord?'

'No, I will not.'

'I cannot resist a challenge,' she murmured, almost to herself.

Sophy closed her eyes and winced. When she opened them, she added a groan for good measure. Tooling a pair of matched if rather showy chestnuts towards them was Lord Tyneham, and his expression was frosty. He drew up, and acknowledged Rothley with the barest civility.

'I had not expected to find you riding unescorted, Cousin Sophronia.'

'Alas, I am as a wraith, invisible,' sighed Lord Rothley, 'or is it that you think they need an escort to protect them from me, Tyneham?' The question was direct, and the smooth voice had an edge to it.

'You are the very last man with whom I would wish them to associate.' Tyneham rose to the challenge.

'I am?'

For one moment Lord Tyneham stared at him in disbelief, and then he coloured to the roots of his hair. Sophy, looking from one to the other, was totally mystified. Lord Rothley was clearly perplexed, and her cousin acutely embarrassed. There was an exchange of glances, one which warned and one which questioned.

Lord Rothley had a slight frown, no longer of confusion, but of displeasure, almost anger.

'Whilst your views must weigh in your sister's case, cousin, I do not see that you have any right to decide with whom I might associate.'

'That, madam, is because you are a member of the more delicate and indeed frailer sex, to whom not everything need be explained.'

'Rot,' declared Susan.

Her brother cast her a look of loathing, and continued. 'By which I mean that there are some things to which it is both unnecessary and undesirable that you be privy. You cannot therefore make an informed decision.'

Sophy wondered why Lord Rothley was now so silent, as if struggling with some inner problem.

'You mean that since I am to be left ignorant I cannot do so. That is most unfair.'

'I think, Tyneham, that you have said enough.' Lord Rothley spoke slowly, and in a voice so devoid from its normal bantering tone that Sophy was stunned.

'But you—' Lord Tyneham jibbed at his horses' mouths unintentionally.

'Enough. I think we should ride on, ladies. The horses are getting cold standing about.' His look to Sophy said not to question but to obey, and without a moment's thought she did so.

'Good day to you, cousin.' She nodded at the now puce-cheeked viscount. 'Come, Harriet, Susan.'

She set the mare to canter, and was soon outpaced by Susan's bay. Lord Rothley drew alongside her.

'Will you explain to me what that was all about, my lord?'

'I regret not, ma'am.'

'You too think there are things I am too "delicate" to know?' She was angry.

'No, but I am uncertain upon several points and without certainty . . . Tyneham cannot keep pace with you, Lady Sophy. Since you are now out of his reach, I crave pardon and ask to be excused.'

The harsh edge was in his voice again, and it made her ask, tentatively, 'I am sorry if I have angered you, my lord. Have I done so?'

He smiled, but the eyes remained untouched by it.

'No, ma'am, I swear you have not. Good day to you.' He touched his hat and wheeled away.

Sophy was glad when they had completed a circuit. Harriet and Susan were discussing what had occurred, but she kept her confused thoughts to herself. Unfortunately, she was returning not to peace where she could ponder, but turmoil.

Lord Rothley rode home, shut himself in his study, and wrote a letter.

CHAPTER EIGHT

THE HILL STREET RESIDENCE WAS IN A STATE OF upheaval, and Sophy, as she had surmised, had no time to think about the events in the Park. Bembridge took her aside.

'Her ladyship's compliments, my lady, and would you attend her immediately in the green saloon. I think she did not mean for you to change from your riding dress, if I may be so bold.' He looked the very picture of the concerned family retainer, which was true enough. The rumour had already run through the house that something untoward had occurred regarding Lady Frances, as was, and he had known her from childhood.

'Thank you, Bembridge, I shall go to her at once.' She saw his worry. 'And Bembridge, I am sure the news is not of the worst sort.' She hoped she was right.

She gave him her hat, crop and gloves, with a wavering smile, and hurried up the stairs. Lady Chelmarsh was in the green saloon, seated at a small writing desk. She looked up as Sophy entered, but did not stop writing.

'Sophronia dear, there you are. Good. I am just writing to Lady Orpington. She will take Harriet and Susan when she presents Cecily at Court. I know that you could do it, my dear, but this is easier and you will have enough . . . to think about. Now, as to which invitations to—'

'Mama, before all else, please tell me why you must leave in such a hurry. What is wrong with poor Frances?'

'No doubt it is first time nerves, poor girl, but . . . She just had news of her dear friend Lady Syre, Anne Gowerton as you will remember her. Died in childbed last week, and the infant with her.'

'Oh no, how awful.'

'Well, it has shaken poor Frances to the core. Tattersett writes that he is terribly worried about her. He has tried, dear boy, to calm her, but he says she is constantly tearful, and shaking and convinced she will die, and fail him and . . . poor child, she needs me there.'

'Yes, yes, I can see that, Mama. You will not be able to return, though? She is not due for six weeks or thereabouts.'

'With all the upset, Sophronia, it is always possible that she might be confined early, and I really do not feel that I dare leave her in such a case. One can never be sure about dates. I well remember thinking your brother would not arrive until mid-May, and yet there he was, in his cradle, by the last day of April.'

'If that is so, then of course you must stay. Oh dear, and there is so much to be thought of with our party only ten days away and—'

'The preparations for our party are all in hand, and Bembridge, you know, has been instrumental in organising such things since before you were born. You need only oversee the last-minute details, and stand in my stead during the evening. Oh, and the flowers, do make sure that you yourself are happy with the placement of the arrangements. Now, I have already made a list of those invitations you must be sure to accept, my love, but you have a sensible notion of how to go on, I will give you that. I am sure that you can chaperone the girls, and people will be understanding.'

'What do I say about your absence, Mama?'

'I doubt they will ask you direct, but you may say that your sister's confinement is giving cause for concern. Selina Orpington has the truth of the thing and I have suggested she let it be known quietly. She will be happy to advise you upon any matter about which you are unsure.' Lady Chelmarsh sighed. 'Of course, it will give little opportunity for you to advance your own cause, but we both know your chances were never very strong, and perhaps Tyneham might yet . . .' She sighed again.

Sophy did not think this the moment to reveal that she thought that particular eventuality unlikely as well as unwelcome.

'I am leaving within the hour. Deeping says there is a

112

full moon and we will reach Stanmore before it gets dark and should get to Aldenham before eight.' She looked at her eldest child. 'I have the fullest confidence in you, Sophronia. It is such a pity that I did not have another few weeks to see how events were unfolding. If only one had some indication of interest. I do not count Bollington as at all certain, as yet, and with his mama in town . . . We can but hope. Do your best, Sophronia.'

'I shall, Mama.' Sophy felt as she imagined some officers must have felt during the War, upon being sent as the Forlorn Hope.

She had of course prepared herself to 'take the reins' for the latter part of the Season, but it had been assumed that, by that stage, if any young gentlemen looked likely to make an offer they would have become apparent and been given an indication as to whether or not their suit might be accepted. Yet here they were with the Season barely fully begun and their guiding hand, with many years' experience, was being withdrawn. Sophy's heart sank.

Lord Rothley spent a long time with his pen not quite making contact with the paper, and had to dip it once more into the ink. There were letters of importance in which the question was quite simple, but phrasing that question terribly difficult. This letter was one such. He had nothing firm upon which to base his question, merely circumstantial evidence, but that evidence crowded his mind. Tyneham was not a man he either liked or

113

respected, but that the man's reaction had been so starkly antagonistic indicated far more than just a vague natural antipathy. Tyneham had actually been outraged, but, being Tyneham, had then behaved like a nodcock. Lady Sophy clearly had as little idea as he himself what had caused this choler, but she was likely to make assumptions. What she would not know was the other half of the tale, and after all, it was most likely not very edifying.

If the answer came back as he expected, and he had little reason to doubt that it would, he was in a predicament. He threw the fourth draft the way of its predecessors, into the flames of the fire which burnt merrily in the grate, at odds with his mood. He drew another sheet towards him, sighed, and began again.

It was twenty minutes later that he achieved something he thought worthy of his signature. He sealed the letter and addressed it, noting the irony of the title, to the Right Honourable, the Earl of Woodhall, at a snug little address in Vienna.

Within the closed circle of Society, information spread like wildfire, whether one wished it to do so or not. Thus, two evenings later, Sophy had to listen to the best wishes mixed with tales of past deliveries, mostly difficult, from a dozen ladies expressing their sympathy for young Lady Tattersett. If all were to be believed, such a thing as a straightforward birth was as rare as hen's teeth. Sophy bore it all with a good grace. After all, everyone was being kind.

That her 'elevation' to permanent chaperone might constrain her own pleasures was accepted. She would be able to dance only very occasionally, and when both her charges had suitable partners. She resigned herself to the gossipy company of the mamas. Lady Orpington sat with her some time, whilst Susan began the very dangerous ploy of trying to make Lord Bollington jealous by flirting with Lord John Hythe, and Harriet was engaged with the Misses Tichborne.

'You need not trouble yourself, my dear. Your mama explained the situation to me, and I assure you the Presentation will be no trouble to me. As for any other little worries you may have, do feel free to consult me as you would her. You are such a sensible young woman, and have enough experience not to be cast into a panic by nothings, but there may be some point where you are unsure how to proceed and, well, you know my direction.'

'Thank you, ma'am, I shall endeavour not to pester you with trifles, but shall most certainly call upon you if at a loss. My biggest concern is one where, unfortunately, I think only my Mama could direct me, and that would be if any gentlemen showed signs of being particular in their attentions to my sister or cousin.'

'Ah yes, that might be difficult for you. Mind you, if Bollington remains as interested . . .'

'Having seen my cousin out of the corner of my eye during our conversation, ma'am, I would not be too sure that my cousin Susan is not at this very minute putting him off completely.'

Lady Orpington's gaze followed Sophy's.

'Oh dear.'

'Yes, if your ladyship will excuse me, I shall attempt to prevent a disaster.'

Sophy rose, and glided over to where Susan was being more than a little obvious. Lord John Hythe was mesmerised, and Sophy had to repeat her question before he gave himself a shake and answered her.

'My sister Cassington, ma'am? Oh yes, she is well, but my niece and nephew both had the croup or some such, over the winter, and it caused her much concern, and she is awaiting a happy event in June.'

Susan glared at her cousin as she steered Lord John into polite conversation about mutual acquaintance, and thereby distracted him from herself. Knowing none of those mentioned, she was set on the periphery of the exchange. Her expression became sulky, but underwent a change as she espied Sir Esmond Fawley and Lord Rothley in conversation a few yards' distant. She waved her fingers at them and smiled. Lord Rothley might have been in her bad books but two days since, but he could still be useful.

'Do we answer the summons, do you think?' murmured Rothley, indicating Miss Tyneham's gesticulations with a small movement of the head.

'What game is she playing tonight, I wonder?' asked Sir Esmond, trying not to smile in a way the young lady would undoubtedly find patronising.

'Bizarrely, she seems to be doing her utmost to put young Bollington off, which strikes me as very odd.' Lord Rothley frowned.

'Found someone better?' volunteered Sir Esmond, acknowledging her with a nod. 'Shall we be brave and find out?'

He moved through the throng towards her, Lord Rothley following. Her smile was, it had to be admitted, the sort that stopped a man in his tracks.

'Sir Esmond,' she crooned, 'and the censorious Lord Rothley, who dislikes scarlet coats.' Her gaze challenged; the words teased.

'What's that? Dislikes scarlet . . .' Sir Esmond looked at Lord Rothley in surprise.

'No, Miss Tyneham, you misconstrue my words. I do not dislike them, I merely advocated that you should not like them so easily.'

'Perhaps you were jealous?' she quizzed him, and flirted with her fan.

'I think not, ma'am, but you see most gentlemen do not suffer from jealousy early in an acquaintanceship. If the lady shows interest elsewhere, well, it would be unchivalrous to stop her. You may well find that is exactly the reaction of young Bollington, for whom I gather this particular scene is being enacted.'

Her eyes glittered, angrily.

'It is no matter to me what Lord Bollington thinks, sir.'

'Really? What has he said to upset you, I wonder?'

'He . . . it is of no concern to you.'

'Quite right, Miss Tyneham,' interjected Sir Esmond, trying to lighten the atmosphere. 'Shall I call this rude fellow out for you?'

'Would you?' Susan looked sceptical but interested. 'I would rather like to have gentlemen to fight over me.'

'Bloodthirsty young lady, are you not,' murmured Lord Rothley, with a wry smile. 'The thing is that Fawley and I have known each other for years, and everyone would guess it was a hum.'

'So you will not offer pistols at dawn?' Susan could not keep the disappointment from her voice.

'Tell you what, we might arrange a compromise.' Lord Rothley's eyes twinkled as he looked at Sir Esmond. 'I am going to Grierson's tomorrow morning to try a new twelve-bore. How about you come with me. Shotguns at say eleven, rather than pistols at six?'

'Thank you, I will be glad to join you. Grierson's, eh? I had a pistol off him four years back.'

'Oh, if you are going to talk men's talk, I might as well go elsewhere,' declared Susan, huffily.

'My apologies, Miss Tyneham,' Sir Esmond bowed, 'that was inexcusable of us.'

'Yes, I think it was,' replied Susan, baldly.

'Yet you will excuse us.'

'I will?'

'Yes, ma'am, because it shows your superior understanding, that men are all . . . just men.'

'That, Sir Esmond, I have known since I was fourteen.'

He looked at her, a little intently. It occurred to him that whilst she did a lot to attract the opposite sex, she really did not like men, not underneath. He wondered why.

Lord Bollington was confused, and piqued. Miss Tyneham had taken umbrage because he had let slip that his mama was yet to be 'won over' by her, even though he had averred that he was himself at her feet. This clumsy admission, which said much for the viscount's inexperience with women, had set up Susan's back, although how his lordship was to blame for his mother's not falling instantly under the 'Susan spell' was not a question she had even asked herself. He had then blundered further by suggesting, very gingerly, that perhaps she might act a little more 'like other girls' when engaged in conversation with her. Susan had glared at him, and then smiled, but not in a nice way. If he even cared what his mother thought, then he was not sufficiently subservient, and needed to be taught a lesson.

The lesson he had learnt, however, was not that Miss Tyneham must come first and foremost, but that she was just as Mama had warned him, 'a fickle little madam without heart and without the maidenly virtues of docility, modesty, and sweetness of temper'. Well, he would dance no more to her piping, though she was so magnificent a creature.

Sophy, who had been trying to juggle conversing with Lord John, watching to see that Harriet knew where she was, and give that damsel a sign to return to her side when possible, and trying to work out how she might deflect Lord Rothley from her charge, at last succeeded in disengaging from Lord John Hythe, and turned a smiling countenance to Sir Esmond. Lord Rothley had the impression that he was less welcome, and wondered if she had come to unpleasant conclusions following the encounter with Tyneham in the Park.

'Is my cousin entertaining you, Sir Esmond, with how well she controlled her horse on our first ride?' She acknowledged Lord Rothley with a lesser smile and the briefest of curtsies.

'Not as yet, ma'am.' Sir Esmond's smile faded. 'I am sorry to hear that Lady Chelmarsh has had to attend Lady Tattersett. I hope the news is not desperate.'

Lord Rothley was suddenly on the alert. He had missed this information.

'It is not, thankfully, but my sister is due her first confinement in a few weeks and has suffered the sudden loss of a friend in a similar situation. Her distress is acute, and my mama's place is with her.'

'Of course. But you do not abandon London, I hope?'

Sophy heard the note of sincerity in his voice, and coloured a little.

'Oh no, Sir Esmond. I stand *in loco parentis*.'

'I am sorry for it,' interjected Lord Rothley.

'Really, my lord?' Sophy was stung. 'Do you think me unequal to the task?'

'Not at all, ma'am, but I regret that you are thereby

both burdened with responsibility and consigned to the ranks of the matrons.'

'If I do not feel "regret", Lord Rothley, it seems . . . unnecessary for you to do so.'

'And I am a burden, am I?' added Miss Tyneham, caught between annoyance and delight at being thought a handful.

'I think, Rothley, old fellow, this is where you admit defeat,' whispered Sir Esmond.

'No, I stick to my guns. Miss Tyneham knows full well that she can be a burden if she so chooses, and I still think it a crying shame that Lady Sophy has to adopt the role of her mama for the rest of the Season.' He was still frowning, and Sophy found this almost as disturbing as his wolfish smile. Was it some form of double bluff for the wolf to pretend regret when the shepherd was called away and the oldest lamb left in charge? His next words gave her cause to think he had every intention of using the situation to his advantage. 'If there is any way, at any time, in which I can be of assistance, Lady Sophy, I am at your disposal.'

He bowed, his expression so serious it would be perilously easy to believe every word.

'At the risk of sounding a pale echo, I also place myself at your command, ma'am, and as a show of good faith offer to risk being shown up upon the dance floor by the twinkle-toed Miss Tyneham.' Sir Esmond smiled in a friendly way at her and then turned to her cousin. 'Will it ruin your scheme, Miss Tyneham, to be seen dancing with me, or will I do at a pinch?'

'Oh, I think I may put you to use, Sir Esmond, and it does a man good to be useful,' she replied, in a purring voice, and offered him her hand.

'With your permission, Lady Sophy?'

'Oh yes, Sir Esmond, with my permission.'

Sophy watched Sir Esmond lead Susan away and quite visibly relaxed. Lord Rothley's frown had not lifted.

'Perhaps with your cousin safely kept from trouble for the duration of the dance, you might consider dancing yourself, with me, ma'am?'

'Ah, but I have another charge, my lord.' She smiled, but past him at Harriet, who was approaching.

'Sophy, may I dance with Mr Stoneleigh?' she asked, a little shyly. 'I thought it best to ask you . . .'

'Mr Stoneleigh? Oh yes, of course. He will not tread upon your toes. Off you go.'

Harriet looked innocently delighted, and threaded her way back to the gentleman.

'But now, Lady Sophy, you are temporarily free, so will you do me the honour of dancing with me?' Lord Rothley held out his hand. She stared at it a moment. 'I am not going to bite you, you know.'

She looked up, shamefaced. His face showed understanding, regret, and a little chagrin.

'Not in so public a place as Lady Funtley's party, at least.' She attempted to lighten the atmosphere, and he smiled, though it did not reach those dangerous eyes of his.

She placed her hand in his, wishing her heart did not leap at the contact, and they took their places in the set.

'Had you considered how you could have refused your sister permission to dance with Mr Stoneleigh without embarrassing her?' he enquired as the music began.

'But Mr Stoneleigh is a very respectable gentleman, sir.'

'He is, but I meant upon principle, and you know it, ma'am.'

'I do not see why you should concern yourself in any way with the problems I face, my lord.'

'Don't you?'

She blushed as the dance parted them. He had not meant to sound so particular. When the steps brought them together again he altered his emphasis.

'You have admitted they are problems, you see.'

'And I am capable of solving them.'

'I am sure you are, ma'am, but at what cost to yourself?'

'That is immaterial, my lord.'

'I beg to differ.' He paused. 'You may think you have cause to stand back from me, Lady Sophy, but my desire to be of help to you is sincere. I have more years upon the Town and . . . sometimes, as Miss Tyneham says, a man can be put to good use.'

Their eyes met, and in that moment she had no doubts about him. She lowered her gaze, a little flushed.

'I . . . appreciate the offer, my lord, but cannot imagine any situation in which I might need the assistance of a gentleman.'

This was perfectly true, but some situations were beyond imagining.

CHAPTER NINE

LORD PINKNEY WAS NOT SOBER. HE WAS AT THE reckless stage where advice would be met with belligerence, and so those who might otherwise have been tempted to remonstrate with him held back. It had not been a good day. He had lost what appeared sound bets upon three horses to the tune of twelve hundred guineas at Tattersalls, and settling day would be a trifle awkward. His recent good fortune had, as it always did, slipped away in the payment of a few of his most pressing debts and the dicing at Watier's, and he was now badly dipped to the tune of a cool eight thousand at the card tables. This mercurial change in his financial situation was not in any way unusual, and most of his acquaintance shrugged and simply shook their heads over it, with mutterings that one day he really would drown in the River Tick.

What percolated through to his fuddled intelligence was that Tyneham, the prosy bore, had been an onlooker for most of the evening, and taken over the Bank at a very late stage, and seemed very smug over holding his vowels.

'No need to look so damned pleased, Tyneham,' he managed, with remarkably little slurring.

'Pleased? Oh no, you mistake. They say fortune favours the brave but tonight you went way beyond brave, Pinkney, into the realm of wildly rash.'

'Going to give me the bunny . . . bunny-fit of your wisdom, Tyneham?' sneered the inebriated peer.

'Let it go, man,' whispered a gentleman at Lord Tyneham's elbow, laying a restraining hand on his arm, but the viscount disliked taking advice.

'I would recommend you don't play after the third bottle.' There was the smug look again.

Lord Pinkney was conscious of a desire to wipe that smug smile from Tyneham's face, but the more pressing urge was to lie down and sleep. He therefore found a sofa and collapsed upon it, and it was from here that he was taken and placed in a cab with directions to his lodgings and a companion who lived close enough by to stroll the last few hundred yards once he had handed over the comatose form to his servants.

It was past noon the following day when Pinkney awoke, and wished, most fervently that he had not. He was generally accounted a man who could hold his liquor well, but vaguely recalled having begun drinking before dinner and had certainly broached a fourth bottle before the end of the evening. His mouth felt dry and disgusting and his head was in danger of exploding. He opened one eye with extreme reluctance, when his man came in upon his summons, then groaned loudly and swore at him for opening the curtains to reveal a painful degree of daylight.

'What is the time?'

'A little after two in the afternoon, my lord,' answered the valet, smoothly. 'Would your lordship care to take refreshment *au lit*, or rise and shave?'

The groan at the mention of food was even more pronounced, and the grumpy peer pulled the bedclothes over his head. Shellow smiled to himself. He was not enamoured of his employer, especially when due two months wages. He returned below stairs to report that his lordship had clearly made a real night of it, as they had thought, and would be unlikely to require food for several hours.

When Lord Pinkney finally emerged from his bedchamber it was in a bad mood, and with an inclination to blame everyone else for his plight. The physical expression of 'everyone', in his mind, was Lord Tyneham. The Viscount Tyneham was self-important, a bore and, what really made Lord Pinkney grind his teeth, so infernally rich that he need not worry if he lost the odd thousand, which made it all the more galling when he won.

The morning through which he had slept had brought more almost polite letters from tradesmen who had heard that he was back in funds and were keen to be reimbursed for their wares. Well, they were too late. He consigned every last sheet to the fire and watched the flames flicker, consuming every word, every neatly written figure. It was a good way to avoid having drawers stuffed with bills, even if he was well aware that it did not remove the debts. He had made recovers before, and he would simply have to do so again. It was purely by chance that he overheard another member of his club mention Tyneham's boast about his sister.

'Rum thing to do, I thought. I mean, he's so flush it stands to reason the sister won't come without a tidy sum, so why make a fuss of it?'

'Perhaps the chit is ugly as sin?' offered the gentleman to his right.

'No such thing. Have you seen the girl? Very tempting, I tell you, before any mention of settlements. Lady Chelmarsh is bringing her out, for there's a family connection. Saw Miss Tyneham at Almack's last week when I did the decent by my mother; skin like porcelain, fine figure and a smile that makes you want a special licence in your pocket, damn me if it doesn't.'

'Disgusting!' An elderly gentleman who had been half dozing behind *The Gazette*, glared at the speaker. 'No way to speak about your mother, sir.'

The younger man opened his mouth to deny the offence but then thought it too difficult to explain, apologised profusely, and sauntered away to see if he could find anyone happy to play billiards.

Lord Pinkney smiled. He did not attend many parties, and far preferred, when he could afford the pleasure, dalliance with young women who had no romantic illusions and an exact knowledge of how best to please a man. Becoming a tenant for life was not on his list of 'things to do', but the thought of a beautiful bride with an even more beautiful dowry was a temptation, especially if that wiped the smile off the face of Lord Tyneham. That gentleman would certainly not entertain him as a suitor for his sister's hand, but, as the saying went, there was more than one way to skin a cat. He sat down, ordered a brandy, and began to contemplate feline skinning.

Lord Rothley and Sir Esmond Fawley met outside the premises of Charles Grierson at Number 10 Bond Street at the appointed hour of eleven o'clock. The shop proudly displayed the superscription 'Gunmaker to His Majesty' though it looked a little tired. The gentlemen shook hands.

'Do you favour Grierson over Manton or Egg, Rothley?'

'Not especially, but I saw this gun when it was in the window the other week and liked the look of it, looked a good balance. Single barrel, twelve-bore, tidy gun. Come and see what you think of it.'

They entered the shop and for the next twenty

minutes argued happily over whether there would be any advantage to John Manton's new V-shaped pan, and whether the barrel length might be an inch or two long. Lord Rothley was convinced, however, that it was just the thing, and arranged for it to be sent round to his address. Having completed his business, the two friends ambled into Jackson's Boxing Saloon a few doors down, exchanged a few words with friends, watched some sparring and then made their way to St James's and luncheon at White's. Their conversation had been sporting, but as they turned down St James's, Sir Esmond brought up another subject.

'A very pleasant morning, Rothley, and I am very glad it was not at six of the clock and with a surgeon in attendance.'

'As am I,' Lord Rothley laughed. 'The depressing thing is that Miss Tyneham was not entirely in jest.'

'No. An . . . unusual young lady.'

'Most certainly. Very hot at hand, I would say.'

'Yes.' Sir Esmond paused. 'Do you rub her up the wrong way intentionally?'

'Ah,' Lord Rothley's smile lengthened, 'I do seem to have that effect upon her, do I not? I won't let her have her own way, which irritates her, I think because she is unused to any opposition, and perhaps I do goad her a little.'

'With an end in view?' Sir Esmond looked sidelong at his friend.

'Yes. I think so.' Rothley did not see Sir Esmond's

smile become rather fixed. 'I would like to prevent her doing something both disastrous to her own position, and unpleasant for Lady Sophy.'

'A further "why" would be . . . intrusive?'

'At this point, my dear fellow, yes. I am not altogether sure how things stand between myself, Miss Tyneham, and indeed her cousin *in loco parentis*.'

'I see, or rather I do not see, which is as desired.' Sir Esmond did not divulge that he too had an interest in the occupants of the Chelmarsh residence, since he was at this stage equally unsure of . . . matters. 'It is a situation where one always feels as if treading upon dangerous ground.'

'It will be if Miss Tyneham becomes even more bloodthirsty.'

'Yet one has to wonder why that is.'

'Yes, one has to wonder.' Lord Rothley frowned, and gave what might have been a sigh. 'Now, Fawley, before we both become as blue as megrim, what dishes catch your eye?'

It had to be said that when Miss Tyneham rode with her cousins later that day she appeared, if a little thoughtful, happy to behave in a seemly fashion. Sophy actually admired the way she was quite fearless upon huge Hugo, apparently confident that what she lacked in strength of muscle was more than compensated for by her strength of will. They stopped to exchange polite nothings with several ladies in barouches, and one lady in a yellow-wheeled phaeton that made Susan wish she had learnt to handle the reins. There was a certain cachet to driving oneself. She found the interchanges rather boring, but revived when they met Sir Esmond Fawley. He smiled, and raised his hat.

'Good afternoon, ladies. How nice to see you out at the social hour. How are you finding your choices?'

'I think we can safely say we are all three of us pleased, Sir Esmond.' Sophy smiled. She had not managed a genuine smile all day. She felt weighed down by an indefinable despondency.

'And Miss Tyneham, you have not experienced vertigo, I hope?'

'Not at all, Sir Esmond. I have no fear . . .' she paused, and glanced briefly at her cousin, wondering if exchanging badinage with Sir Esmond counted as impropriety, 'of heights.'

'I doubt you have a fear of anything, Miss Tyneham,' he commented, smiling, but looking rather intently at her. He would swear there was fear in her, but he was unsure of its source.

'I certainly do not possess one over such things as heights, or mice, or the dark.'

'I dislike spiders,' offered Harriet, shuddering, and, as if at one with her, the shudder ran along her horse's neck, rippling the mane. She laughed. 'And it seems Bramble shares my antipathy.'

'Bramble? Now that is a nice name for a horse.'

Sir Esmond, thought Sophy, spoke to Harriet as if he

were an uncle, even if a young one, and yet he did not do so to her, or to Susan.

'I have named mine Hugo, partly because Sophy's first suggestion was Huge, and in part because I could always claim that "I had Hugo doing just what I told him", which sounds terribly daring.' Susan felt, rather than saw, Sophy's warning. 'Do I shock you, Sir Esmond?' she enquired, frowning very slightly.

'No, you do not. You see, I have resolved not to permit you to do so, and I stick to my resolutions.' He smiled at her in a way she found hard to read. It was in part admiring, part rather too knowing, and part tolerance. The first she liked, the second disturbed her and the third irritated her. He seemed to treat admiring her as a game, knowing that she herself considered it a game.

'Lord Rothley is not shocked by me either, but I do wish he would not act as if I were some sort of . . . entertainment,' Susan remarked.

Sophy felt relief at this comment. She did not want Susan setting her cap at Lord Rothley. It would upset her mama and, secretly, she had to admit it upset her too. If only Mama had not been so sure about him being a man to keep at a distance.

'Sophy, who is the gentleman riding towards us?' Harriet was wondering about a man clearly about to draw up and speak to them.

'That, Lady Harriet,' answered Sir Esmond, before Sophy had time to trawl through her memory, 'is Lord Pinkney, who is a gamester, and not the sort of man young ladies should entertain as a friend.'

'Oh.' Harriet now looked as if Lord Pinkney might kidnap her upon sight, and he noted the trepidation in her gaze as he made his bow.

'Lady Sophronia. I do not think we have met for several years. Servant, Fawley. And who are these delightful ladies?'

Sophy stiffened. She did not need Sir Esmond to tell her the type of man Lord Pinkney was, to be sure. He fitted her image of the rake like a glove.

'Indeed, my lord, several years. May I have the pleasure to present,' the words were so obviously a lie she almost ground her teeth, 'my sister, Lady Harriet Hadlow, and my cousin, Miss Tyneham.'

'My great pleasure, ladies.'

'Sister, cousin, may I present Lord Pinkney.' Sophy did not add anything to the barest minimum.

He eyed her, gauging her disapproval, and smiled. She disliked his smile. Lord Rothley's smile was infectious and a little lupine. Lord Pinkney's was, in her view, reptilian.

'We have not encountered you at any of the parties we have attended thus far, my lord,' observed Susan.

'Why no, ma'am. I tend to find them a bore, but having met such charming ladies, I am sure I will be more often at parties.'

'And less often at the gaming tables, my lord?' Sophy was rarely waspish, but this man raised her hackles.

'Far less, ma'am.' He smiled at her, but it was the smile

of a man acknowledging a foe. 'After all, at the gaming tables one is, alas, likely to lose. Being in delightful feminine company one may only win.'

Susan repressed a snigger. Harriet looked fearful. Sir Esmond looked as if he would like to knock Lord Pinkney's teeth straight down his throat. He controlled this urge, however, and instead spoke in a convivial tone.

'I fear we are delaying the ladies, Pinkney, for they must complete their ride in good time to return and make preparations for their evening's "junketing".'

Sophy gave him a look that expressed her gratitude. Pinkney did not think this statement true for one moment, but it would be awkward to argue about it.

'It would of course be a desolation to think that one had caused such preparations to be rushed. I have no doubt, however, that we shall meet again in the near future, dear ladies.' Pinkney looked most directly at Susan, who was assessing him quite boldly. 'Shall we be on our way, Fawley?'

Sir Esmond made a polite farewell, and let Pinkney trot off beside him. Sophy, thankfully, did not hear what passed between them.

'I am reminded of a dog with a bone when I see you with that trio, Fawley,' Pinkney observed. 'The only thing I do not know is which bone you consider yours, the nervous chit, the tall spinster, or the dark dasher.'

'And you simply remind me how much I dislike you, Pinkney.'

'Account me heartbroken, sir.'

'I would far rather it was your neck, but one cannot expect all one's wishes fulfilled.'

'Alas no, that is so often the case.'

Sophy was glad that Sir Esmond had rescued them from the unpleasant presence of Lord Pinkney. She had no fears for Harriet, since she looked in a positive quake at the sight of him. Be he never so charming, her sister would not fall victim to that particular rogue. With Susan she was less certain, not that she might believe his blandishments but that she might like the challenge of entrapping such a man. Losing Sir Esmond's company was a pity, and having shortly thereafter to spend several minutes being polite to old Lady Norton, who was remarkably deaf, and demanded that every phrase be repeated, was trying to the nerves. Harriet declared her throat was quite sore from having to shout, and Susan said that she was bored. This was a bad sign. A bored Susan meant trouble, and so it turned out.

Susan was rather more alert to the presence of male riders than her cousins, and, whilst they were talking, caught sight of a group of young gentlemen in uniform, catching up with them gradually from behind. She giggled.

'Lord Rothley was very specific that I should not like young men in red coats "so easily". How fortunate then that he is not present. Be sure not to tell.'

Before Sophy had even time to register what she meant, Susan kicked Hugo hard, dropped her reins and screamed, thereby frightening him into a gallop. Apparently out of control, the big bay careered along the trackway. The gentlemen, alerted by her cry, did what any red-blooded cavalryman would do, and charged after her. Galloping in the Park was strictly forbidden, but rescuing a young lady in danger was not. As Sophy gasped, the quartet thundered past them, bent low over their horses' withers. It was as much as Harriet and Sophy could do to calm their agitated mounts. By the time they had done so, the horsemen had drawn level with Susan, and one had grabbed Hugo above the bit and was dragging him to a wide-eyed halt. The two sisters cantered up as a breathless Susan was thanking her 'rescuers' in a tremulous voice.

'I think it must have been a bird in one of the bushes. I cannot imagine what caused poor dear Hugo to take off like that, and once I lost my stirrup . . . I do not know what I would have done without your kind offices, gentlemen.'

The officers, as one, declared themselves only too glad to have been of service and, when she shyly requested whom she should thank, announced themselves as Lieutenants Allerton, Fiskerton and Calke and Captain Lord Edward Wittenham, all of the—

'Oh, I know your regiment, gentlemen. You are in the Life Guards.' Susan gave them a knowing smirk. She looked like a cat who had found the cream.

The cavalrymen seemed even more delighted that Miss Tyneham was joined by two other ladies. Sophy looked at the young men and could not disapprove of them, for they looked fresh-faced and innocent after the leering assurance of Lord Pinkney. The fact that there were four of them also made it more difficult for Susan to cast out lures to any one in particular. They also, very politely, included Harriet in their light-hearted conversation, which entertained them until the ladies had to turn aside to head back to the stables. Only then could Sophy remonstrate with Susan.

'You did that deliberately, so do not attempt to deny it, Susan.'

'There was no harm done, and since it was an "accident" there can be no recriminations about galloping in Hyde Park. It was actually quite exhilarating, and you cannot deny it made the latter part of our ride far more enjoyable.'

'The officers were . . . very nice,' murmured Harriet, tentatively. 'One could not say they were forward or . . . presumptuous.'

'No, but that does not make Susan's behaviour any the better. Have a care, cousin, for your antics are liable to have repercussions you cannot even begin to imagine. Now, remember we want to be at Almack's for nine. Do not dally.'

With which Sophy went to her room, and offered up a silent prayer as she removed her habit that her cousin might not send her grey with worry.

CHAPTER TEN

Sophy chose her gown with care. She did not want to appear too young to be a chaperone, nor yet an ape leader. Now that she did not feel under pressure to attract partners, she had found that she enjoyed Almack's, but tonight, having to watch both sister and cousin alone, she felt too much on duty. She looked at herself in the mirror, and felt she looked 'creditable'. Her grandmama's diamond drops made her look a little more mature and sophisticated, and the deep cream of the silk was set off by gold floss at the hem and upon the intricately cut puff sleeves. She told herself that she must not set out in trepidation, and met her charges in the hallway, where she checked final details and pinned an errant curl for Harriet.

They arrived before the rooms were too crowded,

and Sophy saw Harriet and Susan solicited to dance by unimpeachable partners. She relaxed, and retired a little to one side, where several of the older matrons were enjoying a comfortable gossip away from their progeny. It was not her intention to listen in upon their conversation, and indeed what she heard made her feel a little dizzy.

'Goodness, yes. "Roving Rothley". How often one has heard that name and pitied the object of his affections.'

'"Rake Rothley" is the appellation I recall. You would think his past would make all wary, but did you ever hear of a case where he failed?'

'No, and just think, not all were silly misses.'

Sophy moved away, not wishing to hear more. Her mouth was dry, and she took a glass from a passing waiter with a hand that shook very slightly. She had, like it or not, persuaded herself that Mama had been mistaken in Lord Rothley. She so wanted her to be mistaken. After all, he was received everywhere, and Sir Esmond Fawley, whom she saw as a very reliable gentleman, acknowledged him as a friend. Yet honesty made her accept that men took a very different view of things than ladies. Lord Pinkney was a gamester, and clearly despised by Sir Esmond. Perhaps a man who toyed with women was seen in another light as long as he was not too obvious. The 'tabbies' she had overheard had no doubt about their view of Lord Rothley; he was charming but dangerous, and he did not fail in his objectives. That was quite disturbing, and her evening ruined. When Susan returned to her, she drew her apart and begged her, most sincerely, to have a care in his presence. Susan nodded, but Sophy saw the smile play about her lips and worried. Harriet was in company with several other young ladies and there seemed little chance of warning her. Besides, Sophy thought her sister impervious, for some reason, to his lordship's charms. She therefore spent the next half hour brooding upon her own foolishness, since his charms were all too obvious to herself. However, concern about the dangerous viscount was cast from her mind in an instant when she was confronted by Lady Jersey, almost rigid with anger.

It was not Lord Rothley's habit to frequent Almack's, and he tended to appear there but once or twice a Season, but those who noticed such things, and among the matrons and patronesses there were many that did, ears were pricked. What eluded everyone was which young lady had inspired this change of habit. There were those convinced that Miss Tyneham was his object, and shook their heads over it, for he was well enough liked and Miss Tyneham was gaining a reputation, of the wrong sort. Sympathies were with her cousins, but if things continued they would, everyone agreed, suffer to a lesser extent. A smaller number thought that it was with the tall Lady Sophronia that his ambitions lay, and these ladies sighed, for it would be so nice for 'that poor girl' who had reached the point of being on the shelf.

'That poor girl' was currently attempting to placate a

highly incensed Lady Jersey, who had actually overheard Susan complaining to another debutante that she was being held back from dancing the waltz out of spite. Since this was entirely in the remit of the patronesses, it was against these ladies that a slip of a girl had lashed out in a tantrum, and merely because she had seen another young lady given permission to do so before her.

That Sally Jersey was a friend of her mama was a small help; but that she had been the very patroness who had supplied their vouchers for Almack's added to the insult. Sophy was mortally ashamed.

'There is nothing that I can say, ma'am, except to apologise for my cousin's intemperate and wholly unacceptable behaviour.'

'Easily said,' snapped Lady Jersey, unappeased.

'My mama will be most distressed to hear of it, and on top of her current worries . . .' Sophy hoped that reminding Lady Jersey of the circumstances of Lady Chelmarsh's disappearance from London might reduce Lady Jersey's ire, though it would make her seem inadequate as a controlling force. The truth was that Lady Chelmarsh had feared that Susan would overstep the mark even whilst directly under her eye.

'It is only out of respect for my friend, Lady Chelmarsh, that I do not forbid entry for Miss Tyneham, since it would also preclude you and your sister attending whilst you are nominally in charge of her.'

Sophy bit her lip, and felt a constriction in her chest.

141

'I do try, ma'am. The only thing that I can say about my cousin is that she has never been "with people", never been taught to think of others. It makes suddenly being in the midst of Society difficult for her, as well as . . . us.'

Lady Jersey, relented, a little.

'As I said, my friendship with your mama, and the difficult time she must be having, means that this will go no further. However, I suggest, most strongly, that you take your cousin to one side and explain . . . realities to her. Had Mrs Drummond-Burrell or the Countess Lieven overheard her . . .' Lady Jersey did not need to say more. Had either of those high sticklers become aware of Susan's behaviour, the doors of Almack's would have closed firmly in their faces. Sophy felt rather sick. She murmured a further apology and withdrew to regain her composure and then to take Susan to one side as carefully as she could. She was looking down, trying phrases in her head, when she almost collided with Lord Rothley.

'Oh, I am sorry . . .' she began, and then looked up. There was such a stricken look in her eyes and her face was so pale, he thought she must have received terrible news. His hand went out to steady her.

'Lady Sophy, you are unwell.'

'No, my lord, it is just . . .' Her voice became suspended for a moment, and he led her, unresisting, to a quiet alcove, and pressed her into a seat, sitting beside her. Whatever his reputation, just at this moment he seemed the one firm thing in her maelstrom of emotion. For one moment his reputation was forgotten.

'Do you want me to fetch your sister, ma'am? Should you go home?'

'No, oh no please, do not ruin Harriet's evening also.' She looked away. The urge to be weak and cry, now the shock of how close they had come to ruin sank in, was so very nearly overwhelming.

He had not let go of her hand.

'Have you received bad news, ma'am?' he asked, quietly. 'Your sister . . .'

She shook her head.

'You must think me foolish, sir. Nothing of that magnitude has overset me but . . .' She confided in him, without knowing why, other than that the grasp of his hand anchored her to calm, and his voice was sympathetic. Sophy explained the last ten minutes. The hand hold tightened and if she had not been looking at that hand and her own, Sophy would have seen his expression grow grim.

'The wretch. Has she no notion at all how Society works?'

'No, my lord, in truth she does not. Her mama spoilt her completely, and rarely left Tyneham Court after she was born. I believe, from what little Mama told me, that Lord Tyneham, the previous viscount, treated his wife unkindly, and as good as abandoned her, left her to rot upon the family estate. I think Susan was all she had and . . . My cousin has never mixed with people, had to consider anyone but herself. Her behaviour tonight is part of that.' She sounded resigned.

'It is still unsupportable, and has placed you in a very awkward position. As you say, if a different patroness had overheard her . . . My God, you would all be in the suds.' He paused. 'Let me fetch you a glass of ratafia, and you can regain your colour, and stop trembling.' He squeezed her hand, and got up to secure her refreshment. She resisted the feeling that his absence left her abandoned and, even as she told herself that she should mistrust all he said, she was sure that just now he was not trying to gain her trust for nefarious reasons. He could not be.

When he returned she had at least managed to control the tremor in her hands, and took the glass with murmured thanks.

'I should find my cousin.'

'She was but a moment ago in the company of Lady Orpington, where she is quite safe. You must sit quietly a little longer and then I shall endeavour to bring her to you.' He watched her face. 'This has been most unpleasant but not the catastrophe it might have been. It will not become known.'

'Oh, if only I could believe that! And it shows how pathetic I am as a guide, a chaperone. I have failed Mama, Harriet . . .'

'I think you blame yourself unnecessarily, ma'am. You cannot undo a lifetime of poor upbringing in a few weeks. Has Tyneham no control . . . No, do not answer that. Of course he does not.' He wanted so much to tell her he would do whatever he could to ease her situation. 'Look at me.'

She obeyed.

'Your cousin would be a trial to any woman in this room, however experienced, however grand, or resolute. Have faith in yourself, my dear . . . Lady Sophy,' he added, hastily. 'Now, I am going to get your cousin for you. I may do so via the dance floor so as not to raise suspicions. What would be more natural than to bring a debutante back to her chaperone, yes?'

Sophy just nodded. He smiled at her, rose and disappeared, leaving her mind in a whirl and the pressure of his sustaining hand a memory that warmed her within.

Lord Rothley espied Miss Tyneham, head held high, proud as a duchess. Part of him was so angry he wished he could wipe that supreme self-confidence from her in an instant, and yet there was a part also that admired her self-reliance, the raw courage of her that faced, as she saw it, a world that would crush her, if it could, into being a nonentity. He approached, said a few words to Lady Orpington, made her a polite bow, and requested the pleasure of the next dance in an urbane tone. She regarded him thoughtfully, and assented.

As they took their places, Susan eyed him boldly. Now he was accounted 'dangerous' he was far more interesting to her. Not one to beat about the bush, she did not couch her question in obtuse terms.

'Are you a rake, sir?' She was buoyed up and in an adventurous mood.

'Not particularly.' He leant closer. 'Are you a minx?'

'Oh yes,' she giggled, 'absolutely.'

'It is very dangerous,' he murmured.

'Dangerous talking to a minx?' She gave him a long look from under her lashes.

'No, being one. You see, life is very unfair.' His voice was very calm, very smooth, but there was steel beneath the velvet. 'A man may be a rake and still get invitations to all the best places – well, nearly all. However, if a young lady is a minx, her reputation is liable to . . . slip. Thereafter she is a social outcast. You have come within a hair's breadth of that tonight. You do not complain about the ladies who are the queens of Society.'

'I do not care for what stuffy old people say.' Susan disliked his tone. She lifted her head, challenging the world to condemn her.

'You should when the "stuffy old people" are the Patronesses of Almack's, child, and Lady Jersey is by no stretch of the imagination "old".'

'I am not a child.' Susan pouted, thereby giving the lie to her statement.

'You are from where I am standing, Miss Tyneham.'

'Then, sir, I suggest you stand further away. Derbyshire might be far enough.' Susan was annoyed, and was incapable of pretending otherwise.

Lord Rothley smiled, which infuriated her the more.

'I fear I shall disappoint you, for the furthest I shall remove myself is the width of the set, and leaving the dance floor would get you noticed, yet again, for the wrong reasons.' He paused. 'My advice was genuine, Miss Tyneham.'

'I never take advice.'

He raised an eyebrow but said nothing, and drew back as he had said. She eyed him doubtfully. When they were once again in proximity he continued.

'There is always a first time, Miss Tyneham. We all learn by mistakes. It is far less painful learning by the mistakes of others, but you seem set upon a course which relies entirely upon you making them all yourself.' He was smiling at her, but his eyes were hard. 'You think you are so clever, child, but you show yourself up at every opportunity as a spoilt brat with no more understanding of how to behave in the adult world than a ten-year-old. You think you are admired? Well, yes, you are, until people find out that your looks are of a woman, but your outlook is still in the schoolroom. You very nearly lost everything tonight. Think how many invitations would not come to a girl who was cast out of Almack's. Think also how you would have dragged down your cousin Lady Harriet, and Lady Sophy, who has been exposed to the not unjustified wrath of one of the most powerful ladies in London because of you. If you do possess a heart beneath that pretty gown, miss, think on those things, and when I take you to your cousin, beg her forgiveness.'

Susan had gone pink, and now went pale.

'You cannot talk to me like this, my lord.'

'Someone has to, and it might as well be me.'

'I hate you.'

'That is entirely possible, but it does not lessen the truth of what I have said, nor change the fact that I have done so to help you, if you are not beyond helping.'

'You have no right—'

'You, Miss Tyneham, have no right to trample upon other people for your own ends, ends which will come to nothing unless you learn to consider others.'

The music scraped to a halt. He bowed, with irony in every muscle. She glared at him, a little frightened, and very angry. He took her hand, placed it upon his arm, and then put his other hand over it, pressing quite hard.

'We now go to your cousin.'

She was led from the floor to where Sophy sat, her hands folded in her lap, calm but still pale. Her eyes reproached. Susan felt beset by dislike, and very lonely.

Sophy, who had been covertly watching as much of the dance as she could see, and worrying, in part guessing what was going on, was totally confused. Lady Chelmarsh had been so adamant that she did not want Susan coming into contact with Lord Rothley, and she had herself heard of his unpleasant reputation with the ladies; 'Roving Rothley' had such a callous ring to it, yet he seemed to turn up with alarming regularity to rescue Susan from her own folly or try to take her in hand as if he were her uncle or elder brother. Surely these were not the actions of a heartless seducer? He most certainly did not appear to be one at this juncture. Susan looked like a child berated for wrong-doing, and more likely to hit him than fall into his arms.

'I restore your charge to you, ma'am. I think she might possibly listen, and she ought to have things to say, but perhaps not here, and not right now.' He bowed to Sophy and withdrew.

Susan had said that she did not take advice. She had never done so, and yet, with Lord Rothley's words ringing in her ears and Sophy's face before her, she wavered, wavered enough for cracks to appear in her shell of invulnerability.

'I have done something terrible. I . . . I would not have said it to her face.' Her voice was subdued, but if this was meant to show that she had any notion how to go on, it failed.

'Am I to take that as consolation, Susan? I do not. Lady Jersey could have had you, and us, barred from these rooms. She has made it clear I must speak severely to you, and also explain what you, unlike every other debutante in London, cannot seem to grasp, that you cannot ignore the rules and survive. However, this is not the place to do so, and I am not sufficiently composed to speak without heat.

'I do not want to go home early and advertise that something is amiss, or ruin Harriet's innocent pleasure, but you will stay by me for the rest of the evening unless upon the dance floor, and if – *if* you find yourself next to Lady Jersey, you will make it very clear that you are immensely sorry.'

Susan nodded, and Sophy rose, pleased with herself for no longer shaking. She moved with a stately confidence she did not feel, and with her cousin in her wake. From a distance, Lord Rothley's heart went out to her, and did not return to him.

It was just before the evening drew to a close that Sophy found herself, whether by accident or his design, by Lord Rothley once more.

'You know you do have my sympathies, Lady Sophy. Had you considered a whip and a chair?'

Sophy relaxed a little. He was, she felt it most strongly, 'on her side'. She ought not to want him there, but she did.

'I am sorry, my lord. Was she outrageous?' Sophy managed a querulous smile.

'To use her own adjective "absolutely", but it was sheer bravado. You once told me you did not possess bravado like your cousin. I am sure we are all glad that is so.'

There was a twinkle in his eye. Sophy was disappointed in herself. Mama clearly thought this man dangerous, and yet here she was, wanting to smile at him, and bowled over by the twinkle. Did rakes look in the mirror to check their twinkles, she wondered inconsequentially, and tried to adopt a look of elegant aloofness. Then it hit her. What if he did not want to seduce Susan? What if she herself was to be his 'victim'? What better way would there be than assisting her in curbing her cousin's waywardness?

'I am sorry,' he said, catching the change in her, but

mistaking its cause. 'It cannot be a subject that affords you hilarity since you are burdened with her.' He paused. 'One does not choose one's relatives.'

'Every family has its black sheep, a member whom the rest would prefer to forget,' she responded, and gasped at her own temerity.

'Indeed.'

The twinkle was extinguished instantly, and she knew she had given offence. She blushed. How could she have been so rude, even if he was a rake, and his family's ne'er-do-well.

'Forgive me,' she stammered.

'There is nothing to forgive, ma'am, for it is the truth.' His voice was expressionless. 'If you will excuse me, I perceive Lady Boscobel trying to attract my attention.' He bowed and was gone.

Sophy did not look after him. Lady Boscobel was a woman she considered a 'spider'. She wove a web and waited for juicy tittle-tattle to land in the threads and create a tremor. No doubt she thought a gentleman like Lord Rothley the sort to provide her with just the gossip upon which to feed; would he . . . No, that was an unworthy thought. Were it not for the soubriquet, he was not a man about whom she had heard rumour, nor was he treated coldly by even sticklers such as Mrs Drummond-Burrell. Perhaps he was that rarity, a rake with discretion. Not, of course, that she was interested in him, or his dangerous past.

CHAPTER ELEVEN

HARRIET CHATTED ANIMATEDLY IN THE CARRIAGE as the ladies returned to Hill Street, in blissful ignorance of what had happened. She had been in demand as a partner, greater demand than Susan, in fact, and her general sweetness of character combined with good looks was making her popular. She was not as striking as Susan, but then Susan had a nasty habit of 'striking back' and some gentlemen were quite open in their preference. Susan was disregarding the wavering in her popularity, thus far.

'And Lord Edward Wittenham arrived just before the doors closed. He had been on duty. He was looking for you, really, Susan, but Countess Lieven introduced me as a suitable partner and . . . he was very droll.' In the gloom, Harriet blushed. It did not make Susan feel any better.

When they alighted in Hill Street, Sophy kissed her sister's cheek and sent her off to her bed, with a recommendation that she let her maid tuck her into bed lest she continue to dance in her sleep. This sent her off giggling. Susan began to climb the stairs also.

'The Morning Room please, Susan.' It was not a request. 'Please light two branches of candles, William.' She looked to the sleepy footman, who took a taper and candlestick, and preceded her up to the first floor. Without thinking, Susan stood, hands folded, before the fireplace.

'Is your ladyship wishful that the fire be lit?' asked William, uncertainly.

'No, thank you, William, that is all for tonight. Please, get to your bed now.'

He bowed and retired. The room was chilly. Susan pulled her shawl more tightly about her shoulders, and waited for the outburst. Sophy took a chair by the fire and sat, ramrod straight, the candlelight illuminating one side of her face, which bore little trace of any expression.

'There have never been limits put upon you, Susan, except that you have been immured at Tyneham Court and never seen how the world runs upon compromise, consideration, and socially acceptable modes of behaviour.' It was a simple statement, calmly, made. 'And understanding that you have been unused to conventions, you have been treated very leniently in this house, whatever you may feel. My mama always felt for your poor mother. However, tonight you stepped so far beyond common good manners that I am forced to tell you that you jeopardise any chances both you, and indeed Harriet, have of finding a husband, and that if but one word of this spreads, you will be a social pariah. Do you want to find a husband, Susan?'

'Yes.'

'Then obey the Rules, and try to at least hide your repellent selfishness. You seem keen to attract men, any man in fact, but then treat them as . . . well, as dogs that you have but to snap your fingers at and command obedience.'

'Am I repellent?' There was just the trace of tremor in Susan's voice, then she laughed, an ugly, jangling laugh. 'Perhaps I am. You say I am selfish; I say I am protecting the only person who will look after me . . . and that is myself. My aunt pitied my mama. My mama was a fool, because she let a man imprison her, treat her as an object that cluttered his house and no more. I want to be married, because returning to my "prison" at Tyneham Court is unthinkable. Can you imagine living there with Tyneham? And no doubt with whatever submissive dab he takes to wife? Better I find a new gaol, and a new gaoler.'

Sophy's hands gripped each other, as she listened, shocked, horrified, pitying.

'I am a beauty, as my mama was, I think. It did not save her but it will save me. Men,' and she almost spat the word, 'are so very visual. They look, as a child does at a table laid with cakes and pastries, and then they want. Well, if they want me they have to do as I want, yes, like a dog. They are no better than slavering dogs. If I can get a husband who will do anything to keep me happy, then I will have freedom. I will run my own home, but I will run my own life too. I shall decide what I do, where I go, whom I take as friend,' her eyes glittered, 'or lover.' Her cynicism was total. 'You think me cruel to men. I say I am paying them back for the way my father treated my mother.'

There was silence in the room, where swathes of shadow encroached to distort the image of the two young women. Sophy thought very hard before she responded, and her voice held sympathy, though Susan heard it as pity.

'I am sorry, Susan, very sorry, that you, at nineteen, have so dark a view of life, and love.'

'I have not mentioned love. I do not believe in it. The only love I ever saw was my mother's for me, and that was weakness.'

'Then what you aspire to is not living but existing. You want to keep people out because they may hurt you. That is a risk, but only when we make ourselves vulnerable can we benefit from the strength of love, and love, of husband, children, relatives, friends, is what living is about.'

'But even if that is so, love and marriage are not the same thing. How many of my peers will marry for love?'

'A few. Many will marry with attraction, affection, admiration, and find love, perhaps not passion, but comfortable love, companionship of sorts, and not being alone. You want to marry yet remain alone. You have no experience of people beyond the tiny world in which you grew up, and it has slewed your perceptions. When a woman marries she becomes the possession of her husband in law. That is fact, but she gains his protection, she gains someone to stand alongside her against the world if it does come banging at the door, armed and angry. You talk of wanting a husband who will obey you. You would look down upon him. Well, I am past the age when it is likely I shall find a husband, but I would want a man to whom I could look up, respect, admire, not slavishly but be proud to be his companion, and given the chance I would want love, real love, with all its vulnerability. I do have more years in the world, Susan, grant me that.' She smiled, a little sadly. 'You say you want a husband, even if upon terms I find appalling. In that case, listen to me now. If you disobey the conventions of Society, you will not get a husband, of any sort, which leaves living with Tyneham. I happen to agree that anything would be preferable to that.' She did not say Lady Chelmarsh thought she was the 'submissive dab' he might pick as a wife. He might pick her, but she most certainly would not accept. If she ever—She banished the fleeting image of 'Rake Rothley' from her mind. 'If you want a husband like a lapdog, then remember you can only kick a dog so often and then it will turn and bite you or run away. You have pushed Bollington away, aided by the fact that his mama regards you with horror as uncontrolled and uncontrollable, and likely to bring ruin upon them. If you have a gentleman who singles you out and whom you would consider being your "gaoler", have the good sense not to try and make him jealous before his ring is upon your finger.' She stopped for a moment, and her voice softened. 'I may, in my mother's place, demand a standard of behaviour from you, Susan. I cannot demand you find a heart. I can implore you to think upon what I have said, however, and try to see that marriage is not about victory or defeat, not if you have warmer emotions involved. I once told Mama the best thing for you would be to fall in love with a man who did not reciprocate your feelings, a rake who would be more cynical than you yourself. That was wrong of me. I would wish that you found a man you could love, and would love you in return, not abjectly, but honourably, and could teach you to . . . really feel.' Sophy sighed, and passed a hand over her eyes. 'Enough has been said tonight, Susan. Go to your bed, and include in your prayers one for self control. We can only hope that the young lady before whom you made your outburst tonight was too shocked to tell anyone else about it. If you repeat such behaviour, I will not permit you to attend social functions. Goodnight.'

'Goodnight, cousin.' Susan curtsied, as she would to her aunt in such serious circumstances, and left.

Sophy sat for a moment, and having concentrated upon her cousin, slowly found herself contemplating not only Susan's folly but her own. She covered her face with her hands. Susan ought to be her only worry, and here was she, actually excited by the thought that Lord Rothley might want her to fall into his clutches at the same time as she was determined that he must fail. She wished her mother were here, but even more so her father. Depressed and worried, she then sought her own bed, where she did not sleep until near dawn.

Lord Rothley did not sleep, but then he did not seek his bed until dawn. He would not hear from Vienna for perhaps ten days, but he did not need a reply to feel responsible. Susan was a problem child, and child he thought her still, wilful, if not actively contrary, and Lady Sophy suffered because of it. When he had seen her tonight he had wanted so much to hold more than her hand, give more than advice. He had wanted to hold her, take her troubles, bear her burdens. He laughed out loud at himself. He sounded like some chivalric knight in such tales as little boys read. He would be wanting next to slay dragons for her. Susan might seem, if not a dragon, then at least a serpent, but he could not slay her. Somehow he had to try his best to protect her also, though how eluded him. When he lay in his bed, when he closed his eyes, there came not rest but a revolving in his mind of how he might deal with this complicated situation, and no good answers.

If the matchmaking mamas watched Lady Sophronia and saw her troubled, they sighed sympathetically, and shook their heads, blaming it upon her cousin. None of them would want to have charge of the wayward and wilful Susan, even without the knowledge of what had happened at Almack's. Susan's behaviour there became more restrained, even as she privately railed against the prohibition on her dancing the waltz, which remained, clearly as a punishment, for another two weeks. This bottled-up anger found expression elsewhere. She went out of her way to flirt with Lord Edward Wittenham, who appeared the day after the Lady Jersey incident with posies for all three ladies, though Sophy could see that two were but covers for the third to be acceptable. She thought his eye had actually been taken by Harriet; after all it had been she who had danced with him, and she coloured very prettily when she received the flowers, but Susan dazzled him, intentionally trying to cut out her quieter cousin. It was cruel. Sophy was not sure it was totally successful, however, since Lord Edward cast several slightly desperate glances at Harriet, glances which seemed to convey that he was being unwillingly sucked into the quagmire of admiration. Thereafter he was seen at more parties than previously, and though he gravitated to Harriet by inclination, the magnetic attraction of Susan almost always won. Harriet was sweet, laughed at his mild jokes, looked up at him as if adoring a demi-god. She made his heart sing softly. Susan did not bother to appeal to his heart, but to a rather different part of his anatomy. He wondered sometimes, as he lay in his bed, if she was the true form of a witch. He did not like her, let alone love her, but the stirrings of his heart for Harriet could not compete with the stirrings in his loins when Susan purred at him, drooped her heavy eyelids and fluttered her eyelashes at him. It was enthralment in the truest sense. He was ashamed but exhilarated.

Harriet was unhappy. She felt inadequate, and did not blame the cavalry officer. After all, Susan seemed to only have to snap her fingers and men fell at her feet. She only hoped that she would be allowed to pick Lord Edward up from the floor at a later date, for she had noticed that gentlemen did not remain as enamoured of her cousin as she perhaps hoped. Harriet had found his open, engaging manner and slightly dashing looks striking from that first moment when she had seen him, already looking at Susan. She was always going to be the one looking at men already looking at Susan. When her cousin was not close, as when she had spent that delightful evening at Almack's and he had danced with her and then obtained refreshment for her and talked to her and . . . it counted as one of her best evenings ever.

She knew why she had come to London, to find a suitable husband. It was what one did, what one was expected to do. She knew how deep her mother's mortification had been that Sophy did not 'take' and had returned home unattached, unsought. At the same time, one dreamt, dreamt that romance and practicality would prove one and the same thing. Several gentlemen had shown a little interest in her, but they made her feel that they were doing just that, taking an interest in making a purchase, like a horse. Lord Edward Wittenham did not make her feel that way at all, possibly, and loweringly, because he was totally uninterested in her. She knew that she was terribly interested in him. The only good thing about him watching Susan was that she could watch him, unobserved, notice that the very tip of the ring finger on his right hand was missing, that his smile was always fractionally lopsided, that in candlelight there was a flash of copper in his brown hair, and that although Susan mesmerised him, he did not look happy with her.

So Harriet lost a little of her appetite for food, and jollity, and Sophy, strangely shy about asking after her youngest sister's heart, still had the wit to see the problem, and know its cause. Susan did not want Wittenham, she wanted to show her cousins she could have him at her feet if she wished, wanted to make Sophy pay for the constraints that she felt were being put upon her by making the innocent Harriet miserable.

In this Sophy was only partially correct. Lord Bollington had cooled, and Susan wanted freedom as soon as possible. The youngest son, even of a duke, who had blood and lineage but little to inherit, would not normally interest her, but making her cousin pay for treating her as a foolish child was entertaining and, as she had said, she would marry anyone to escape a return to Tyneham. She was unsure of her next move, however, for there was an alternative to Lord Edward. Lord Pinkney would make her a countess, though one who lived hand to mouth if the tales were true. However, his lordship was not an easy fish to land, and this intrigued Susan. Wittenham was so very easy, but Pinkney sometimes looked lazily at her lures, and smiled, and at other times acted as if she had him upon the hook and all she had to do was reel him in.

Sophy knew her words fell upon deaf ears when she warned her cousin about him, and even thought it spurred the foolish Susan on, and she knew the uncharitable thought that when her cousin was busy ensnaring him, she at least had less time to work her wicked magic upon Lord Edward.

As Sophy watched her cousin, so Lord Rothley watched them both, and became increasingly frustrated that he could not be of assistance without revealing a secret that was still supposition on his part. When he next encountered the three ladies after the night at Almack's, Susan had treated him to a display of icy coolness, which had been mirrored by Lady Sophy when the younger girls had been led onto the dance floor by suitable partners.

'Surely I do not have to assure you ma'am, that the events of the other evening will remain cloaked, and private, between us only.'

'Between us only'. Sophy flushed. Oh, how alluring were those words, the declaration of a bond, a shared secret. Yet how often had he captivated a lady by making her think just as she was thinking now? Had he looked as sincere to a score of ladies before?

'It is better forgotten, by everyone, my lord, the entire evening.' She spoke stiffly, and lowered her eyes.

'Lady Sophy, what have I done?'

Seduced too many credulous females before me? She could not say that.

'Nothing, my lord. I . . . I am, as you well know, struggling to keep my cousin under control and . . . short of locking her in the house, I wonder how that is to be achieved.'

'I did suggest a whip and a chair, ma'am, but, as you have consigned that evening to oblivion you may not recall it.'

'I . . . have not forgotten, Lord Rothley.'

'I wish you would trust me.' It was such a simple statement.

'No doubt you do, my lord.' There was sharpness, which he did not comprehend, and she half turned away. If she trusted him, he would have her in the palm of his hand, and in such a place she would be crushed, and yet his hands had held hers, sustained her, aided her without any attempt at wicked seduction. 'I trust that you have no intentions towards my cousin, at least, since you now know her faults so well.'

'You say "at least" with relief.' There was that regret again.

She stole a look at him and found him regarding her as if he might read her mind.

'I am at your service, ma'am, in all things. Command me, and I will endeavour to do it.' He sounded so sincere it would be easy to treat it as the truth.

'And if I commanded you to leave us, keep from our problems, our affairs?'

'Ah, that is the one thing I would not be able to do.' His voice dropped to a whisper. 'Is it what you wish, truly?'

She ought to say yes. She could not say yes, for it was so great a lie.

'I wish you might help me keep my cousin from the dangerous clutches of Lord Pinkney, without resort to calling him out, of course.'

'Now that is another way in which you show yourself so very different from Miss Tyneham, ma'am. She was rather keen that Fawley call me out so that she might say men had fought over her. Or possibly she wanted me in a bloodied, lifeless heap at the time.'

Sophy was shocked from her self-absorption.

'She did not, surely?' She paled at the mental image.

'Oh, she did. Ask Fawley if you . . . do not trust me.'

'No need, my lord. I know my cousin and have to admit she would say just that, and mean it too.'

'She also suggested I should retire to Derbyshire.'

'Derbyshire, my lord? Have you estates there?' She blinked.

'Oh no, she just thought it far enough away from her person.'

Sophy gave a low laugh at that, despite herself.

'Then it is a good job that you have no intentions towards her, for she, for one, is resistant to your charms.'

'You say that as if I possessed a multitude of them.' He frowned, but had noted the 'for one'.

Was he going to deny them, and play the innocent gentleman? That was a step too far.

'Far too many for one of simple tastes like myself, my

lord.' It was the response of an instant, and she gasped at her own temerity.

'Then I ought to remove them to a safe distance for you, ma'am. I hope Derbyshire is too far since from there I can be of no assistance with Lord Pinkney.' There was an edge to his voice.

He bowed, and withdrew, leaving Sophy Hadlow prey to myriad emotions.

Obeying Lady Sophy's command with regard to Lord Pinkney was not as simple as it might appear. Confronting him directly was out of the question, since Pinkney might, with every good reason, question his right to do so. His approach had to be tangential. He observed Miss Tyneham, both working upon Captain Lord Edward Wittenham, and then upon Lord Pinkney, who, like himself, saw her tricks for what they were.

'Are you attempting to make me jealous, Miss Tyneham?' murmured Lord Pinkney, when she released Lord Edward from her toils for the evening, a few nights later.

'Might I not, my lord?' she twinkled up at him.

'Not with someone as boringly worthy as Wittenham. Bore you in a week. You, madam, need someone far more adventurous.'

'Any suggestions, my lord?'

Lord Pinkney's eyes widened a fraction. He was unsure whether she was simply the innocent acting the courtesan, or possessed the soul of one in a body that had lineage. He drew a bow at a venture.

'Many, Miss Tyneham, but none that would be suitable for Lady Swaffham's ballroom.'

She looked puzzled, then belatedly arch. She knew that what he had said was too daring, but not what the suggestions might include. He read her face like a book. So the little Tyneham was not as experienced as she pretended. She was very pretty. Teaching her would be . . . enjoyable.

'I meant, wicked Lord Pinkney, whether you had any other gentlemen in mind.'

'Depends how gentlemanly you want them to be, Miss Tyneham. I, for instance, am a lord, but many will assure you that I am not a gentleman. Does that scare you?'

'No,' she lied.

'Are you sure?'

'No.' She giggled.

He smiled, and it was an anticipatory smile. Lord Rothley saw it, and his hand clenched. He took a glass of champagne from a servant bearing a salver, and made his way nonchalantly so that he passed the pair of them, and as he did so he tripped slightly and sent part of the contents over the skirt of her gown.

'Miss Tyneham, my profound apologies. Your cousin will know if anything should be applied. I am terribly sorry. She was with Lady Castlereagh a minute ago.'

Susan looked exasperated, and excused herself to Lord Pinkney.

'That was very careless of you, Rothley,' remarked Pinkney, casually.

'Yes, was it not. Remarkable how careless one can be upon occasion. Mind you, having a care is something everyone seems to forget occasionally, even yourself.'

'Indeed?'

'Yes, it would be the act of a careless man to think Miss Tyneham was er, unprotected.'

'Though not necessarily by Tyneham.'

'Correct.'

'One wonders why another man – you, for instance – might choose to champion the young lady. Not self-interest?'

'Not directly. You might say I aim, er, higher. For the rest, well, one would have to continue wondering.'

Lord Rothley thought a blatant lie too obvious. He patently did not want Susan Tyneham for himself. If he was to be effective he had to give another reason, and hints at interest in her cousin, whilst containing an element of risk, would be credible. Pinkney raised an eyebrow.

'Need our purposes be mutually exclusive, Rothley?'

'Alas, I think they might.'

'How novel, to have a rival, whilst for a different woman.'

'But just as . . . dangerous.'

'That, my lord, we shall see.'

CHAPTER TWELVE

WHILST IT COULD NOT BE SAID THAT LORD Pinkney withdrew entirely, he certainly chose his times to approach Miss Tyneham with care, avoiding both her relatives and Lord Rothley. However, being a gambler, it did add an extra element of risk which he rather enjoyed, and he thought there might yet be spokes he might thrust in Lord Rothley's particular wheel and leave him far behind, freeing Miss Tyneham for his seduction. When the letter from Vienna arrived, Lord Rothley was so absorbed in the situation that it took him by surprise. He took it to his bookroom and requested that he not be disturbed. For a minute or so held it in his hand, lost in thought. The handwriting was not unfamiliar to him.

My dear Rothley,

I read your letter, and my first reaction was to damn your impudence, demanded as it did, and yes, there is no better term for it, to know details of my past private life which ought to be no concern of yours. However, I do concede that if Tyneham knows, then a little clarification may be in order.

Of course it was all so very, very long ago, and to be honest I had forgotten the entire episode. Clarissa Tyneham was a very beautiful woman in her prime, and Tyneham was a boor, as it seems is his son. He neglected her shamefully, and made her unhappy. She was a woman who thrived upon affection, and it was a pleasure to show some towards her, but I never pretended that it was more than amusement; my reputation was well known, and I never mentioned her leaving Tyneham. She was the entertainment of a Season, no more. That she took things to heart showed she was a fool.

As for the child, Tyneham showed some sense at least, and kept quiet. After all, it only turned out to be a girl and there would be no problem with the title if anything happened to the heir. All in all, it seemed a very satisfactory conclusion to a pleasant interlude.

Rothley ground his teeth. Satisfactory, yes, to a man with no responsibility and seeking new amusements. He had no consideration for the life he had left to Clarissa Tyneham, or the embarrassed shame of his own wife, who must have known the *on dits*, even if not in Town. Some 'kind friend' would have been bound to tell her, as they had with the others.

I can see that the situation might be difficult for you with the chit residing with Lady Chelmarsh, but memories are very short, really. I had to think hard to recall the affair myself. There may be a few old tabbies who remember if, as you say, there are actually similarities, but of what consequence is that, since it is to Chelmarsh's girl you are attracted with a view to being leg-shackled?

That the 'Tyneham' chit is a beauty, knowing her mother, is not a surprise. That she shares characteristics with you in colouring is a compliment to me. Your mother always said you looked like me, but I think she was exaggerating. You are not a bad-looking fellow, but if you had seen me in my prime, my boy . . .

His lordship scoffed. Of course, there had been very little chance of seeing Viscount Rothley 'in his prime' since he rarely visited his estates, and took no more interest in his son than sending him money at school, along with the practical, if rather shocking advice to a thirteen-year-old, that he should always make sure the women he 'played with' were clean. As paternal advice it was limited. His grandsire had been his role

170

model, and the old earl was of such different metal to his son that he could not comprehend what had gone awry in him. Restrictions upon his purse strings only worked when his gambling was unsuccessful, which in those days was rare, and the best the elderly Earl of Woodhall could do was stand by his son's wife and heir.

Grandfather had died when Rothley was in his last year at Eton. The old man had left what he could to his daughter-in-law, the Dower House for her lifetime, and a good annuity, and as much as he could in Trust for the new Viscount Rothley, but that still left a considerable portion to the profligate, whose luck had eventually nose-dived, and the new earl had chosen to live, more economically, abroad. This may also have had something to do with the fact that there were gentlemen in England who had designs upon his health as a result of his peccadilloes with their wives. Not all men were as sanguine as old Tyneham.

I hope this clears the situation for you and wish you well of the Chelmarsh girl; about time you thought of setting up a nursery, and I do not disapprove of the family, good stock.

That was rich, coming from him! He simply could not see that it might be Lord Chelmarsh who did not think Woodhall's son was 'good enough stock' to marry his eldest daughter?

Teresa sends her regards, though of course all her warmest are reserved for me. Just try to remember our Marston family motto, 'Life is to be lived' and stop thinking like a parson. Morality is for the weak. With which sound advice, Rothley,

I remain your affectionate parent,

Woodhall

If it was not so appalling it would be almost funny. There was his father, the aged Lothario in his foreign bolthole, with his latest, perhaps last, and none too young, inamorata, telling his son to be more like him. Well, Lord Rothley knew that his father was the aberration. The Marston heritage was of good management of their estates and decency regarding their own spouses and those of other men. Saints they might not be, but sinners of his father's magnitude they were not either.

He thought of his mother. She had been a quiet, loving woman, with gentle eyes that were always haunted by sorrow. Her misfortune was never to have fallen totally out of love with her errant husband, and she had spent her life, as long as her son could remember, in a state of semi-widowhood. She had never displayed any public awareness that her spouse had 'abandoned' her. She had lived quietly, acting as chatelaine in her father-in-law's house, doing every good work that might be expected of a lady of good breeding, so that when she died after two years of declining health, there had been crowds outside the church who could not get in to hear the service. He did not regret his father's absences, but he did look upon those two years with sorrow. After all she had put up with, it seemed cruel that she should be afflicted as she had been. In those two years he had not come up to Town for more than the odd appointment with his tailor, nor been upon the circuit of house parties and visits. She had almost had to force him to spend a couple of weeks at his hunting box in Leicestershire, and make the occasional visit to a friend. She had always been there for him, and love and duty meant that he had felt the least he could do was be there for her.

It had been one of her last wishes that he re-establish more than written contact with his father, and so he had travelled to where his father had finally settled, in Vienna. There he found him ensconced in a baroque residence with rather too much peeling gilding, and a lady he described as 'the Gräfin Teresa', who appeared to be a middle-aged widow with enough money to cover his lack of it, and an eye to an aged rake.

His father was not, on the face of it, a bad-looking man for his age, and had an even greater sense of self-importance now that he had inherited his father's title. He clearly felt 'the Earl of Woodhall' would be advanced more credit by tradesmen than a mere viscount. He had steely grey hair now, and a thickened figure, but still appeared 'distinguished' until you looked more closely, and noticed the marks of dissolution. Presumably Teresa was short-sighted, or he still had that magical 'something' which made women adore him. He had no scruples about living off her, indeed seemed to think he was doing her a service by 'giving her his protection'. He was, in short, the same man he had always been.

His son tried, for his mother's sake, to find something in him that he could like. The man was totally unrepentant, said nothing about his wife other than 'pity the poor soul suffered so long' and then brushed it away as unpleasantness he would rather not face. Rothley soon saw this was his father's basic attitude to life. He did what he wanted, and if anything unpleasant intruded, he turned away and ignored it. That was how he had ignored the consequences of his actions. He did not gloat over the women he had used, he simply forgot them, as he did his debts, his mistakes and his failings. He was completely and utterly selfish.

The worrying thought occurred to Rothley that perhaps Susan Tyneham had inherited that as well as the glossy dark hair, and he hoped it was untrue.

He had stomached his sire's company for four months, and then made his way back to England via Paris, of which his grandfather had spoken in the days before the French had removed the heads of their aristocrats. It was, he thought, a place still haunted in odd places by blood, though it had a bustling *joie de vivre* about it. If he did not see his father again he would not be distraught. He had little thought that the sins of the father would influence the future chances of happiness for the son.

It sounded histrionic, but since meeting Lady Sophy Hadlow, he had felt different. That first time he had put it down to interest, in the sense of wanting to watch what happened with the unpredictable Miss Tyneham, and there was a peculiar draw to her, which he could now see as vaguely familial. It was the tall, so very tall for a lady, form of Lady Sophy, however, with her alert mind and willingness to spar light-heartedly, that had made him contemplate a permanent attachment for the very first time. There had been the odd liaison in the past, it was true, of a mutually advantageous nature and with ladies who understood business, but he was, by the standards of his peers, far from being a ladies' man, unlike his disreputable parent. Certainly, there had never been a woman who appealed to mind and body as Sophy Hadlow did. He wondered at a fate which had meant that when she had been in London for the Season he had been absent. He must have noticed so statuesque a young lady, and yet a voice told him he would not have appreciated her then, and something in her demeanour spoke to him of expecting the world to ignore her. She found compliments difficult to accept, as if none could be true. Perhaps, at eighteen, she had not dared to stare the world in the face and defy its unkindnesses, since the unusual was always prey to them. He remembered her words, 'I am too tall to "take", and I have not my cousin's . . . bravura.' Yes, she was not in the common mould. Now, at twenty-three or four, as he guessed, she was past worrying what the world whispered. Sadly, this also meant that she listened to him with scepticism. Some of his words were pure jest, but if he as much as added a term of honest appreciation to a comment, she treated it as foolery. Persuading such a lady of his bona fides was not easy. At least he did not possess his father's sullied reputation, but if Tyneham revealed his relationship to Susan, would the Chelmarsh household not hold him at a distance?

Suddenly a thought occurred to him. What if Lady Sophy assumed that his character must be akin to that of his sire? Everything made sense in that context, her comments, the way she pulled back from him.

He gazed down at the letter in his hands, and his lip curled. His father had so very much for which to answer.

Lord Tyneham did not jump to conclusions. In fact, jumping was a thing he never did. He prided himself on being methodical, organised. He had begun the Season intending to make an offer for his cousin Sophronia, an offer she would of course accept. These last few weeks, however, his certainty had been severely shaken, and from the most unwelcome of sources. Sophronia was not to know, how could she do so, that any form of 'friendship', and he put it no higher, with Rothley was out of the question. It irked him. Rothley had appeared to be in ignorance when he had encountered him, so very at ease with the ladies, in the Park. That might have been true then, but the meeting must have raised his suspicions, given him cause to find out. He must know how things stood, must know what lay between the two families, how unacceptable he was. When Tyneham had been unsure of this he had wondered if, by a quirk of perversity, Rothley had his eye on Susan. That, were it not offensive, would almost be funny. He had imagined, several times, the satisfaction of revealing the truth to the pair. However, more recently it had become obvious that Rothley wanted to fix his interest with Sophronia. Women were notoriously unreliable, and much inclined to prefer danger to reliability, until their fingers got burnt. For some reason, Sophronia's efforts at repulsing Rothley were lacking in self-belief, and he showed absolutely no sign of doing the honourable thing and withdrawing from the lists. Instead, he was pursuing her. It was no use, Rothley must be warned off, once and for all. Sophronia must be saved from her own feminine weakness, and he would forgive her. With this view in mind, Lord Tyneham went in search of his 'rival'.

Lord Tyneham ran his lordship to ground at White's, where he found him perusing a periodical.

'Ah, Rothley. Just the man I was looking for.'

'Really, Tyneham?' Lord Rothley lowered the newspaper with a soft rustle and looked at him without enthusiasm but with mild interest. 'Forgive me for being surprised. I can think of no possible reason why you could be looking for me, not even to buy a horse, since nothing I have in my stable could be up to your weight.'

'I don't wish to buy a horse,' declared Tyneham, a little flustered. He had expected Rothley to understand instantly why he might want words with him, and be evasive but not bored, and his lordship sounded distinctly bored. 'It is a more delicate matter.'

'If you had your eye on the fair Hyacinthe at the opera, let me tell you she is damnably expensive and way above my touch, whatever rumour may have to the contrary.' He sighed. 'I think I only have to look at a woman and the gossip begins. It is amazing how easy it is for some people to assume that the vices of the father are those of the son.' The voice had hardened. 'Besides, I am not a man for flaxen beauties.'

This last was said looking Tyneham straight in the eye.

'No, my lord, perhaps you are not. Let us say that certain darker ladies are also outside your . . . scope.'

'Do you really think so, Tyneham?' Lord Rothley raised a quizzical eyebrow, and regarded the increasingly choleric peer sardonically.

'I would have you know that I consider any acquaintanceship between you and my sister repellent, and my cousin, Lady Sophronia Hadlow is as good as betrothed.'

'You do of course have a say in whom your sister meets on terms of friendship, though sadly you clearly have no control over her behaviour.' Lord Rothley ignored the implication about Lady Sophy and the viscount.

'And where do you think she gets her waywardness?' Tyneham ground his teeth.

'Oh, I think we both know the answer to that, don't we,' Rothley said, and though there was a smile upon his lip, his eyes glittered. 'However, had it been dealt with when she was younger, there would not now be the need for someone to take her in hand.'

'It shall not be you, Rothley.'

'I regret that since you have clearly done nothing, it is me, will be me. You see, I do understand fraternal responsibility.'

'Good God, you would tell her!'

'No, and for heaven's sake keep your voice down, you fool. I would not tell her at this juncture, but leaving her as a burden upon Lady Sophy and watching from the wings as the chit sets all and sundry on end is not the action of a brother, even, Tyneham, a half-brother.' He let Tyneham digest this information before continuing. 'As for Lady Sophy . . .'

'Her name is Sophronia,' Lord Tyneham interjected, most put out, and increasingly flushed of cheek.

'Yes, and one can perfectly understand why she abhors it.'

'But—'

'I take it that "as good as betrothed" means you mean to make her an offer?' Lord Rothley laughed, softly. 'If you think that Lady Sophy is yours for the asking then you are deluding yourself. She will refuse you, Tyneham.'

'You cannot possibly know that.'

'Ah, but I can. You are far too great a prosy bore, and not nearly tall enough for her.'

'Unlike you?'

'Now you mention it, unlike me, though I am not sure she may not dream of an even taller lover.'

'Lover. How dare you!'

Rothley's eyes gleamed.

'One who loves, Tyneham. What were you imagining?'

Lord Tyneham's flush of anger became a scarlet blush of embarrassment.

'I don't have to listen to this.'

'No. The simplest expedient would therefore be to go away. I was really rather interested in that article on . . . the increase in agricultural labour force since the Peace.'

Lord Rothley was quite deliberately insulting. Short of making a very unpleasant and public scene, Tyneham had no course but to withdraw, fuming. He could not see that Rothley was doing likewise beneath the cool exterior.

Tyneham had abrogated responsibility for his sister, and although he knew she was his half-sister that responsibility existed. He was thus leaving his cousin to deal with the problem. Without revealing facts of which Susan Tyneham and her cousins were unaware, Lord Rothley wanted to help, and he would not be kept at a distance by a prig like Tyneham.

Whilst he told himself it was the least he could do for a young woman as close to him as she was to her acknowledged brother, by blood, and in part to make up for his father's failings, he knew that his prime reason was to lift the burden from Sophy Hadlow because . . . He smiled, wryly, to himself. 'Love' was a word so often used and so little understood. He had never anticipated that love would feel this way, or be so damnably difficult. If he had thought about it at all it had been a vague assumption that it would be a mixture of physical desire and happiness on both sides. The desire was certainly there for his part, and that indefinable glow of happiness which erupted into flame when near her, but she held him off even as her eyes told him that his feelings were reciprocated. There were unguarded moments when he no more doubted her affection than that the sun would rise in the morning, and then the veil would come down and she would withdraw, unwillingly, he thought, but determinedly. He was almost sure that she did not know of Susan's paternity, and even if she did, he saw no reason why it should preclude her accepting him, so his love was surely keeping him at a distance because she had heard that his line were predatory, and feared his motives? Damn his father.

CHAPTER THIRTEEN

SUSAN WAS A YOUNG WOMAN WHO BLEW HOT AND cold because it was more exciting, and she liked to see men suffer. She was not altogether sure that Lord Pinkney would go so far as suffering, but she thought she might yet slip a barb beneath his armour if she showed herself very keen upon her uniformed admirer. Lord Edward Wittenham was as putty in her little hands, even though he sometimes dreamt she was squeezing his heart until it burst, not in the sense of loving but so that it might not follow its own inclination.

When he saw Lady Harriet that heart gave a little skip. Had it not been for the malign presence of Miss Tyneham, he would be determinedly fixing his interest with that damsel. He knew he was not the greatest catch, but he could keep a wife in comfort, assure her of moving in the highest circles and had a snug little estate from an uncle where he might settle once he sold out, and the army was far less interesting now there was peace in Europe. Not that having Polish Lancers attempting to skewer one counted as merely interesting, and there were odd nights when in his dreams he still parried the blow from a French cuirassier that thus did not slice off his arm but merely slid down his own lunging blade and neatly removed the tip from his right ring finger. He could hold his head up as not just a fancy soldier for London parades, and if you were going to have been present at any battles, Vitoria and Waterloo were undoubtedly the ones which would be remembered by everyone. He was twenty-six, and had no need to settle as yet, and no pressure from having to secure a succession, yet thoughts of a cosy home life did now intrude. He imagined that comfortable life with Lady Harriet, not Miss Tyneham, about whom his unconscious thoughts were more frequent, but located only in a bedroom.

Lord Rothley, who did not blame Wittenham for his infatuation, but pitied the man, wisely refrained from giving him the hint to stand down. He thought the fellow would see sense soon enough and would be left with nothing worse than an embarrassing memory.

Sophy, despite the added stresses, had always enjoyed the ball her mama held in the Hill Street house, even the awful year of her own debut. She wondered whether it was because it was one time when nobody announced her name. If it had not been for the tangle in which she found herself with Susan, and her worry over Harriet, she would still have enjoyed it this year, once she had got past the 'day-before panic'. Bembridge was a fount of good sense and respectfully avuncular calm, whose veneer only cracked when Sophy took his hand and averred that without him she would have taken to her bed and hidden beneath the bedclothes, quaking in horror, until the event was cancelled. This reduced him to a blushing mumble for a full three minutes.

She thrust any thoughts about her cousin, and even her sister, to the back of her mind whilst there were practical tasks to check or oversee. She recalled her mama's stricture to look at the positioning of the floral arrangements for herself, and double-checked that there was a sufficiency of hams, and additional patisserie from Gunter's supplementing the output of the kitchens. It was only as she dressed for the evening that she wondered how the pair would fare. Harriet was not inclined to chatter with her cousin as she had been used to do, but had not done anything so ill-bred as refuse to speak to her. She need not fear a receiving line that gave off a crackle of mutual antipathy.

She had avoided the potential of one problem by the simple expedient of not sending an invitation to Lord Pinkney. She had also omitted Lord Rothley from the list, though she did not account him as disreputable as that peer. She told herself it was what her mama would have wished, even though it had not been decided at the point of her departure. She also told herself that the pang of regret it cost her was actually indigestion. At least the first was true.

Lord Pinkney's absence would of course mean that Susan would, Sophy knew instinctively, devote as much time as she could just this side of propriety, to Lord Edward Wittenham. She had been tempted to omit him from the guest list as well, just for peace and quiet, but Harriet would miss him if he did not appear, even if she was forced to suffer seeing him in the clutches of her cousin if he did. Sophy hoped he might be Duty Officer, but this was not to be.

Sir Esmond Fawley would be present, and upon him Sophy could rely, and even foresee a few minutes of entertaining conversation. He might also be useful, being privy to Susan's intemperate behaviour, if there were 'emergencies'. She had the maid set a diamond crescent in her hair to match the diamond necklet about her white throat and the bracelet that glittered about her wrist over a long kid glove, and surveyed herself one last time in the mirror. The galling thing was that the thought uppermost in her mind was that it was such a shame Lord Rothley would not be there to see her in all her sparkling glory. She gave herself a mental shake, and the maid, seeing her expression, assured her mistress that she looked a treat. She tweaked the zephyr shawl that was draped with studied carelessness, and went out to take a final look at the public rooms, and then take her place at the head of the stairs. It occurred to her as she did so, and awaited Harriet and Susan, that this might be the only time in her life that she held this position, as the lady of the house greeting the guests. It was a rather depressing thought on which to commence the evening.

Lady Chelmarsh judged her parties by how hot it became and how fast the ladies' fans wafted to and fro. By these criteria Sophy could safely report this one could be added to the list of successes. By half past ten the rooms were crowded and Sophy had sent Harriet to circulate among the guests. Susan she kept by her side, largely because she did not trust her. She therefore remained under duress and her smile was fixed. This was especially true because Lord Edward Wittenham had arrived a little after ten o'clock and she assumed Harriet would do just as she would have in the situation, and made every effort to find him and keep him 'attached'. In reality Harriet was perfectly aware where he was, as if threads led from him, but she was too well brought up to be obvious or select people she would talk to upon her own wishes. She was therefore speaking to the most elevated of the guests, and the nearest she got to talking to him was to glance in his direction, catch his eye and smile. He smiled back, and she thought her evening made.

Sir Esmond Fawley was among the last guests to arrive, and smiled apologetically as he climbed the stairs towards his hostess.

'Lady Sophy, am I in your bad books for my tardy

arrival?' He bowed over her hand, and then looked up.

'That depends upon your reason, sir.'

'Now that puts me in a quandary. Should I be honest and say I arrived late to make my preparations, having been on a very enjoyable drive to Richmond and back, or do I improve upon it and say that I was visiting my old nurse, and could not drag myself away because of the tears in her aged eyes?'

'You could have said you were visiting your aged horse, and combined the two, Sir Esmond,' suggested Susan, drily.

'Now that is ingenious, Miss Tyneham, but I will have to use that next time.' He paused, bowed over the gloved hand she extended, and when he straightened, his eyes were full of merriment. 'Did the horse have tears in its eyes?'

'Oh yes, otherwise there would be no feeling that you had done something that made the horse happy rather than yourself.' The fixed smile had become real.

'I shall remember that.'

'And I, being magnanimous, will forgive you this once, Sir Esmond, but if you arrive late at a party I organise in the future, a whole stable of weeping equines will not save you from opprobrium.' Sophy could at that moment forgive him anything for improving Susan's mood.

'I have thus been warned, ma'am. Will you dance at your own ball?'

'Oh, I shall be led out by the most high-ranking gentleman present for the first dance, and I fear that will be the Marquess of Donnington, who is known to dance about as well as I sing.'

'Have you a good voice, Lady Sophy?'

'Cannot hold a note.'

'Then might I only say that if your feet survive the encounter intact, I would consider myself honoured if you would dance with me later in the evening.'

'If you see me limping you will know I am *hors de combat*.'

'When I was young,' murmured Susan, mistress of nineteen summers, 'I thought *hors de combat* was the French for 'warhorse'.

'A perfectly logical mistake to make, Miss Tyneham.' He bowed, and moved away into the throng.

Sir Esmond having apparently turned Susan's sulk into something approaching good humour, Sophy felt brave enough to send her among the guests for a while, though she tried hard to keep her eye upon both her and Harriet as best she could. She had explained that they had 'duties' tonight, and would be expected to think of their guests more than themselves. When she looked at Susan she wondered if the girl even understood the concept of 'not thinking of herself'.

When the dancing commenced, Sophy sacrificed her feet, and let Lord Donington, whom, she found out, had clammy hands as well as being a lumbering dancer, lead her to the floor. After these purgatorial few minutes, she was able to wander among 'her' guests, feeling less and less nervous and more assured that anyone to whom she spoke would be enjoying the party. Whilst the reason for the Season was to see Harriet and Susan established, the most important event to Lady Chelmarsh, other than the Presentation, which was so formulaic Sophy had not feared Susan might behave outrageously, was their own party, when house and occupants would be on full show. If she could report that it went smoothly, if friends wrote to her to say that it was 'a terrible squeeze' and that they had an excellent evening, then she would be able to look Mama in the eye.

By one o'clock she had not noticed any great thinning of numbers, so was confident that people were not drifting away to put in an appearance elsewhere. She relaxed enough to enjoy herself. Sir Esmond renewed his request that she dance with him, and she accepted, little knowing that among some of the matrons this was seen as significant.

'This is how I like to see you, ma'am,' he commented, as they performed the first figure.

'Dancing?'

'Well, you dance very well, but no, I meant at ease. You get precious little time for enjoying yourself.'

'I have in part engineered this, though, Sir Esmond,' she confided, smiling. 'You see,' she dropped her voice to a low whisper, 'I avoided trouble by not inviting Lord Pinkney, so Susan could not play off him and poor Lord Edward Wittenham against each other.'

Sir Esmond's expression became serious.

'Wittenham is a nice enough young fellow, but Pinkney . . .'

'I know.'

'Does Miss Tyneham look with ambition at either?'

'Oh, I do not know. I see flickers of humanity, as when you arrived, but for the most part Susan is so coldly, scarily, cynical, she might do anything she thinks will achieve her ends.'

'Which are?'

'Escape from incarceration at Tyneham Court, and her brother. Other than visiting us as a child, I do not think she has ever left it, nor been part of even local society. She actually said she was looking to exchange "one gaoler for another". She—' Sophy coloured. 'I am sorry. I should not talk about her so personally. I blame you, Sir Esmond, for being such a good listener, and . . .' she paused for a moment and looked at him squarely, 'might I say such a good friend to me, to us.'

'I am honoured if you do so, Lady Sophy, and would have you know you may command my services at any time.'

Her colour became even more pronounced, but for a reason he could not know. He echoed Lord Rothley's words so closely, the absent viscount intruded very forcibly into her thoughts, and there remained, lurking.

It was nearer the end of the evening when her pleasure unravelled, and Lord Rothley found no room in her mind. She had been with Bembridge, evaluating whether they needed to bring up additional champagne from the cellars at this late stage, and had temporarily left her duties as chaperone in abeyance. She did not see Susan dance with Lord Edward or lead him, when they left the floor, down to the courtyard garden, which Lady Chelmarsh grandly termed her 'Italian Garden'. Harriet, however, did, and though she knew she would regret it, slipped out onto the iron balcony from which they had descended, and observed, gripping the railing ever tighter.

Susan had been 'good' all night, comparatively speaking, and now wanted to please herself, which translated as wrapping Lord Edward about her little finger. He was not a challenge like Lord Pinkney, but it improved her mood, She flirted just within the bounds of decency throughout the dance, and by the end he was 'hers' and let her take him, unresisting, onto the balcony, and thence, with only a weak 'Are you sure?' down to the privacy below. Susan was very sure. The strains of a waltz filtered down, and she held herself in pose.

'Dance with me here,' she commanded, with just a touch of pleading in her voice.

He took her in hold, rather nervously, as if about to waltz with a tiger. She smiled.

'It is but dancing, sir.'

Technically, she was correct, but dancing in the semi-darkness and alone with her, made him feel distinctly uncomfortable and simultaneously exultant. They twirled in silence for a minute or so and then she stopped, so abruptly he could feel her feminine shape against his body. She looked up. In the low light he could not read her expression, but her voice told him everything.

'Kiss me, Edward.'

He obeyed. Somehow there was no possibility that he would not obey. For a moment his body was triumphant but her mouth was 'dead', as if she did not care whether it was him or any other man. Her coldness repelled, and he pulled back.

'Have I shocked you?' she purred.

'Yes.' There was constricted horror in his voice, when she had expected amazement.

Susan made a rapid recovery of her situation.

'I have shocked myself, my lord. I beg you will forgive me. I think it was the champagne and the intoxication of your nearness. Permit me to retire and compose myself.'

She flitted away, leaving him standing as if turned to stone.

Sir Esmond was contemplating retiring for the evening. He had danced with the few ladies with whom he always found it a pleasure, and several out of compassion for those who knew that their days of being first choice as partners was waning. It was a hot evening, and he stepped out through an open window onto the balcony and took a good lungful of cool air. It was the light catching upon Miss Tyneham's gown that drew his eye down. He saw her dancing; he saw her stop dancing. One hand clenched. He saw the embrace; and then he heard the stifled sob. Controlling his emotions admirably, he turned and found himself looking along the balcony at the half-shadowed figure of Lady Harriet Hadlow, whose stricken face was illuminated like that of a distraught ghost.

'Lady Harriet, I . . .' Two large tears rolled down her cheeks, and his generous heart went out to her. The struggle within proved too much for her and, with his sympathetic gaze upon her, Harriet crumbled. He stepped forward and put his arm about her, and she wept upon his broad chest. After a few minutes, and wary lest they be discovered and entirely erroneous conclusions drawn, he led her back into the house and to a gilded chair set back in an inconspicuous corner.

'I shall fetch your sister to you, Lady Harriet. You need her.'

He squeezed her hand, and went upon his quest. He found Sophy in some agitation, having lost sight of both her charges, and knowing that they were neither taking refreshment nor among the dancers.

'Excuse me, ma'am, if you seek your sister, I can take you to her.' He looked very serious.

'Yes, Sir Esmond, I . . . It is so very difficult when one is meant to be chaperoning two girls.'

'I can, with some regret, tell you where Miss Tyneham was a few minutes ago, at the least.' As he led her to Harriet he explained what he, and she, had seen.

'Oh, poor Harriet. Susan is too provoking. She has no more feeling for Lord Edward than, oh, than her hired horse. Not that such behaviour should be condoned, but if her heart were engaged . . .'

'Miss Tyneham has a heart?' Had she not been so upset for her sister, Sophy would have heard the edge of bitterness in his voice.

'I hope so, Sir Esmond. The thing is, I do not think she has ever felt it beat, except perhaps for her mama, and then not in a blind and unalloyed way. If she did but discover it, there would be her salvation.'

Sir Esmond took some small comfort from this, and nodded, but did not reply. He guided her to where Harriet sat, shoulders hunched and head still bowed.

'Harry?' Sophy knelt before her tearful sister and took the hands that were crushing a lace-edged handkerchief.

'I wish I were more like Susan,' sobbed Harriet.

'What? Harry, dearest, how can you possibly say that in view of what she has done?'

'Oh, I do not wish I was wicked, but . . . Susan knows what she wants and is prepared to act to get it.'

'I rather think that her problem is the opposite. She thinks she knows what she wants, but having got it, finds it hollow.'

'I am too timid. I have hung back. I never let him see . . .'

'Darling Harry, you behave beautifully, and I am very proud of you. If Lord Edward has not seen—'

'It is not his fault. She bewitches them.'

Sophy could not deny the truth of this, and Sir Esmond appeared engrossed in the study of a marquetry cabinet. He wondered how it came about that he, who knew the girl was playing games, still felt the power of her spell. Bewitchment, yes, that certainly covered it very well.

'Look at me, Harry.' Harriet lifted a tear-stained face, and in that moment Sophy hated her cousin. 'Have you any reason to suppose that Lord Edward prefers you to other ladies, other than our cousin?' She thought she knew the answer to this, but wanted Harriet to consider it.

'No, and yet . . . Yes, yes I have, because he was not at any party we attended until we met him in the Park that day, and since then he has only been absent when his duties precluded it. He told me that he was finding the Season uncommonly pleasant this year. And he has danced with me whenever he has been able, although probably that was because *her* dance card was full.' Harriet caught her breath on a muffled sob once more.

'If Lord Edward is worthy of you, dearest, then he will break free of this "bewitchment". Gentlemen do. You must have seen that. And if he does, then his thoughts may well centre upon you. He . . . he has stirred feelings, yes?'

'It is not that I have fallen for a uniform,' Harriet murmured. 'It . . . I think he is the nicest man I have ever met.'

Sophy did not comment upon how low that figure had been until the last few weeks. She squeezed her sister's hand.

'Then do not give up hope. I hate to say wait for Susan's cast-offs but . . .'

'Oh, I always knew that was the way it would be. You see, I am very ordinary.'

Sir Esmond, embarrassed at being privy to sisterly conversation, found that this was too much, and looked down at her, unsmiling but not unfriendly.

'Lady Harriet, you do yourself a great disservice. You are not "ordinary" at all, but only think so because you compare yourself to your "extraordinary" – and I do not say so as a compliment – cousin. You are a well brought up young lady, she is . . . farouche. Do not regret that you are unlike her.' He frowned. 'If you would permit, ladies, I would take my leave of you now. Lady Sophy, thank you for an excellent party, despite . . .' He left the sentence unfinished.

Sophy thanked him, and suggested to Harriet that she might be able to slip upstairs and remove her tear stains in time to bid other guests farewell. Sir Esmond left the house still frowning, and found himself right behind a gentleman in uniform. Lord Edward Wittenham turned at the sound of the firm footsteps. For a fleeting moment Sir Esmond knew an urge to knock him to the floor for the misery he had just caused, but the look upon the younger man's face, reflected in the downcast light of a lamp, gave him pause. Lord Edward was very pale, as though he might be physically ill, and his eyes stared in semi-recognition.

'Fawley?' His voice was unsteady, and Sir Esmond took him by the elbow. 'My God, Fawley, I have been such an almighty fool.'

CHAPTER FOURTEEN

SOPHY DID NOT SPEAK TO HER COUSIN UNTIL THE NEXT day, in part because she did not trust herself not to hit her, and at least attempt to wipe the calculating smile from her lips. Harriet did not appear at breakfast, even though it was late, and Sophy hoped that her sister might rest long enough to awaken at least physically refreshed. Susan was likewise absent, and so Sophy ate alone and in silence, feeling her bottled-up emotions rising within her once more. She wanted to at least sound calm, but at the moment that seemed impossible. She resolved to clear her head by going out for a ride, and so went upstairs to change into her riding habit. As she left she asked Bembridge to inform Miss Susan, if she came downstairs before her return, that she wished to see her at two o'clock, in the library. Bembridge wondered, looking at his mistress's sombre expression, what new problem Miss Susan had caused.

Accompanied by a groom, Sophy made her way the short distance to Hyde Park and there set her horse to an easy canter, which enabled her to feel a breeze upon her cheek and was less likely to encourage other equestrians to engage her in conversation. She tried to empty her head of rancour, but had difficulty in doing so. So lost was she in her own thoughts that she did not even hear the sound of a horse gaining on her, or look to her left until the grey was parallel.

'Good morning, Lady Sophy.' Lord Rothley nodded a greeting in view of the pace. 'Blowing the cobwebs away?'

'If only it were cobwebs, my lord.' She sounded calm, but her mind was suddenly jumbled. Lord Rothley was the very last person she wished to encounter, and yet also the one whose appearance lightened her deep gloom.

He glanced more closely at her, noted the shadows beneath her eyes, the crease between her brows.

'Did your party not go as you had expected, or perhaps did it go as you had expected in an adverse sense?' He was conscious of the groom's presence.

Sophy coloured. Of course he knew about the Chelmarsh party, who did not? Did he wonder why he had been omitted from the list of guests or was it the sort of thing that rakes took in their stride?

'More the latter, sir.'

'One hardly need guess the source.'

'No, one hardly need guess.' She looked straight ahead and her voice was flat.

The horses, without encouragement, had drifted into a trot and now slowed to a walk. He was caught in the position where he could not reveal why he felt he had not just a right, but an obligation, to take a hand in the matter, but then how he might improve the problem was equally insoluble.

'You cannot be blamed, you kn—'

'Oh yes I can. And with justification.' Sophy cut him off, brusquely. She was near the end of her tether, and bland assurances were of no help to her.

Lord Rothley wondered what had occurred, but plainly could not ask.

'Is there anything I can do?' It sounded ridiculous even to his own ears. Without being privy to events, without being trusted, what could he do?

'What had you in mind, my lord?' snapped Sophy. 'Making her fall in love with you instead?' She kicked the mare back to a canter. 'Good day to you.'

He pulled up, stung as if she had struck him with her crop. Had they been alone he would have ridden after her, demanded to know more, demanded to have his innocence accepted. She thought him a Lothario upon the evidence that his father's reputation was . . . disreputable. That was unfair, and also illogical, so why did she believe it? And when she said 'instead', did she mean make Susan Tyneham fall in love with him instead of having other men fall in love with her, or did she, just possibly, mean instead of herself? He rode on upon a loose rein, turning various possibilities over in his mind, lost in a brown study, and only at the last moment noticed Sir Esmond Fawley riding towards him, his face grim.

'Fawley. You look as bad as I feel.'

'I am wondering why I am such a damned fool.'

'So am I. About myself, not you, that is.'

They exchanged looks, and knew they were united in the incomprehension of the male about the female.

'Rothley, you said a few weeks ago, I might not ask about . . . about Miss Tyneham and Lady Sophy. Is that still the case, since I have to confess an interest?'

'There is one thing perhaps above all you should know. It clarifies many things, and in fact whilst I was in ignorance of it, among the matchmaking mamas it is known, even if half forgotten.' He took a deep breath. 'Susan Tyneham is my half-sister.'

Sir Esmond's mouth opened, and then closed. 'Your . . .'

'I suppose there were always less likely things. After all, my father debauched his way about Society for the best part of fifteen years before he took refuge abroad. I probably have a number of half-siblings littering the Ton. It isn't edifying, but then, my sire's behaviour never was. I therefore feel a degree of responsibility, not that he would.'

'Yes, I can see that.'

'It is not helped by the fact that I am damned sure neither she nor Lady Sophy, and of course Lady Harriet, have a clue that Tyneham was not her father. Brother

Tyneham is well aware of it, however. He had the audacity to warn me off, and off Lady Sophy too, whom he regards as his preserve, the fool.'

'And, just to be clear, you would far rather she were your preserve.'

'Yes. However, she seems to keep me at arm's length because of my papa's reputation, and looks upon my protestations of a desire to help her in the light of nefarious seduction.' A thought struck him. 'Our, er, interests do not conflict?'

Sir Esmond shook his head.

'I should be clapped in Bedlam for it, but the "awful Susan", if you will forgive me being honest, draws me to her. The oddest thing is that I am one man she does not play the full power of her tricks upon, so I have not the excuse that she has, to use Lady Harriet's term, "bewitched" me with intent. There is something about her, and it is not her beauty, and certainly not her wilful, selfish and unbelievably wild behaviour, but something I think, I hope, that lies beneath. Just once or twice I think I have glimpsed it and then she misbehaves as she did last night and . . .'

'I gathered she had, from Lady Sophy, whom I found out riding earlier. She would not say more, but then her groom was close by, so even had she trusted me . . .' Lord Rothley shook his head.

Sir Esmond gnawed his lip.

'Since we are, in a sense, upon the same side, and I can assure you I wish you well with Lady Sophy, an excellent young woman, perhaps I may enlighten you. It will help you see her problem and er, ours.'

Lord Rothley listened in growing horror.

'Oh my God, no wonder . . . Poor little Lady Harriet, too.'

'I think that is what has really cut up Lady Sophy, that not controlling her cousin has meant hurt for her sister. But as I say, I think Wittenham had the fright of his life and will run a mile if Susan Tyneham as much as smiles at him again. It was a pretty sudden dropping of the scales from his eyes, and he was shaken to the core.'

'Why did she do it?'

'Because she was bored, because she only feels safe when in control, I think, and because she has never learnt to think of anyone else's interests but her own. Oh, and I think she wants men to suffer.'

'And yet you . . . ?'

'I do.'

'I did wonder, when I found out for sure, if she had simply inherited my father's remarkable selfishness.'

'Possibly, but instinct tells me there is a reason that she . . . Lady Sophy said she had told her she wanted to marry to escape a return to imprisonment at Tyneham and would "exchange one gaoler for another". Not a nice view of life for a young woman whose only "crime" is her existence, and one with no more understanding of Society than a fourteen-year-old still stitching samplers.' He shook his head. 'And Wittenham babbled about how when she kissed him, or rather got him to kiss her, he thought it clinical, as though she took no pleasure from it.'

'Wittenham ought to have had the decency to keep silent. I thought better of him.'

'Oh, he would, my friend, but for the fact I told him I had seen them. I also told him Lady Harriet had seen them too. Should have seen how green he turned then. Felt sorry for the poor fool, but better he knows the worst.'

'So, without having any apparent "right" to do so, we have to protect the wild Susan from setting London upside down, at least any more than she has already. Then you have to find her deep-seated loathing of the male of the species and turn it to affection, and I have to woo a lady who thinks everything I say to her part of a cunning plan to make her fall in love with me so that I can then abandon her to ruination. Make that two cells in Bedlam, Fawley.'

Having parted at odds with Lord Rothley, Sophy arrived home in no better mood than she left it, for all her good intentions. She went up to change and then went down to the library, detailing Bembridge to alert Miss Susan to her return. She looked at the ormolu clock upon the mantelshelf. It lacked fifteen minutes to two o'clock. She tried yet again to form sentences in her mind which did not sound simply aggrieved, let down and angry. She failed, because that was just how she felt.

It was five past the hour when the door opened, and Susan walked in. She did not look submissive or afraid, but rather combative. Her position was indefensible and yet she was going to stand her ground.

'You demanded my presence, cousin.' Susan's head was held high.

'In effect, yes. You cannot fail to understand why when I say that you were seen last night behaving in a manner more usually found among the muslin company.'

'Servants can be prudish.' Susan shrugged.

'You were not seen by a servant, but by Harriet.'

'Was she spying upon us? I doubt not she mistook the matter.' She would brazen this out.

'She did not. I know this because you were also seen by Sir Esmond Fawley, who reported to me both Harriet's distress and, from necessity, the reason for it.'

Susan's colour drained away. She told herself that Sir Esmond was merely a talebearer and she did not give a fig for the fact that it was he who had seen her with Sir Edward Wittenham. She did not quite convince herself, however.

'Are you going to send me back to Tyneham?' Her self-confidence wavered for a moment.

'It would be in many ways the easiest course. However, it would occasion remark, and, in addition to the gossip about your behaviour, which is almost certainly already in circulation, would confirm what Society already whispers, that you are unfit for decent company. It would also disappoint your aunt, my mother, who wished to do whatever she could for you for the sake of her late sister.'

'So I was always a charity case.'

'No, but many people have been charitable towards

you when you do not deserve it, since you came to London. Let us not beat about the bush, Susan. Having behaved with scant regard to your good name, or that of this family, you have now shown yourself to be lacking in modesty, morality or with any thought to anyone but yourself. You are not going to claim, I take it, that you were suddenly overcome with passion for Lord Edward, and, since I know full well who led whom, you cannot say he persuaded you into wrong-doing.'

'It was but a dance, and a kiss.'

'A dance in private, in near darkness, and a kiss you ought never to have offered. You are not betrothed to Lord Edward Wittenham, nor even in expectation of him making you an offer. If that were the case, well I am not so unreasonable as to think that no exchanges of tokens of mutual affection may not be exchanged.'

'"Tokens of . . ." Listen to yourself,' sneered Susan. 'Are you jealous because you are on the shelf and no man has ever wanted to kiss you? Well, let me assure you, it is not that exciting. And kisses, I am not afraid to use the word at all, are just . . . kisses.'

'Kisses lead to . . . other things.'

'Things you know nothing about, cousin.' The riposte was swift.

'More to the point, do you, Susan? Are you stronger than a man? If you encouraged him to think you are without morals and would not object to the liberties a man might take with some Covent Garden opera dancer, you would need to be.' Sophy had done what she had been determined not to do; she had lost her temper.

'I am the Viscount Tyneham's sister. Who would dare take liberties?'

'Oh Susan, you little fool. There are you saying men are simple, easy to entrap, and yet you cannot see that if you act like . . . like a lightskirt, that is ultimately how a man will treat you, and not think of who your brother might be.'

Susan stared at her cousin, as if this was impossible.

'You are not to be trusted, Susan, in company. I have no alternative but to instruct that you do not leave this house without my permission, or if Harriet or I are not with you, and be assured that from now on I shall remain within sight at all times if we are at a social function. I dislike making you a prisoner here, but until such time as you can comport yourself like a decent young woman, that is how it must be. You may go.'

Susan looked grim, made her cousin a flourishing curtsey that was designed as an insult, and stormed out of the room. Sophy sat down, her hands trembling, and then wept. Once the tumult of her emotions had waned, she took several deep breaths, and went in search of her sister.

Harriet was in what they termed the sewing room, a small, cosy chamber which had a large enough window to catch good light, even if northerly facing. She was hemming a handkerchief, but looked as though she had also been using one.

'Oh Harry, please do not be miserable.'

'I am sorry, Sophy, I did try to be positive, but whenever my mind wanders . . .'

'Then we must ensure that it does not wander, my love. I . . . have spoken to Susan, made it clear that what happened cannot happen again or she goes home in disgrace. I have also said she may not leave the house unless you or I are with her.'

'Oh dear, she will not like that, feeling a prisoner.'

'No, but it is more in the notion than the reality, since how often has she gone out without us before? The thing is that I must also keep the strictest eye upon her when we are at balls and parties, which means I cannot be there to guide you as much. However, you have been about long enough now to know many people, and I have absolutely no doubt that you can deal with any situation. If not, you must find me.'

'And your Season?'

'My Season, Harry?'

'What about you having enjoyment? There is Sir Esmond, who makes you smile, and Lord Rothley, who makes you smile even more and—'

'We did not come to London for my benefit, Harry. You know that I did not even wish to come at all. There was never any intention that I should be seeking a husband. I am too long in the tooth to be a debutante, my dear. I came to assist Mama, and see you be a success.' She smiled, but this made Harriet sigh once more. 'I think perhaps you have been letting yourself sit in lonely gloom too long. Come upstairs and put on that new pelisse Madame Clément had to adjust. The weather is good, and you and I can have a comfortable walk together in Green Park if you do not wish for too much bustle.'

Harriet set aside her stitchery.

'That would be nice, just us.'

'Just us, Harry.'

She forgot that they might meet someone, and fate decreed that it should be Captain Lord Edward Wittenham. He was alone, and did not look, thought Sophy, as if he cared whether the sun rose on the morrow or not. Harriet, when she noticed him a second later, took a gasping breath, and gripped her sister's arm more tightly.

'Let us turn about and go the other way,' she whispered, her cheeks turning parchment pale.

Sophy patted the hand upon her arm.

'No, dearest, be brave. You cannot avoid him forever, you know, and far better to get this meeting out of the way, do you not think?'

'Yes.' She coloured, flustered. 'No. Oh, I am not sure.'

By this time recognition had pierced whatever despondency afflicted the captain, and he too paled, then blushed, and finally swallowed convulsively as he drew near enough to make his bow.

'Good afternoon, my lord.' Sophy's voice was very calm.

'Good afternoon, ladies.' He looked at Sophy, and then at Harriet, and his poise deserted him. 'Lady Harriet,

I . . . might I call upon you, tomorrow perhaps? There are things . . . Must explain . . .'

'No, please no.' Her response was instinctive, and in that moment Sophy, who had entertained very uncharitable thoughts about this foolish young man overnight, even if he was technically her senior in years, felt desperately sorry for him. His face fell. 'I will not be receiving visitors tomorrow,' Harriet managed before biting her lip and looking away.

'Then the day after? Lady Harriet, you must permit me—'

'I am not sure that "must" comes into it, Lord Edward.' Sophy murmured.

'Not must, no, but I implore you . . .'

'Will you be attending Lady Cleobury's rout on Friday?' Lord Edward blinked. The question threw him.

'Yes, I believe so, but—'

'Then I think we shall see you on Friday evening, my lord.' Sophy hoped he was not slow in taking her meaning.

'Yes, but—'

'On Friday evening, then. Good day to you, my lord.'

'Friday. Oh, yes, Friday evening.' He tried to give Harriet a speaking look, but she did not raise her eyes. He saluted them and passed on, not quite sure whether to be hopeful or even more gloomy.

CHAPTER FIFTEEN

Sophy had thought it good fortune that the evening was one of the few when they were not engaged elsewhere. After the tumult of their ball, she had anticipated it would be good to have a quiet evening and early night. In view of what had actually taken place this was even more the case, except that dinner was a ghastly and embarrassing affair. Harriet could scarcely bear to speak to Susan, who therefore addressed her as frequently as possible, upon subjects which were perfectly bland, but simply a way of making her more uncomfortable. She was also pointedly avoiding conversation with Sophy. If she felt the slightest remorse, there was no sign of it.

None of the three ladies did justice to the dishes set before them, and Harriet begged to retire before the tea tray was brought in, because she had the headache.

Susan remained, determined not to slink off. She sat quite upright, playing patience, knowing her cousin found her presence a trial. Well, if her life was to be hemmed in, she would not make it easy for those who did so.

Sophy looked at the clock, wondering if Susan would continue until the small hours just to prove she would not be the first to 'give in' and retire. She returned to the book she was not reading, not even bothering to turn the pages, and tried to imagine how she was going to explain these weeks to her mama. Harriet's plight was, she prayed, temporary. The haggard look of her errant beau should have taught her one thing, at least; he was feeling as terrible as she was. Sophy had no doubt that Lord Edward wanted to beg forgiveness, and, if forgiven, might well seek to secure Harriet's hand both as a sign of his commitment and to make him feel comfortable again. She was almost sure Harriet would forgive him, and forgiveness was needed, even though she kept saying she did not blame him. Her reaction today had been still full of upset, but by Friday she might have reached a state of calm. She might speak to her sister about giving him the benefit of the doubt. It had been male folly, but in the catalogue of sins, very small, if Harriet could come to see it that way.

'Benefit of the doubt' brought her own situation to mind. She had told Harriet she had not come to London to find a husband, and it was true. She had certainly not come to London to fall in love, but she very much feared she had succumbed to it, like an attack of the measles.

Why could she have not fallen in love with Sir Esmond Fawley? He would be a lifelong friend, a gentleman with whom she could laugh, and whose perspicacity would never fail to surprise her; yet she felt nothing more than friendship. She was convinced he felt the same way about her. Had there not been someone who had touched her heart, they could have made a very contented match; but someone had. Lord Rothley haunted her dreams, and intruded into her waking thoughts. When he was close by, her skin tingled, her chest felt tight, and when his eyes met hers she trusted, totally, foolishly. When apart she could, just, resist him, but in his presence her resistance was overcome. This is what it was like to be seduced by a rake. She had considered herself so sensible, yet here was every fibre of her being wanting to be cherished by him. Only her sensible brain stood, if not firm, then at least still only teetering on the edge of succumbing to those eyes, the smile with that wolfish twist, the voice that made her yearn to tell him all the troubles that beset her.

Her heart put up the valid question; why should a rake set his sights upon her? She was at her last prayers by the standards of the debutantes about her, and she was memorable for her height, not her beauty. Heart's answer was that, be he never so dangerous a rake, he was drawn quite genuinely to her by some unfathomable attraction. Head responded that she was just a different sort of challenge.

Susan had taunted her about being a woman no man had kissed, had even wanted to kiss. She had thought herself to be of a dispassionate nature, because this had not concerned her in the past, but oh, if Susan did but know how that had changed. She did not want to know how it felt to be kissed, she wanted to know how it felt to be kissed by Lord Rothley. When they had danced, when she had been so close in brief moments that she could imagine being taken into those arms, it had given her senses enough that she could imagine a kiss also. That was how dangerous Lord Rothley could be, so dangerous a decent woman could dream of his kisses upon her lips, his arms about her.

She turned a page for the first time in a quarter hour. Susan yawned, and let the cards spill from her hand.

'Are you going to set a guard at my chamber door, cousin?'

'Of course not. You are not a prisoner, whatever you may think.'

'And my thoughts may not be bound.'

'You ought not to perceive me as your enemy, Susan, I am simply charged with keeping you from so great a faux pas that you will thereafter be excluded from the Ton. I did not seek the role, nor do I relish it, but that is my duty and I will fulfil it. Now, shall we retire?'

Susan, bored, and with the germ of an idea in her head, nodded.

Lord Rothley found himself in an awkward position, as he had explained to Sir Esmond Fawley, and, with a valid reason to return to his estates to view the completion of renovations to the stable blocks, withdrew from Polite Society for a week to work out how he might logically solve the insoluble. If Sophy Hadlow did not know of his relationship to Susan Tyneham it would be dishonourable to reveal it, with all its ramifications. If she believed him to be some rakish fellow setting out to lure her into falling in love with him, he could not tell her that he did not follow in his father's footsteps. Following their last meeting, he was inclined to think that Lady Sophy would avoid him where possible, and hold him very much at arm's length when this proved impossible. This would also preclude his relieving her of at least some of the burden of the wilful Susan. However he looked at it, his chances of winning her hand seemed remote. His staff wondered why their normally cheerful master seemed preoccupied, and if his valet had an idea that it might be an affair of the heart, he said nothing.

The estate had come to Lord Rothley upon the death of his grandfather, who had stated quite openly that though the title would go to his reprobate son, he had no intention of the 'ancestral home of the Marstons being sold off to pay foreign whores, and an assortment of tradesmen'. Thus, the responsibilities and income of an earldom rested with the young Viscount Rothley, whilst his father, the ignoble earl, managed upon a begrudged inherited allowance. It had seemed strange at first, but after six years, Rothley disregarded the unusual situation, and at thirty-one no longer felt callow and out of his depth. His retainers were happy, without fear of finding themselves turned off in times of straitened circumstances, or having the hallowed corridors the haunt of scantily dressed Paphians. This would not have appealed to the very conservative rural Worcestershire worthies who had served the family man and boy, or girl and woman, for generations.

While Lord Rothley's mind was working in honourable circles, Lord Pinkney's was aiming straight but with every possible dishonourable intent.

Lord Pinkney had no knowledge of what had gone on at the Chelmarsh ball, but he too was a man with plans, plans which centred upon Miss Susan Tyneham. However, since Lord Rothley had declared himself Miss Tyncham's covert guard dog, it would be as well to ensure that this particular canine's teeth were drawn before he made further overtures. Rothley, inexplicably, was interested in the tall and rather severe Lady Sophronia, and if he had her ear, and at this point Pinkney smiled in a lascivious manner, at least her ear, he might make things very difficult for him. Pinkney was under no illusion. Lady Sophronia thought him a spendthrift fortune-hunter. This accurate appraisal did at least prove she was not without wits. It would be advantageous if he could make Rothley appear in as bad a light. What was difficult was getting into a position where he might drip his poison in her ear, and also be believed. She had a tendency to give him a basilisk stare and turn away. Mighty high in the instep was the Lady Sophronia Hadlow. Well, she would not feel so high and mighty when he was related to her. He could add discommoding her to the pleasure of upsetting the insufferable Tyneham.

It proved even more difficult than he had anticipated, because he did not have unlimited access to the houses of Polite Society. Some were inclined to omit him from their guest lists altogether, and many only included him when they held their largest parties. In the general run of things, this did not concern him, but financial matters were pressing, and the tables were consistently against him when he attempted a recovery by means of rattling dice. He needed Miss Tyneham's dowry in the very near future, and could not obtain it without contact with the young lady herself. The news of Rothley's removal to the shires was useful, but until he espied the tall form of Lady Sophronia at the Duchess of Rutland's ball several days later, he was powerless to play his advantage.

Had Sophy not been engaged in conversation with Lady Hornsea, she would have noticed his approach, but it was too late when he made his bow and smiled ingratiatingly at the voluble countess.

'Lady Hornsea, what a pleasant surprise.'

Lady Hornsea actually looked as if she would prefer a surprise involving being trampled to death by wild horses, but returned his smile with one just as fake.

'My lord. Surprise it is indeed. I had thought you in a debtors' prison these months past, and yet here you are, hale and oh so hearty.'

His smile wavered only for a fraction of a second.

'I have a knack of survival ma'am. Like a bad penny, I always turn up.'

'Ah, but hardly as legal tender.'

Sophy nearly choked, and changed her opinion of Lady Hornsea. What she did not know was that once, some years past, Lord Pinkney had come close, but not quite close enough, to seducing the then Lady Cecilia Cosford. Her eyes had been opened, just in time, by her seeing him at the Opera, when he had no notion she was there, in company with a highly painted young woman whose attractions he seemed to find far more interesting than the singing, and all in a box opposite. Since he had earlier spent the better part of an hour in the Park protesting that without his divine Cecilia his life was dross, that lady became very sceptical of his utterances thereafter.

Lord Pinkney's eyes sparkled.

'Sometimes the illegal is so much more . . . exciting, ma'am, but then you would not know.'

'My husband is a connoisseur of fine art, sir, and he would say that a fake always betrays its cheapness if one looks beneath the obvious. I have always found you so very obvious, my lord.'

'Not quite always, my lady, not quite always.'

Lady Hornsea coloured a little, and snapped her fan tight shut. She was at that moment spotted by another acquaintance, and turned away. Sophy would have done likewise, but Lord Pinkney addressed her directly.

'Cecilia Hornsea is an admirable woman, but very damning. I am used to it, of course. Those who live upon the shores of the River Tick, must perforce accept the cutting words of the permanently well-heeled. But, you know, Lady Sophronia, there is a certain honesty to even such as I, the gamester.'

'Really? I had not noticed it.'

'But you, like Lady Hornsea, admire solvency and uprightness. I have to say that it surprised me that you have chosen to be seen with Rothley in attendance with that being the case. Some men gamble with dice and horses and cards, others gamble with hearts, and virtue.' Pinkney very carefully did not actually state that Lord Rothley was one such, but the implication was clear. He did not expect Lady Sophronia to take his bait as easily, but was very pleased with himself when it became clear that she did.

'I do not think that Lord Rothley's . . . propensities . . . are of any interest to me, my lord.'

'Are they not? I am so relieved, ma'am. One would hate to see virtue hoodwinked by vice.'

Sophy, feeling hollow in the pit of her stomach, was at the same moment prey to the near overwhelming urge to strike the satisfied smile from Lord Pinkney's face.

'Except at cards, I take it?'

He laughed. 'Ah there you have me, ma'am. Definitely "except at cards".'

Lady Harriet felt distinctly uncomfortable in the role of 'guardian' over a girl who was the better part of two years her senior, but understood that it was unfair on her elder sister to bear the burden alone. When Susan bemoaned the fact that she had not even been able to change her reading material at Hookham's Library, a few days later at breakfast, she therefore offered to go with her. To avoid it looking as if this was a burden, she invented the excuse that she had been recommended a novel by one of her friends, and would like to search for it before the title left her head. Sophy gave her sister a grateful look.

They arranged to depart at eleven o'clock and would return in time for a light luncheon. Susan left the breakfast table looking more cheerful than for a week past, and Sophy reached across and took her sister's hand.

'Thank you, Harry. You are the best of sisters.'

Lady Harriet blushed and demurred.

Just before eleven, Lady Harriet knocked upon her cousin's bedchamber door, and was invited to enter. Susan was just closing a small tan valise. Harriet frowned.

'We are taking a maid with us, so I thought perhaps after Hookham's we might stop in Conduit Street. The servant can carry this.'

'What is it?'

'A valise,' giggled Susan. 'I am sorry Harriet, that was facetious, was it not. Actually, it contains a gown, that one I wore last week with the floss trimming. I am sure the arms are too tight when I dance, and I would hate to think of a seam ripping in the middle of a quadrille. Think how embarrassing that would be.'

Harriet nodded, though secretly wondered if Susan knew the meaning of embarrassment.

Susan placed her bonnet on her head, tucked a

recalcitrant ringlet into place, and smiled at her cousin.

'I think I am ready to depart. Let us go.'

The two young ladies, accompanied by a maid carrying the valise, and three slim volumes, stepped out into Hill Street, and turned left towards Berkeley Square.

'Are you sure you would not prefer to visit Mme Clément first, Susan?' enquired Harriet, helpfully.

'Ah, but if we are delayed there, Harriet, we will find the library far too busy, and with far less chance of taking out the books we would care to read. No, let us go to Conduit Street on our return journey.'

This seemed a sensible plan of action, and so the trio made their way to Hookham's Library, and Susan handed back the books, of which she had not actually bothered to read more than the first and last chapters. The gentleman who took them from her gloved clasp received a smile which brightened his day.

Harriet, cudgelling her brain for the name of the author of the novel her friend had recommended, scanned along the shelves and was, in a few minutes, engrossed. The maid stood back respectfully, and wondered at the point of reading things that were not true, but then she came from a family where the only book ever quoted was the Bible, and that not by actually reading its pages. Susan relieved the girl, with a kindly smile, of the valise.

Whilst Harriet searched for her book, her cousin moved to another line of shelves, taking out the odd leather-bound book, until she was near to the door, and out of Harriet's sight. Then Susan, her valise in her hand, and a secret smile of triumph upon her lips, slipped out of Hookham's Circulating Library and stepped the few yards to Piccadilly, where she boldly hailed a cab.

She directed the jarvey to the Knightsbridge Barracks where the Life Guards were lodged, and then realised that she had a problem. However little she cared for public opinion, a young lady with a small valise knocking upon the door and requesting to speak to a particular officer would not do. She paid off the cab, and stood, feeling rather conspicuous upon the other side of the Knightsbridge Road, and for once in her life wished she had a maid with her. A man passing by touched his hat respectfully, but the look that accompanied it made her stiffen and glare at him. A faint feeling of panic made her stomach turn over. Then she saw a lad sweep a crossing for a lady some hundred yards along the road. She fumbled in her reticule and found three pennies. That was surely enough? She walked with every appearance of assurance to where the youth awaited further employment and raised her hand. He approached and tugged his forelock.

'I do not wish to cross, but I have three pennies if you will take a message to the Guardroom for Captain Lord Edward Wittenham.'

'Captain Lord Edward Wittingham, miss.'

'Wittenham. Be sure of the name. You must tell them it is a matter of extreme importance, and await him.

221

Then tell him Miss Tyneham wishes to speak with him immediately. If he is upon his duties elsewhere,' she hoped most fervently that he was not, 'come back and inform me of it.' Her tone softened, and she gave the lad, who was perhaps a few years her junior, a wide-eyed look. 'I am depending upon you, totally.'

With the thought of this stunning young lady depending upon him, and three pennies for his pocket, the crossing sweeper was prepared to risk having his ear clipped. He crossed the road and disappeared into the entrance of the barracks. Susan waited, at first pleased that he had not come back to say the gentleman was at Horse Guards, and then worried that he was out upon his own business. However, after a long five minutes, the scrubby youth reappeared, followed by the smart figure of Lord Edward Wittenham, who was frowning.

'Miss Tyneham, but . . . Ma'am, what are you doing here?' He waved the sweeper away. Susan thought that he did not sound delighted to see her. She took her handkerchief from her reticule and dabbed at her eyes.

'Lord Edward, I am so very sorry, I do know it is perfectly scandalous that I should be here but . . . Oh, sir, if you but knew my predicament.' She stifled a sob, and Lord Edward looked about him, even more uncomfortable.

'Really ma'am, I am sure—'

'There is no other person I can trust, none to whom I can turn, orphan that I am!' Miss Tyneham was a great loss to the theatre. She stared up at him with great wet eyes, and it would have taken a stronger man than Wittenham to resist them, even though his instincts were telling him he was being bamboozled. 'My brother Tyneham, he has told my cousins that I must marry Lord Pinkney, and unless I do so I am to be kept almost a prisoner. I may not even leave the house without one of them. I . . . I was deceived by Lord Pinkney, but now I have seen more of him, he frightens me.' She finished the sentence in a very little-girl voice. It made her sound as if being thrown to a wild beast.

'But everyone knows Pinkney hasn't a feather to fly with.' Lord Edward frowned.

'Ah yes, but he has some relation who has died and is now about to become really rather wealthy.'

'Still does not stop him being a dashed loose screw.' Lord Edward spoke and then coloured. 'Not that I should use such language before a young lady. I cannot credit it.'

'You think I would make such a thing up? Risk everything by escaping the house, coming here, alone, in a grimy cab, to turn to the only man in London who can protect me?'

Good sense told him she would do exactly that.

'No, of course not, but—'

She could see him wavering, and played her ace.

'If you do not assist me, sir, I shall have no alternative but to . . .' She blinked away a tear. 'The Thames is fast flowing, I believe.' She looked the picture of tragic virginity.

Cornered, the worried captain assured her such a fate could not be hers, and that he would help her.

'But you cannot stand about here, ma'am, on the

public thoroughfare. Let me find you a parlour and coffee at a hostelry while I . . . make arrangements. I can say you are my sister, so all will be right and tight.'

He took her elbow and guided her to the nearby Halfway House, and there bespoke a private parlour until his return. Susan regarded him with a little suspicion.

'You will return.'

'Upon my honour, I will return.'

Lord Edward was thinking on his feet. His first thought was that he had to see his colonel.

'I have to request leave of absence, upon . . . compassionate grounds, sir. It is my sister, Amelia, Lady Holt, in Buckinghamshire. Holt died suddenly last November, and I am the only member of the family available at the present.'

'Of course, Wittenham. Any idea how long you will need?'

'Only a few days, sir, to sort things, I think.'

Had Miss Tyneham heard this, she might not have sat drinking her coffee with a smile playing at the corners of her mouth.

His lordship then changed into civilian clothes so that he might be less obvious, had his batman pack a small valise, and hailed a cab to take him to a posting house where he was unknown, and he could hire a post chaise and four. It was in this equipage that he drew up at the Halfway House an hour later, and collected Miss Tyneham, who was just beginning to fret.

CHAPTER SIXTEEN

HARRIET RETURNED HOME WITH HER BRAIN IN A whirl. She had initially thought merely that she and Susan were, in effect, playing hide-and-seek between the bookshelves. She felt a little guilty, since interest in a volume had meant she had not noticed Susan move away. However, it seemed ridiculous that she ought to have to gaze at the same titles as her cousin, so Harriet was not concerned. When neither she nor the maid could find her after methodical searching, and a word with the gentleman issuing the books had discovered he had seen a lady such as her ladyship described walk out some ten minutes since, Harriet panicked. It took all her self-control not to lift the hem of her skirts and run all the way back to Hill Street, and she arrived having walked as fast as possible, with the maid keeping up as best she could. As soon as the door was opened, Harriet fled up the stairs calling for her sister.

Sophy was finishing a letter to Lady Chelmarsh, a difficult letter to compose, in that hiding recent events was wrong, but that telling her about things she could do nothing about would only distress her at a time when she might have enough problems.

'Harry, what is it?' Sophy turned from the desk, and saw her sister's heaving bosom and trembling lips.

'Oh Sophy, I am so sorry, so very sorry. I could never have imagined . . . I mean what possible cause was there and—'

'Harriet, sit down, take a breath, and tell me what has happened, slowly.'

Harriet obeyed, as far as the part about speaking slowly. Then Sophy had to concentrate.

'She was in the library with us, and I was just hunting for that book that Corinna Lewisham recommended and—'

'She.' Sophy had a sinking feeling. 'Susan. Of course, it had to be about Susan.'

'Yes, yes. We went to Hookham's Library though I had suggested we went to Mme Clément's first to have the gown altered, and she said no, we could do it afterwards . . .'

'What gown?'

'When we went out, she gave the maid a small bag, a small valise, to carry. She said there were alterations that needed to be made.'

226

Sophy ran a mental check through her cousin's wardrobe, and could think of nothing that could need any alteration at this point in the Season. Harriet would not have questioned further, since she had no reason to assume anything out of the ordinary.

'So you went to the library and she left whilst you were choosing a book.'

'Yes. Oh Sophy, I am so very sorry. I know Susan had to be accompanied, but I thought it was just so that she did not make some scandal . . . except this will be an even bigger scandal, won't it?'

'Harry, I have no idea. We need to find out where she went but how can we achieve that other than sending servants to the major posting houses and asking after a young woman of her description carrying a small valise. I cannot say that I feel that is likely to be successful, but what else . . . Oh dear. I ought to inform Cousin Tyneham.'

'Must you? I cannot face him, Sophy. He will look at me just so and—'

'Do not worry, Harry. You may retire before he arrives.' Sophy tried to think. 'Which maid accompanied you?'

'Lucy.'

'Well, she is a dependable sort. Bembridge will try and keep the gossip within the house. The staff cannot fail to notice that you went out with Cousin Susan, and returned in some distress without her. Where could she have gone, though? I would hope she could not bribe any of the servants to take a message for her, but there was no specific ban on her doing so, so perhaps . . . I shall ring for Bembridge.' Harriet bit her lip. 'Harry, dearest, this was not your fault, remember that. Now go and remove your pelisse and bonnet and try to be calm. You could always sit at the pianoforte for a half hour, with that sonatina you liked. Do something to distract yourself.'

Sophy rose, smiled reassuringly at her sister, and pulled the bell-rope. Harriet gave a wavering smile in return and blinked away a tear. Bembridge, under no illusions about what must have occurred, appeared before Harriet even reached the door, and bowed her out. He turned a troubled face to Sophy.

'Yes, Bembridge, I know. We are, in the popular phrase, "in the suds".'

'I could not but surmise that, my lady, when Lady Harriet returned in such a state and without the young lady.'

Sophy noticed how he distanced himself from Susan. Susan was not 'part of the family', she was a guest, and a troublesome one at that.

'Indeed. Well, there is no point in trying to disguise the fact that Miss Susan has run away. However, for all our sakes, it is important that this does not spread beyond this household. I am trusting you to make that clear to the staff. Should she be found, it may yet be possible to keep this from making us the talk of the Ton for all the worst reasons. I need not tell you how much it would upset my mother, and reflect upon the Chelmarsh family.'

Bembridge nodded, looking grim. Sophy knew he would protect the family name as a soldier upon ancient battlements, to his last breath. He had been born upon the Chelmarsh estates, started his service as a lad at their country estate, and come to the London house before her parents were married. There was nothing he would not do, perhaps short of burying Susan in the garden, to keep the Chelmarsh name from being besmirched.

'You can be sure that I will make that clear, but I will say, my lady, that I am confident that none within this house would let out so much as a word, unless it were perhaps after too much ale, which is the only risk I perceive.'

'Very good. The next thing is to try and find out where Miss Susan has gone. You must find out if any of the servants were given a note to deliver, to a house, to a posting house, perhaps, these last few days. It is possible that she went off with no idea where she might go, but it would be an act so desperate, and she seemed quite calm at breakfast.'

'I shall endeavour to find that out, my lady. Is there any young person with whom she has perhaps formed a friendship at social functions, some other young lady . . . ?'

'Miss Susan does not have friends among the other young ladies, I am sorry to say, Bembridge. I fear if anything she might have turned to a gentleman of her acquaintance. Sir Esmond Fawley would bring her straight here, I have no doubt of it, and,' she paused only for a moment, 'the same is true of Lord Rothley.' Would a rake reject a ripe plum falling into his clutches? He might not, but whatever had been said, Sophy could not quite believe the Lord Rothley they had come to know would act in such a manner. 'I will write to them if I must, in case they should hear something, but later. Lord Bollington . . . No. Sir Edward Wittenham I can also discount, but . . . Lord Pinkney, oh if any missive has gone to him then I fear we know where to seek her.' Sophy was talking more to herself than the family retainer, and remembered his presence with a slight flush. 'I am sorry, Bembridge, my mind is disordered. Would you please send tea up to Lady Harriet's room, and send Thomas here to await a note I must send round to Lord Tyneham, immediately. Then see what we can find out. If there is no knowledge of Miss Susan writing a letter or note to anyone, we must send manservants to the most notable posting houses, and starting points for the mail coaches, with her description and that of the valise.'

Bembridge went to set these things in motion, and Sophy set aside the letter to her parent, and taking a deep breath, began to write to her cousin, Lord Tyneham. She felt that what had happened was best explained in person, so restricted her missive to a request that he come as a matter of urgency to speak with her.

Lord Tyneham arrived some considerable time later, in response to her urgent request, having been neither at his lodging nor his club. He was expecting to hear something reprehensible about Susan, but was understandably shocked to find out that she had actually disappeared.

'How could a young woman in your care just . . . wander off?'

'I hardly think she did anything as aimless as "wander off", cousin. You make her sound like some dreamy infant. The truth is that she planned whatever she has done, since she had a ready answer to any questioning about why she had the maid carry a small valise with her.'

'She left with a valise?'

'A small one. She said that after visiting Hookham's Library she wanted to take a dress for alteration to the dressmaker in Conduit Street, and that she wanted to be present so that it could be fitted to her. My sister had no cause to think this untrue. How could she guess that Susan was planning to run away?'

'It should not even take a few weeks, let alone two months, for you to discover that anything is possible with that girl,' snorted Tyneham. 'Despite this, you let her out with only a chit of a girl and a maid for company.'

'What would you have preferred, my lord? A troop of dragoons?' Sophy was in no mood to be conciliatory. Had her cousin seemed even slightly concerned for his sister's welfare it would have been different, but he was not.

'You should have kept her indoors, except under your own supervision.' He shook his head. 'I hold you responsible, Cousin Sophronia, though it grieves me to say so.'

'Oh yes, you have stood back from the moment we arrived in London, simply waiting to look important and give your consent when my mother, or latterly I, myself, managed to find a suitable husband for her.' Sophy made no attempt to hide her contempt. 'You have not been responsible at all. In fact, the only thing you did was most irresponsible, and that was flaunt her dowry to every fortune-hunter in Town so that we have had the likes of Lord Pinkney swooping in like crows to carrion.'

There was a knock, and Bembridge entered, with a missive.

'No reply is requested, miss,' he said, sympathetically.

Sophy did not recognise the writing, which was in a neat, but rather small hand. She almost tore open the sheet and then sat down rather heavily.

'Thank goodness! Bembridge, we need not send to the posting houses, after all.'

'No, my lady. Might I say as that is a blessing.'

As the butler closed the door behind him, Sophy looked to Lord Tyneham.

'She is safe. Lord Edward has taken her to his sister, the widowed Lady Holt, at Gerrards Cross. It seems Lord Edward is not as easily brought about Susan's finger as she thought him. According to this, Susan threw herself upon his mercy, with a tale of being forced into marriage with Lord Pinkney, whom she has now come to fear, and with nowhere else to turn. She even threatened to throw herself in the Thames if he did not "save" her from her plight. He was not convinced by the tale but was unsure of what to do. I can only assume that Susan believed that throwing herself at him would mean him taking her to Gretna and marrying her, little fool, but instead he is taking her into Buckinghamshire and Lady Holt. By the time they made the first change he was completely certain that what she had said was a complete hum, and sent this by messenger. Lord Edward describes my cousin as "having a dangerous combination of ignorance and guile", which I frankly consider generous, and requests that a member of the family collects her, since he has no faith in his own ability to return her here without her absconding, and if he did so and was seen, it would be considered most peculiar. Indeed, it was that which prevented him returning with her immediately. He is quite right, for heaven knows what manner of faradiddle she would have concocted to persuade strangers that he was coercing her. It is a great relief,' Sophy sighed, 'though how I wish he had seen her in her true colours much, much earlier.'

'He will have to marry her, of course.' Lord Tyneham frowned.

'No such thing. The world does not know of this, nor shall it. Poor Lord Edward was put in a very difficult situation and acted as a man of honour.'

'As a man of honour, he must marry her.' Lord Tyneham sighed, heavily. 'I had hoped for better. A mere youngest son.'

'Better? You mean wealthier? Lord Edward Wittenham deserves far better than Susan. I can scarcely imagine a better man in such circumstances. Besides, do you really think he could control her, cousin? Oh, I know you would like to wash your hands of her, but she will always be your sister, and if she married him, I would give it six months before she created a wild scandal. Now, I shall make immediate preparations to go to Gerrards Cross. I take it that it is not so far distant that I may not travel there and back before dark?'

'No, it is perfectly possible. I will call here at ten this evening and await your return if you have not done so already.'

Sophy noted that his lordship did not leap to offer to accompany her. She would not wish to have him beside her all the way to Lady Holt, nor indeed see what would happen when he and his sister met, since the chances of them remaining civil, even before strangers, was slim. However, his washing his hands of her, and no doubt enjoying a decent dinner before coming to Hill Street, irked her intensely.

It was in an aggrieved mood with all those who bore the Tyneham name that Sophy set out, bearing the address of Lady Holt at Gerrards Cross, half an hour later.

Sophy had wondered how she was going to face Lady Holt, but in fact that lady made things very easy for her. She greeted her without Susan being present, and sat with tea things as if this were a standard morning call. Amelia, the Dowager Viscountess Holt, had been in black for some seven months following her husband's unexpected death upon the hunting field. She was some ten years older than Sophy, and not so old that she felt any inclination to treat her as anything other than her peer.

'I am sorry that you had to travel out so far, and at such short notice, Lady Sophronia, only I do not think any other alternative would avoid the sort of scandal one would wish to avoid. My brother is currently "on guard" outside the parlour in which Miss Tyneham is, well, confined.' She poured tea from an elegant silver teapot. 'I have not a huge admiration for my brother Edward's understanding, but I think in these circumstances he has actually done quite well. It is amazing what seven years in the army has done for him.' She smiled in a sisterly way. 'Do you have male siblings, Lady Sophronia?'

Sophy was thus led into talk of brothers before the difficult subject of her cousin arose once more. Lady Holt explained what had happened very calmly, and when Sophy brought Susan away, an hour later, she was conscious of a feeling that Lady Holt was a person whom she would like to know better. Her short interview with Lord Edward had been rather more embarrassing. He had been desperate that she understand he had not wanted to be with her cousin, but had felt there was no other course open to him. He had explained the exact manner in which he had been pressed into what he conceded must look a disreputable act. What was clear to Sophy was that he wanted Harriet to know that he had not acted out of choice, and that at no stage was he 'running away with Miss Tyneham'.

'I was in the deuce of a fix, ma'am, with her threatening to throw herself into the Thames if I did not help her, and I thought if I put her in a cab and brought her home, well, as soon as she saw the direction she would have jumped out, and haring after a young woman in Hyde Park would be as harmful to both her reputation and my regiment's, since I was in uniform and highly conspicuous.'

'So you brought her to Lady Holt. I have already thanked her ladyship for her aid, and apologised.'

'Well, I cannot see how apology comes into it, Lady Sophronia, since it was not your fault she arrived upon her doorstep. It was me who had a peel rung over them,' he blushed, 'as is not uncommon with older sisters.'

'She certainly seems to have the measure of my cousin, Lord Edward.'

'Yes, I have to say Amelia always was a downy one. My mother wanted her to return home when Holt died, but Amelia said no, she wanted her children to remain in their home, their father's house, especially with the eldest, George, off to Eton in the autumn, and having seen them, she was right. To be truthful, though, ma'am, I think this,' he paused, unsure how to describe what had happened, 'incident, has given her the chance to look outside her own four walls and family for the first time in months, having been in heavy mourning.'

'Well, I hope she sees it in as useful a light.' Sophy looked at Lord Edward, thoughtfully. 'I think I have the right to ask, my lord, before this happened, were you hopeful of what I shall term a "reconciliation", with my sister?'

'You have a right, and I will be quite frank about it. I would very much like to make Lady Harriet an offer, but I fear that, having already been in a precarious position, after this she will not exchange as much as the time of day with me, let alone accept my proposal.' He looked dejected.

'Then listen to me. I know my sister very well. Of course I do. She has been very hurt, and that is because her feelings are engaged. I can see that Susan's absconding was not your fault, and that you acted throughout as a man of honour. I will try and help Harriet see that. She is confused, and she is unhappy. I think, indeed I believe, that you could reverse this, but it may require you to be . . . assertive.'

'Assertive, ma'am?'

'Yes, Lord Edward. When you get the opportunity, you have to be persistent, so that Harriet will let you make your case. How you do so really must be your decision, but your future lies in your hands. She would not agree to see you when we encountered you unexpectedly in Green Park, and we must cry off from the Cleobury's, but there will be other opportunities for you to tell her your true feelings, I am sure. You must seize the chance, Lord Edward.'

'I would not force her, ma'am.' Lord Edward looked slightly shocked.

'Of course not, but you saw how she was in the Park. That was her fear of being told how much you admire her cousin. She feels second best.'

'But she is the best, the best by far.' Lord Edward averred, and Sophy could see he meant it. If Harriet could but see him at this moment, she would have no more fears.

'So you have to find a way to tell her that. It is in your hands, sir.'

She had been as clear as she could, and for her sister's benefit. It might not yet be too late to see her happy, and see Mama happy also, before the end of the Season. Given what had occurred, securing a husband for Susan was an impossibility. As for her own position, Sophy sighed.

Once bowling back towards London, Susan's opening gambit, which described Lady Holt as disagreeable and hard, left her cousin cold. Sophy did not want an argument in the chaise. She therefore simply told her cousin that she had no intention of discussing the matter until they were back home.

Harriet did not choose to greet her cousin when they reached Hill Street a little after nine. Susan was aware of the servants' eyes upon her, and disliked it. Only by a direct command to remain could she be forced to await her brother at ten, and when he did arrive, a few minutes before the hour, he launched into a tirade which, Sophy acknowledged, was justified but most unhelpful. Susan herself stood in the middle of the room with all the aloof hauteur of a Christian about to meet, quite willingly, a martyr's fate. She did not speak whilst her brother went on at length about her iniquity and stupidity.

'You have disgraced the name of my family.'

Sophy shook her head. He was as selfish as his sister, for here was he saying 'my' name. How much more obviously could he say he wanted her to have it no more, want her gone. At least she would not be distressed by his rejection.

'It is not a name I cherish, I assure you. In fact you can see the lengths I would go to change it, brother mine,' Susan spat back at him. She was, at heart, disappointed, and struggling to come to terms with her plan being so summarily foiled by a man she considered weak.

'Such a method would not occur to a young woman with a spark of honour.'

'Honour? Where does that get you? You thought I would sit with folded hands until some *man*,' Susan enunciated the word as if she meant 'vermin', 'happened to think me suitable to adorn his house? You think I want to be handed over like one of your ghastly pots?'

'Susan, you look upon this with too cynical an eye.' Sophy attempted to lower the heat of the exchanges.

'Do I? Well, that is rich, coming from one who has sat and waited in vain for *any man*.' Susan was in a mood to lash out at everyone.

Sophy flinched, but persisted. 'And yet what you attempted was hardly an improvement, was it? You tried to get Lord Edward, for whom you admit you have no *tendre*, to run away with you, presumably with the aim of becoming his wife. How did you envisage your life with a man you had tricked into marriage?'

This had not actually occurred to Susan. She simply thought that once the knot was tied, she would twist him about her finger and he would be happy as long as he did as she desired.

'And how do you think their graces, your new parents-in-law, would react to you? Welcome you with open arms, would they? Invite you to all their house parties? I think not. It is possible he might one day be forgiven. You would never be.'

'It matters not now, does it? Anyway, I am glad it came to nothing. He was useless. I hate him,' declared Susan, roundly. 'I had thought him at least bold enough to take me to the Border but no, he took me to his sister! He did not even try to make love to me. The fool.' With which she flounced out of the room.

Sophy stared at the door.

'You know, I think the opposite. I never imagined Lord Edward had so much sense.' She pursed her lips.

Tyneham spluttered.

'She will have to be sent back to Tyneham,' he declared, forcefully.

Susan, one foot upon the stair, froze and listened.

'Oh yes, and put an announcement in the *Morning Post*

to accompany it? You might as well. For goodness' sake, cousin, show a little sense. Yes, it sounds the easy course, but under how much constraint would she be there? Are you going to stay there and be her gaoler? I would far prefer not to have the worry, I assure you, but there is no alternative to her remaining here, and at least visible enough not to occasion remark.'

'But you have not prevented this . . . this disaster.'

'Short of chaining her to my wrist, there is little more that I can do, Tyneham.' Sophy almost shouted. She was threadbare. She had spent nearly twelve hours of worry and self-blame, which was not the same as having her cousin berate her. 'At least she has learnt that nothing will come of playing off hoyden tricks upon a man of honour.'

Susan still scowled as she trod softly up the stairs, but her eyes glittered. She did not hear the next exchange.

'Frankly, I no longer care if she is locked in her room and meals handed in to her.' Lord Tyneham was feeling bruised, as much by his cousin Sophronia's lack of feminine subservience and respect as Susan's shameful behaviour. She openly questioned his judgement, indeed went further and condemned it as ill-considered. He had maintained his self-belief that by the end of the Season he would simply have to offer for his cousin and she would accept him, with the relieved best wishes of her parents. The Sophronia he was seeing today made him realise both that this was unlikely, and that, in fact, marriage to such a woman would give him no peace. This was, naturally, Sophronia's fault. She had deceived him.

'That is hardly a brotherly feeling.'

'Why should it be? He snapped. 'She is not my sister.'

Sophy gaped at him as if he were mad.

'You cannot—'

'She is my mother's daughter, yes, but that is the extent of our relationship, and how much I resent even that much shared blood.'

Sophy went white, her brain making a rapid review of what little she could remember of her Aunt Clarissa. She had never come to visit them for more than a few days, and had seemed a pale, hollowed-out woman, whose love for Susan had a protective desperation about it. This gave good reasons why that should have been so. She wondered at what point the father had told the son. She blinked owlishly at her cousin.

'Yes, you may stare indeed. My father was very generous. He let her keep the child and even defied the gossip and said it was his to spare her shame.'

Sophy thought it more likely that the real reason had been to save his own face, and not be marked out as a cuckold. Her own memories of her uncle were of a man who spent most of his time with his cronies. He had never shown any outward sign of misery, or heartbreak. It made sense of what Susan had said about her mother being as good as neglected, but it was a mind-boggling revelation. If this stunned her, his next words made her sit down suddenly.

'I also shall not condemn my mother for her folly. She

was, after all, my mother, and,' Tyneham's voice dripped sarcasm, 'she was seduced by an expert. She would not listen to sound sense and gave her heart, and more, to probably the most notorious rake in London. I dare not consider how many more progeny of "Roving Rothley" litter Society.'

'"Roving Rothley"?' Sophy whispered, breathlessly, as her stomach turned over.

'Oh yes. The father of the current Viscount Rothley, whom you have most unfortunately permitted to be seen in your company rather often, and who wishes to interfere in family affairs.' It was a snide comment.

'So it was his father who was the rake.' She spoke to herself.

'I have no interest in Rothley's affairs, of course. He may be as licentious as he pleases. His father eventually had to flee the country and live abroad, even after inheriting the earldom. No doubt many men would like his blood, even after all this time.'

'His father was the rake,' repeated Sophy, her fingers white knuckled where she clasped them tightly together.

'Yes, that is what I just told you.' He made a grumbling noise in his throat. 'So do not thrust lack of family feeling at me, cousin. My father and I are the ones who are wronged. Susan has done very well by us.'

'You will not tell her.'

'That remains to be seen. If, at the end of the Season no man will take her, I am minded to make a small settlement upon her when she reaches one and twenty and inherits her mother's meagre portion, and let her live alone where and how she pleases as long as it is far from Tyneham Court.'

Sophy could not believe what he was saying.

'Alone? You do not seriously think that she would do that for long, do you?' Sophy reddened, both in embarrassment and anger. Her cousin did not care if his half-sister ended up among the demi-monde. Well, her behaviour might make that seem a natural progression, but . . . Could Susan not be 'rescued' even now, and become a woman who at thirty would look back and shake her head at her wilful youth? 'I think you have made your position plain, cousin. Should a suitor present himself, I will of course inform you, but otherwise, until my mother returns, I see no reason for you to visit. Good day to you.'

She needed to be alone. She felt sick and a little faint. This was more than she could assimilate quickly, both concerning Susan and, the part about which her heart was beating erratically, the innocence of Lord Rothley. Tyneham might hint that he could be 'licentious', and Lord Pinkney had hinted that his 'vices' lay with women, but there was no proof of either, and her own instincts were strong. Had she not overheard the alliterative epithets, had Mama not been so determined that he must be kept at a distance, for a reason, now clear, that was his name and not his person, she would have had no qualms about . . . about making it obvious that she enjoyed his company, that her affections were, yes, engaged.

How ironic, that it was in part through Susan, who mocked her so much for not attracting a man, that she had held off from the one with whom she might have found happiness. This was making the assumption that he liked her, but he had, surely, hinted at it often enough, and shown hurt at being rebuffed so unjustly.

Lord Tyneham departed, with chill politeness. After a few minutes there was a polite knock, and Bembridge entered. He saw his young mistress pale and distrait, and assumed it was reaction to the traumatic events.

'I was wondering whether you might not like a nice cup of tea, my lady, as a restorative. Very restoring is tea, after a nasty shock, and you have had a bad day, my lady, a bad day.'

'Thank you, Bembridge, that would be very nice.'

If only a nice cup of tea would mend matters.

CHAPTER SEVENTEEN

IT COULD NOT BE SAID THAT THE HOUSEHOLD SETTLED immediately after this upheaval. Harriet was quiet and kept to herself as much as possible, and when she was, perforce, in the same room with her cousin, it was clear that she did not relish the company. She might, she told Sophy, have understood a little if Susan had fallen madly enamoured of the Life Guards officer, but she had not. She had simply used him, wound him about her finger as she did with men, and he had gone along with it. It had not been hard for Harriet to see his actions in taking Susan into Buckinghamshire as noble, but she blamed Susan for putting him in a difficult situation, and for effectively trying to ruin his life by making him marry her.

'How could she be so heartless, Sophy? And she

knows that I am . . . very partial to him. It is cruel.'

Sophy made no attempt to deny this.

'The scales are most certainly lifted from his eyes, though, Harry. You can be in no doubt that he feels in no way inclined to Susan.'

'No, no, he cannot. But . . . How will I face him? I am sure I will not manage a single word.'

Sophy hoped that words might be unnecessary.

Lord Edward was perfectly used to obeying orders, and as he saw it, Lady Sophronia's words to him had been just that, a set of orders. However, in order for him to 'not go away' he had to actually see Harriet, and for several days both she, and the other two ladies, were 'indisposed', according to the hostesses to whose invitations Sophy had sent hastily penned apologies. Without anyone knowing the origins, one reason put forward was that the indisposition was the result of putrid sore throats, whilst another suggested dubious crab meat in a course at dinner. Whilst Lord Edward had more reason than most to guess the truth of the matter, he still sent round a bouquet, carefully worded to apply to both Hadlow ladies, wishing them a swift recovery and in the meantime paid a visit to his father.

His duties, and the independent attitude that the army had fostered, meant that Lord Edward might meet his sire in his club, and his mother at parties, but he was not a frequent visitor to their house in Grosvenor Square. He was made a very adequate allowance, which he did not exceed, and his grace would have been surprised at the arrival of his youngest son upon his doorstep had not his eldest daughter given him a very accurate representation of the current state of affairs, minus certain 'Susan aspects' immediately after his visit to her. Discussion with his duchess had confirmed that Lady Harriet Hadlow was an unexceptional young woman who was regarded as sweet-natured and neither irritatingly ignorant nor unpleasantly bookish.

'I think she will suit Edward very well,' declared his duchess. 'The Chelmarshes are a good family, even if her father has this rustic obsession with livestock, and it is not as though, with two elder brothers, it is vital that Edward marry dynastically. There is the Tyneham chit, who seems set to try and tarnish her cousins' good name with her own, but . . . No, Edward could do a lot worse, and you never know the sort of women that army officers can meet. We must consider ourselves fortunate his choice has fallen upon a young woman of breeding and class.'

The Duke therefore greeted his son with affability, invited him to take a seat and not stand as if about to make a report of troop movements, and to ring for a bottle of burgundy.

'So, you have decided to get leg-shackled, eh?' He laughed, as his youngest offspring stared at him as though he had performed an act of clairvoyancy. 'Come, my boy, you have a sister and mother. Such things cannot be kept hidden from the distaff world.'

'Ah, I suppose not. The thing is, sir, that I thought I would speak to you first, not that I require your approval, but . . . I think it the decent thing to do, and I would like the approval so that if accepted, I could be sure of Harriet's reception.'

'If? You are in some doubt of the young lady's affection?'

'No, and, temporarily, yes.'

Reluctantly, Lord Edward explained the true state of affairs to his father, who remarked, sapiently, that if the chit accepted him after all that she was besotted.

'I am rather hoping she is, sir. I . . . I am, despite what may have appeared to the contrary. Harriet is the sort of girl who is generally happy, affectionate and makes a fellow feel . . . comfortable with life. That may sound damning with faint praise, but there is a great deal to be said for the warm glow of . . . feeling like that. I want to cosset and care for her, see her happy, that sort of thing. There are women like her cousin who could never do that, not for me. To be honest, I can see us being very happy. I thought I may sell out, actually live on my estate at Staythorpe, set up our nursery, and generally settle into domesticity. The army has been tremendous fun and all that, and I have seen a bit of action, but now, with peacetime, the ceremonial palls after a while and—'

'You need say no more, my boy. I understand perfectly. All I need say is that if your Harriet accepts you, your mother and I will be exceedingly pleased. I would offer my felicitations, but at this juncture they might seem precipitate.'

'Yes,' sighed Lord Edward, his face falling, 'I just hope I can persuade her to see how I really feel.'

Perhaps his message or the bouquet of flowers were efficacious, because two evenings later Lord Edward saw the object of his affections at a party at Bedford House. At least, he saw Lady Sophronia, and he could not imagine that she would have come alone. His next problem was to get close to Lady Harriet without seeing, or being seen by, the disgraceful and disgraced Miss Tyneham. He therefore did what was really more the task of light cavalry; he reconnoitred. Miss Tyneham, stunning in jonquil silk, was stationed at Lady Sophronia's side. She was not there out of choice, he thought, seeing the look upon her face. Lady Harriet was not present. He worked upon the principle that she must therefore be upon the dance floor, and his opportunity lay in 'ambushing' her as the current dance ended. He made his way to the forefront among the onlookers. Lady Harriet was dancing with Lord Bollington. If she did not look as stunning as her dark-haired cousin, she looked, to him at least, infinitely prettier, though her cheeks were a little pale as though she had indeed been ill. A wave of guilt swept over him. Had he made her ill through upsetting her? It was a chastened Lord Edward Wittenham who approached her from the blind side as she left the floor. He bowed.

'Your servant, Lady Harriet. Evening, Bollington, I believe our hostess was looking for you a moment ago. I would be glad to escort Lady Harriet back to her sister.' With this barefaced lie, which he salved to his conscience by terming it a *ruse de guerre*, he managed to get the charming Lady Harriet to himself. She kept her eyes very slightly averted until he addressed her directly.

'I wondered if I might have the honour of the next quadrille, Lady Harriet?'

Harriet looked reproachfully at the supplicating cavalry officer.

'Why, sir? Has my cousin filled her dance card already?' She sounded bitter, and he was both taken aback and hurt. She dropped her gaze, flushing at her own temerity.

He had expected reproach, but not words so sharp. He was stung, and responded far more firmly than he had intended.

'I have no idea, ma'am. I did not ask her. I am asking you.'

She was looking at the floor, but at this she raised her eyes back to his face, and the flush became pallor.

'I . . . I am sorry, I did not mean . . .' She swallowed rather hard. He looked so very serious, and offended, and suddenly everything was a jumble and she wanted to cry. She bit her lip, and his expression changed instantly, and he grasped one of her hands in a tight clasp.

'Your cousin means nothing to me. What happened was not at my instigation, you must believe that. I thought, briefly, she was beautiful, but . . .' He spoke hastily, afraid that she would not listen to his heartfelt words.

'Susan is beautiful.' Harriet sighed.

'Only in her features. There is no beauty within her.' Lord Edward's voice dropped to a passionate whisper. 'Not like you.'

Harriet now turned a shade of deep pink.

'I did not think you the sort of man to flirt with me. I do not care for it, sir.'

'I am not flirting, Harriet, and you know it.' It was not lover-like; it was not romantic in the way Harriet had always imagined, but Lord Edward was undoubtedly sincere.

'Oh.' He had used her name, and it made her heart pitter-pat.

'Now show me your dance card.'

She did so, and still unsmiling, Edward Wittenham wrote EW in a flourishing, if small, round hand beside a quadrille, and then the waltz. In the face of this masterful behaviour, Harriet's anger melted away.

'I shall return to claim . . . my dances.'

She nodded.

Sophy, who had permitted Susan to join the set of the next country dance with a youthful peer whom she knew was far too young to be seeking a serious relationship, saw the exchange, and reading it by their expressions and the ebb and flow of Harriet's colour, gave a heartfelt sigh. Her sister looked about her, seeking her, and came towards her a little dazed.

'Sophy, he . . . Lord Edward . . .' She held up her dance card, and her face glowed. 'I . . . If he should wish to speak to me, in private I mean, might I . . . What he said, the way he looked . . . Oh Sophy, Papa would not refuse him permission do you think, because he will not inherit a grand title?'

'Harry, you goose, of course he would not. Lord Edward is the sort of man he will approve of mightily, although if he sells out do not be surprised if Papa starts inculcating sound land management in him or suggests he have a herd of prize Jerseys.'

'Oh, he would.' Harriet giggled.

'If he wishes to . . . find out if an offer would be acceptable to you, I have been in this house often enough to know that there is a small chamber two doors beyond the card room. The young ladies of the house use it for their drawing class because there is good light in the daytime. Just do not go there hand in hand. Dearest Harry, this makes me very happy.' Sophy leant and kissed her sister's cheek.

'You . . . you do not feel that I am fickle, do you? Because I said I did not wish to see him again?' Harriet looked at her hands. 'For in truth that was not true. I mean it was only true then. I did not want to see him just at that time, you see, for I felt very low . . . despondent, but I . . . oh, I am making no sense.'

'Sense enough.' Sophy laughed, softly. 'Now go and

await your dashing soldier claiming his dances.'

'Perhaps I am expecting too much. Perhaps he does simply want to dance.' Harriet was suddenly uncertain.

Sophy shook her head and pushed her away. So delighted was she, and so lost in thoughts of how the interview might proceed, that she did not see that the dance had concluded or that Susan was being escorted to sample the ices by Lord Pinkney.

Lord Edward returned, ostensibly to lead Harriet into the quadrille, but his head was so full of the declaration he was about to make he thought he would forget all the steps. He had found a glass of claret and a quiet corner, and rehearsed what he considered suitable ways to ask a young lady to marry him. It was rather more unnerving than waiting for the trumpeter to sound the charge.

'I . . . Would you be offended if we did not actually take our places in the set, Lady Harriet? There is something very particular I wish to say to you.'

'Not offended at all, sir. If . . . If it is "very particular", I believe there is a little chamber, where the ladies do watercolours and such, towards the rear of this floor. We might be more private . . .' She blushed, and he took her hand and gave it a squeeze.

'I will meet you there in a few moments, yes?'

She nodded, withdrew her hand, and flitted away. Her fear, as she opened the door, was that some other couple might also know of this secluded spot for a tryst. It was dark, but the curtains were not drawn, and the light from the flambeaux upon the terrace below gave enough illumination if one did not stand too far from the window. Without quite understanding why she did so, she removed her long gloves. Her heart beat fast, and although she was expecting him, she gave a squeak as the door opened, and the uniformed figure entered the room.

'Harriet?' His eyes were not adjusted to the gloom.

She stepped forward with a rustle of her skirts, her hands held out and trembling. He took them firmly, carried them to his lips, and then went down immediately upon his knees.

'Before all else, forgive me,' he implored.

'Is there so much to forgive, my lord?' she asked, softly.

'Your cousin, I . . . I have lusted after her, there is no nicer word for it, but never, never, my darling, have I thought of her with love, as I do you, and now it seems so wrong to want you, who are so much better, so sweet, so pure . . .'

She looked down onto the top of his head, bent over her hands, and for a moment felt completely in control.

'Plain lust should be banished, but love cherished, and physical desire is a part of love, surely? I . . . I cannot see that wanting me is wrong, as long as you never again want her. But can you, truly, want me? Me?' There was modest disbelief in her soft voice.

He half scrambled to his feet in his urgency to take her in his arms and prove that he did. His arms went

255

about her and she lifted her face for his kiss, and as his mouth closed over hers he knew that the memory of Susan Tyneham's kiss was obliterated, that he would never look upon her with desire again, because his Harriet's lips were soft and full, and trembled with her emotions, and having her in his arms was so much better than any thought of her cold, manipulative cousin.

'I want you,' he breathed, between kisses. 'I want you to be my wife, Harriet, darling Harriet. I love you, only you, want only you. Marry me, please, marry me.'

She melted in his arms, and her 'Yes' was both an assent and a request that he continue. Only when the need to claim a breath overwhelmed them did they part, trembling, and laughing a little guiltily at the power of their passion. He kissed her hands once more, the backs and then, more sensuously, the palms.

'I shall get leave of absence from the Colonel and post into Suffolk immediately.'

'Not this minute immediately, I hope, sir. It is dark, and besides, I like you with me.' She blushed at her own daring, and then, abandoning herself to shamelessness, took his right hand in her own, raised it to her lips, and kissed the misshapen end of his ring finger. 'Was it something very brave?'

He laughed again, shakily, for the small intimacy thrilled him.

'No, sweetheart, mere self-preservation.'

'I am so glad, so very glad, you were not wounded

more severely, but had it been so, I would still have fallen in love with you.'

'Say that again,' he whispered, huskily.

'I would still have fallen in love with you. Oh, Edward, I love you so very much.' She blinked away a tear and was taken into his embrace once more.

When Lady Harriet took her place with her beau for the waltz some minutes later, one elderly lady, who disapproved of such a licentious dance, pointed her out.

'See that chit, see the look on her face. "Dancing" you call it? Might as well have 'em kissing and caressing to the scrape of fiddles. Disgusting!'

CHAPTER EIGHTEEN

THE NEWS THAT LADY HARRIET HAD RECEIVED A proposal of marriage was greeted with pleasure below stairs in Hill Street. This was both because she was considered to have always been a very nice young lady, even from when small, according to such worthies as the housekeeper, the cook and Mr Bembridge, and also because it must surely put her thoughtless cousin's nose out of joint. Miss Susan was not well liked.

The 'thoughtless cousin' was indeed piqued, and congratulated Harriet in such a way that it sounded as if Lord Edward was better than nothing, but only just, and that if he had been more impressive, Susan would have secured him for herself. If Susan hoped to irritate Harriet by this she failed signally, since Harriet was inhabiting a private cloud of joy so elevated as to be beyond cousinly barbs. Sophy noted the words but said nothing. After all, the proof was there to be seen; Harriet's hand had been sought and Susan's had not. If Susan went about with a private scowl, Sophy could not care the less.

For her own part Sophy felt herself relax a little. She could not be said to have failed her mama if Harriet's betrothal was assured, and to a man whose lineage could not be faulted. Mama could see how succeeding with Susan was an impossibility, and would merely sigh over it, and say that some things were beyond achieving.

With Lord Edward's return from East Anglia, bearing Lord Chelmarsh's benison and a few wise words upon the importance of good animal husbandry, the announcement was made public. Whilst Harriet herself received congratulations, Sophy was actually rather surprised to receive so many herself, from the matchmaking mamas amongst whom she had become a temporary member. Lord Edward was not so great a prize that any felt his attaching himself to Lady Harriet Hadlow had lessened their own progeny's chances of achieving a stunning match, but at the same time it was acknowledged that he was an excellent young man with the finest of connections and an easy competence, comprising a very pleasant estate in Nottinghamshire, and one also in Leicestershire, inherited from his maternal grandfather.

Harriet had been quite surprised to find that she was not going to be a wife who might at any moment be called to follow the drum, and confessed to her sister that she was more comfortable knowing that she had no need to learn how to bandage wounds or skin a rabbit. Her face was so serious that Sophy laughed.

'I am sorry, Harry, but the idea that you might be whisked away upon some foreign campaign is so . . . outlandish. You might rather have become bored, with a husband whose duties meant residing in London outside the Season. However, I think your Edward's decision to sell out will be to your advantage, since you can be together and make his house a home.' She paused. 'I will miss you, Harry, but after all, it is not as if Nottinghamshire and Suffolk are so far apart that I may not visit you occasionally.'

Harriet opened her mouth, but thought better of it, and simply said nothing. The idea had occurred to her that her sister might not be travelling from Suffolk at all. Worcestershire was, thankfully, as far as she could remember from her lessons in geography, about the same distance from Staythorpe as Suffolk.

Whilst engrossed in her own happiness, Harriet had still found time to wonder why Lord Rothley did not feature in her sister's plans for the future. She had little doubt that Sophy liked him extremely, or that he was taken with her, although of late they had not been so much in company because his lordship had been away from London on those Worcestershire estates. She liked Lord Rothley, although she found him a little too needle-witted for her tastes, and sometimes had to ponder his witticisms, which Sophy did not.

* * *

In fact, Lord Rothley was occupying a vast deal of her sister's waking thoughts, and her dreams also, but not in an entirely pleasant way. She wondered whether his withdrawal to the country, which she had discovered had coincided with her last sharp comments to him, had been in response to estate matters or her treatment of him. She also recalled those things which she had said which he might think referred to his character in a slighting way. Such thoughts were lowering. Many hours were spent in her bed rehearsing various ways in which she might make it clear that she had been in error, misled by circumstance, and had only with extreme reluctance thought the worst of him. Telling a man one had believed him a heartless Lothario was not, however, at all easy, especially if one also wished to intimate that in reality he was almost constantly in one's thoughts and inspired the most tender of emotions.

It was therefore inevitable that their first encounter upon his return to London would be marked by awkwardness. He had discovered the news of Harriet's engagement via both the notice in the *Morning Post* and from Sir Esmond Fawley, whom he had encountered whilst dining at his club on his first night back in the Metropolis. Sir Esmond, who had been the recipient of mild confidences from Harriet in the manner of an uncle, which, he declared wryly, made him feel terribly old, was able to flesh out the bare facts, and also reveal 'the elopement that never was'.

'I am telling you because I know you will keep the

confidence, and because I need someone to tell me that I really ought to give up on a girl so lacking in common decency.'

'But do you think she had any idea what she was doing, beyond escaping "incarceration" and cocking a snook at Society?'

'No, I don't. From what I gather, her planning extended to throwing herself at the only man she thought she could persuade that she would do away with herself if he did not assist her, and then marrying him to spite everyone. The cold realities of what that entailed almost certainly never entered her calculating little head. I daresay that if he had set off towards the Border with her, she would have been not just outraged but violent if he had not engaged separate bedchambers, for a start. I have no proof of that, it is merely a fool's instinct.' Sir Esmond sighed. 'At least you can be assured that Lady Sophy is not so stressed now that Lady Harriet is safely betrothed, and whatever bumble-broth Miss Susan tumbles into, it cannot ruin her sister's chances.'

'That is true, not that I have discovered any likely method of re-establishing myself with the divine Sophy. However, I shall use the news of Lady Harriet's approaching nuptials as an excuse to pay a social call, and the worst she can do is have the aged butler throw me out upon my disreputable ear.'

This calamity did not, however, befall him, although Lady Sophy was not at home when he presented himself, and he initially found himself facing Lady Harriet, who used her cousin Susan's presence as chaperonage.

'I came to offer my congratulations, Lady Harriet, though I ought really to be offering them to Wittenham, for finding just such a lady as would make any man happy.'

Harriet blushed at this encomium, and murmured her thanks, shyly. Susan, he noted, curled her lip, as though she privately thought any man who would be happy with her cousin must be a very miserable specimen.

Making polite small talk beyond the obvious about the plans the newly betrothed had for their future was laborious, and Lord Rothley had just about given up and decided that he must leave without seeing Lady Sophy, when she entered the room, dressed for walking. Her cheeks paled a little, but she came forward and offered her hand calmly enough.

'I am sorry, my lord. I have been out making purchases and was only told of your visit as I returned.'

'It was a spur of the moment decision, ma'am,' he lied, 'so you could not have anticipated it. I hope you were successful?'

'Successful?'

'In your shopping expedition.'

'Yes, oh yes, quite.' She felt a little flustered. 'It was merely fripperies.'

'So you have not been followed home by a train of footmen labouring under heavy loads.' He smiled, and she could not help but respond in kind.

'Not at all. The sum of my success is contained in two

small packages that I was able to carry for myself, my lord.' She paused. 'Have you been offered refreshment, sir?'

'Oh, I am so sorry!' Harriet put a hand to her mouth. 'I completely forgot to do so, chattering away as I have been.'

'Then rectify that omission by ringing for . . . would tea suffice, sir? Good, then tea, Harriet dear, and if you would be so kind as to permit me to change, I . . .' Sophy took a deep breath and looked at his lordship very straight, 'I would be grateful of the opportunity to have a few words with you, Lord Rothley.'

He could not tell from her expression whether these words would please him or not.

Sophy withdrew without undue haste, but rang for her maid with unusual vehemence, and was indecisive when asked which gown she chose to wear. Her voice was agitated, and she changed her mind three times before eventually deciding upon one in a soft blue with a simple appliquéd chevron design at the neck and lower edge of the bodice. It was a dress in which Sophy felt comfortable, knowing it suited her. She 'revived' her hair since it had been crushed by her bonnet, but did not linger. After all, the gentleman was waiting for her.

Therefore, it was only ten minutes later when she returned to the yellow saloon, to find her sister attempting to sound like the lady of the house and proffering the tea, whilst telling Lord Rothley that her intended was going to take her to visit his mama for a whole afternoon on the morrow, and that she had received a charming letter from his sister, Lady Holt. This had the unfortunate effect of reminding her of Susan's recent escapade and made her blush and stumble over her next words. Lord Rothley pretended not to have noticed.

Sophy tried to look serene herself, but could imagine just how Harriet felt. She was about to engage in something far more embarrassing.

Lord Rothley rose as she entered, but she bade him be seated and drink his tea.

'We are all,' and she smiled in an inclusive way at Susan, 'delighted that my sister has found a gentleman who will make her very happy and with whom she is well suited.'

'Lord Edward is the fortunate one, ma'am.'

Sophy wondered if she was just imagining a hint of regret in Lord Rothley's voice. He certainly felt that the cavalryman had contrived to emerge from the 'war' victorious, having done the equivalent of losing every battle on the way.

There was polite conversation, in which Susan took no part beyond the occasional response, but Harriet did not need the speaking look from her sister to know that whatever words Sophy wished to say to Lord Rothley, she wanted to say in private. Harriet, therefore, finished her tea and 'remembered' that she really must go and write a note to Miss Welling, their former governess.

'She wrote to me as soon as she saw a copy of the

Morning Post. Do please excuse me, my lord.' She rose and added, 'Come, cousin, we have things to do,' as Rothley made his bow.

Susan stared at her, frowned, and then, as he inclined his head to her also, gave up, though she was heard to whisper to Harriet as they left, 'I do not see that it is any more permissible that Sophy should be alone with a man, in spite of her age.'

Lord Rothley's lips twitched, despite everything. The door closed, and he faced a flushed Lady Sophy.

'You need not be concerned, ma'am, your decrepitude is not obvious, at least to me.'

She smiled, though only for a moment.

'There are times those two do make me feel ancient, however. Please, my lord . . .' She indicated that he should resume his seat but herself then rose and clasped her hands in front of her like a child forced to apologise before adults.

'Is what you have to say so difficult?' He smiled, trying to be encouraging, but it made her feel the more wretched for having thought the worst of him. 'I feel distinctly uncomfortable sitting down whilst a lady stands. Please, do sit down, Lady Sophy. I am not, really I am not, your father about to hear of some mild misdemeanour.'

'I . . . I think the more pertinent thing, Lord Rothley, is that you are not *your* father.'

'Ah.' He paused. 'Had you assumed that the sins of the father were those gleefully perpetrated by the son? I did wonder. What was it that gave you cause, ma'am?'

His smile remained, though it was fixed, and his eyes questioned.

'Nothing that you did, sir, but my distrust of myself, and a misunderstanding of . . .' She stopped. Did he know that Susan was his half-sister? If he did not, would it be right to tell him? She spoke a little cryptically. 'My mother was vehement that we should not be seen in frequent company with you. I found this confusing, since you are everywhere received and, forgive my bluntness, mamas do not hide their vulnerable offspring from you.'

'No, I have to say they do not. There are occasions when I almost wish they would . . . but I interrupt.'

'Yes, well you see now I understand why Mama held this belief. I should also say I heard two older ladies discussing "Roving Rothley"', "Rake Rothley", and jumped to a very wrong conclusion. I am very sorry for it, my lord. I have been uncivil and . . .'

He waved away her apology and concentrated upon the important fact. 'You understand why Lady Chelmarsh thought as she did. I see.' He paused. 'We share colouring, but I hope little else, you know.' He saw her patent relief and laughed. 'Yes ma'am, I am aware of the relationship between myself and your cousin. I was not until that day when Tyneham met us all in Hyde Park and then . . . well, the suspicion made me write to my disreputable parent and ascertain the truth. I have been cudgelling my brains how to intimate to you that I was not the reprobate you thought me without revealing what I thought you did not know, and it turns out you have been labouring under the same difficulty.'

'Only since Lord Tyneham revealed it to me when Susan . . .'

'Absconded?'

'You know? Oh, my goodness, if it is common knowledge . . .'

'Have no fears on that score. I had it from Fawley, who would no more reveal it than I would. He, er, is aware that I have, shall we say, a brotherly interest in Miss Tyneham, and thought it only right I should know. I believe he had the tale through things Lady Harriet let slip. He says she treats him like an uncle, which is both charming and very lowering, as you can imagine.'

'Oh yes, poor Sir Esmond,' Sophy responded, without really concentrating. She was coming to terms with the enormous relief of knowing that Lord Rothley was privy to the same awful secret, and the feeling that somehow it lessened the burden.

He was watching her closely, seeing the emotions, however well contained, flicker across her face and linger in her eyes. His manner became more serious.

'I take it that Tyneham has not made his sister's true parentage public. Does she know, herself?'

Sophy shook her head.

'I do not think he wishes it in the public domain to "protect" his father's name, but he has said he may tell Susan when the Season is over, and pay her to leave Tyneham Court and his life, when she reaches full age.'

'Charitable of him,' declared Lord Rothley,

sarcastically. 'Lady Sophy, let us be open with one another. I cannot act as I would wish, cannot involve myself publicly in your cousin – and my sister's – affairs for fear of unwelcome revelations. However, you are not alone when having to cope with her. If there is, at any point, a way in which I can assist you, you have but to say it. I offered as much some time since, but I think then it was misinterpreted.'

Sophy nodded, and coloured.

'Part of me so wished that I might trust you, and yet . . .'

'That does not matter now. I would also say that Sir Esmond Fawley is also with us on this, and can be equally trusted.'

'Sir Esmond is a true gentleman, and I do trust him.'

'Should I aspire to that same level?' His brow rose in interrogation.

'There is not the need, my lord. I have never distrusted you upon my own instincts.' She looked at him, a little shyly, and extended her hand.

He took it, wondering for a moment if he might carry it to his lips and make the depth of his feelings clear, but instead he clasped it strongly, and shook it. There had been enough disclosures for one day, and it did not feel the right time.

'Since we are being open with one another, I would also like to say that I believe the sole care of your sister and cousin has been a heavy burden upon you, ma'am, one which you have borne admirably, but one which is now lessened by Lady Harriet's betrothal and by no longer standing alone to "guard" Miss Susan Tyneham. You might therefore permit yourself a little time to consider yourself, and what your aspirations might be.' He still had hold of her hand. 'I would hope that you do not look upon me as less than a friend, and would ask you to—' He suddenly stopped, for the words left him.

There was a short silence.

'You are right, my lord. I have had no opportunity to think of myself these last weeks, and would appreciate the chance to do so. I would ask a little time, to be clear in my own mind.'

It was odd, he thought. They were talking of the same thing, yet both afraid to say it openly, as if to do so would place some curse upon it. He sensed that she was inclined to favour him, and certainly wished to count him a friend. He was sure of his own mind and heart, but if she needed time he would give her that time. He would give her anything in his power. And besides, his sister had committed virtually every folly possible, so there was little worse she could do.

This only proved that he knew his half-sister not at all.

CHAPTER NINETEEN

L ORD PINKNEY COULD NOT BE SAID TO HAVE HAD
much opportunity to beguile the wild but naive Miss
Tyneham, since she was, as she described it, shackled to
her cousins. He had expected that he would need to be at
his most suave and charming to get her into the frame of
mind where she, however full of bravado she may appear,
would contemplate that ultimate indiscretion for the
Society debutante, an elopement to the Border. However,
her antipathy towards the world in general, and her cousins
in particular, seemed to be providing enough incentive for
her to do something truly outrageous without him having
to pay excessive court to her.

This was both a relief and slightly unnerving. Somehow,
the idea of fleeing to Gretna Green with a young woman
who was not in his toils, and willing to do anything for

'love', seemed slightly indecent. That her attitude should be as calculating and pragmatic as his own did not fit. It was therefore almost out of a need to fulfil the 'rules' of elopement that Pinkney made the effort to gain her affection. That meeting her was so difficult, and was reduced to swift, covert conversations and smouldering looks, added a little spice. He could not rid himself of the thought that she treated it all as a game.

After the attempted flight, Harriet had at first refused to go out alone with Susan, both out of dislike and fear of her doing something wayward yet again. However, with her happiness assured, she relaxed a little, and was even prepared to promenade in the Park with her cousin when Sophy had other duties demanding her attention. Harriet was not to know that in this way she played right into her cousin's hands.

A murmured exchange the night before at a rout party had seen Susan assure Lord Pinkney that she would try her best to be in Hyde Park the following afternoon at the fashionable hour, and that if he could but observe her and show himself to her but not her 'gaolers', she would contrive to slip from under their noses, for a few minutes at least. He had not held out much hope of this succeeding with Miss Tyneham under the watchful gaze of both the Hadlow sisters, but when he saw that Susan Tyneham was only accompanied by Lady Harriet and a maid, he smiled. Had that been good fortune, or Miss Tyneham using her wits?

Lord Pinkney was a great believer in Lady Luck,

although he freely admitted she was a capricious mistress. Today she smiled upon him so much he was inclined to try his hand at cards again, come the evening, which might even obviate the need for a clandestine marriage at all.

Lady Harriet and Miss Tyneham had exchanged pleasantries with several young ladies, and Susan, on the alert, had noted Lord Pinkney sauntering some way behind them, when Harriet espied her Intended on a converging course. From that moment, Susan was thrust to the back of her mind. Lord Edward was in fact returning from a visit to his bootmaker, and merely stepping the comparatively short distance through the Park to his barracks rather than taking the Knightsbridge Road, since it was far more sociable. Once he caught sight of his beloved waving a gloved hand, he amended his pace to fall in with her, and he then noticed, with a feeling of some awkwardness, Miss Tyneham.

The conversation between the betrothed couple effectively excluded Susan, and she used it to advantage, claiming that there was a hole in the seam of her reticule, and she must have dropped a half guinea that she had been keeping in it.

'I am not so fortunate as to be able to waste money upon nothing. I beg you will let me at least retrace our steps from where we entered the Park. If I dropped it in the street, no doubt some itinerant has already taken it up, but here . . . I will catch you up as soon as I have checked the path.'

She sounded so reasonable, and neither of her

companions were enjoying her company. Harriet agreed readily enough, requesting only that Susan should not engage in conversation with strangers, and dithering over whether the maid should remain with her or her cousin.

'But I am not to meet anyone, cousin, and you are with a gentleman. I see your quandary, but surely the answer is obvious. She must remain with you.' Susan sounded modesty personified, and had her listeners not been so absorbed in one another, they must have been highly suspicious.

Thus it was that Harriet did not think to question why her cousin was being so helpful, and nodded. Susan therefore began to retrace their steps, ostensibly looking at the pathway. Her cousin and swain were too engrossed in each other to see Susan step aside to some shrubbery, where she joined Lord Pinkney. She was flushed with success rather than ardour, but did present a most fetching sight, and, instinctively, Pinkney smiled and lifted her little gloved hand to his lips.

'You are a very clever conspirator, my dear.'

'Yes, I think I am, my lord. However, when together we risk discovery, and I have important things to discuss with you.'

It was quite amusing, hearing this slip of a girl so serious. He quelled the urge to smile at her, realising she would not care for his mockery. However, her next words had the power to stun him.

'Would you like to run away with me, Lord Pinkney?' It was posed in quite a matter-of-fact way, as if he might care to escort her to the theatre or to see the beasts at the Tower of London.

'What a question to ask, ma'am.' He stalled, since either answer could be seen as the wrong one.

'It is an honest one, sir. I find myself in a predicament, and you, I believe, have a different one, which might be solved if you solved mine at the same time.'

He frowned, a little confused by this.

'You are lacking in funds. My brother will effectively pay a man to take me off his hands. At the same time, you are not a gentleman whom he, or my "dear cousin Sophy" would look upon with favour. I have been told that no man of honour will offer for me, so I look to a rogue, dear sir, which sounds to me far more exciting. And if you did run off with me, Tyneham would be mad as fire.'

'And might call me out, ma'am?'

'Ha! Not my brother! He will pay up my dowry if he can avoid scandal, and to avoid any possible violence. I never knew a man so desirous of maintaining his own health. In short, we blackmail him, sir.'

Lord Pinkney was taken aback both by her daring and her coolness.

'If, Miss Tyneham, I can be of any service to you . . .'

'And to yourself, do not forget, my lord.'

'And, incidentally, to myself, I would be glad to do so.'

'So you agree?' She sounded gleeful, which shook him.

'I, er, agree.'

'Good, then this is what we do.' Miss Tyneham had A Plan. In truth, it was not a bad plan, and Pinkney could see that it might be their greatest chance of success. He made some slight alterations, where Miss Tyneham's knowledge was, perforce, a little thin, but otherwise everything was agreed upon. Miss Tyneham offered her hand, not to be kissed in a romantic manner, but to shake upon the conclusion of what felt like a business transaction. It was remarkably disconcerting, and as he watched the young lady hurry away, he became lost in thought, wondering not least whether she had even the haziest idea what her life would be once her brother had handed over the dowry. He was still contemplating this as he rejoined the main pathway, and did not hear a man leading a horse come up beside him.

'You know, Pinkney, there are a few depths to which I had, mistakenly, thought you would not stoop.' Sir Esmond Fawley's voice was superficially disinterested, but his lordship detected steel within it.

'It never pays to underestimate me, Fawley.'

'I might say exactly the same.'

'Oh, I do not think I have ever underestimated you.'

'Perhaps until now, my friend.' The appellation might be amicable, but the tone was now clearly menacing.

'Are you warning me off? Do not tell me you have an interest in the refreshing Miss Tyneham.' Pinkney very nearly sneered.

'I shall not tell you that, merely that if you think to play upon her . . . lack of experience . . . you will find yourself wishing you had limited your interest in chance to cards and horses, and not "gambled" with your life.'

'That sounds so very like a threat, Fawley.'

'Not at all, Pinkney. It is, in fact, a promise.'

'Promises, ah, they can be so notoriously difficult to keep.'

'So I have heard, in your case.' Sir Esmond's eyes glittered.

Lord Pinkney's hands clenched at the insult, but he refused the bait.

'You ought not to listen to tittle-tattle, my friend.'

Sir Esmond, upon whom the rigidity of Lord Pinkney's smile had not been lost, smiled back.

'And you, my friend, should pay attention to friendly advice. Good day to you.' Sir Esmond touched the brim of his low-crowned beaver, mounted his bay, and trotted away.

Lord Pinkney frowned in a thoughtful manner. Sir Esmond Fawley was not noted as an aggressive man, but exuded the air of one whom it was unwise to anger. However, Pinkney was a gamester to the core, and cast caution aside. This was just another risk to add to his list. It made the future look rather exciting.

Sir Esmond Fawley left Town the following day to visit his aunt, his father's eldest sister, which led to speculation in some quarters that Lady Cottingham must be at her last breath and Fawley was hoping to inherit. In fact, that lady was in her customary stout health, much to Sir Esmond's pleasure. His parents having departed this life within three years of each other during his twenties, his Aunt Cottingham was his closest relative of an older generation, and Sir Esmond had a mind full of questions which only someone of an older 'vintage' could answer.

'Hmmm, I thought there must be a reason for you to abandon the dubious delights of the Capital in the Season and come to visit an old fidget like me.' Lady Cottingham was a bird-like lady whose apparent physical fragility hid the fact that she was as tough as steel and as sharp as a needle made thereof.

'You make me sound a very scimble-scamble fellow if all I care about is the social whirl, ma'am, and I was hoping, really I was, that you would be pleased to see me.' His eyes danced but he managed to look crestfallen.

'Jackanapes.'

'I protest. I am the most staid of men, so staid I am contemplating matrimony.'

She sat more upright in her chair and her claw-like fingers gripped the arms.

'And you want my approval of the chit?'

'Hardly, ma'am, but I do want your knowledge.'

'I know nothing of modern misses, sir. I stay cooped up in this rat hole from one year's end to the next.'

He understood her arthritis must be bad, for the 'rat hole' was a very comfortable dower house ·into which she had removed those pieces of furniture she particularly liked from the main house, along with the elderly butler, five maids, a cook who knew her likes and many dislikes to perfection, and a coachman with an equipage that was as old as it was grand.

'I would like to know not about modern misses, but old mistakes, ma'am. To be specific, I want you to tell me all you can recall about Rake Rothley and Clarissa Tyneham twenty years ago. You would have been visiting Town in those days, I swear.'

Lady Cottingham pursed her mouth and narrowed her eyes, concentrating. A slow smile dispelled the wrinkles.

'You make it sound as if I must have already been decrepit. Hmmm.' She gave him a severe look, but her eyes twinkled. 'Now Rothley was a careless man in the true sense of the word. Made no difference if you warned a woman about him, he still took what he wanted and then discarded them. Clarissa Tyneham was a fool, but a very lonely fool.'

'Do you recall her marriage to Tyneham?'

'Oh yes. Her mama crowed about it, but to my mind her younger sister Honoria made a better match when she hooked Chelmarsh.'

Sir Esmond smiled wryly, wondering if he himself was just another fish. 'Just so, ma'am.'

'Tyneham had wealth and wasn't a bad-looking man, but Miss Clarissa Northam was the sort of beauty who needed love and adulation, and that type of nonsense. Tyneham put himself out long enough to take her to the altar and then ignored her, especially after she presented him with a son. So she pined and grew even more willowy and then, several years later, she managed to persuade him to let her join him in London for the Season. Then he watched as Rothley made a fuss of her. Easy meat she was, for a man like that. Everyone shook their heads, but she was blinkered, right up to the point where he abandoned her. I think she honestly thought he would run away with her. Rothley! Not his style at all.'

'And there was a child.'

'Oh yes. Left her with a broken heart and a mewling memento, he did. Tyneham bluffed his way through, not out of kindness, of course, just to save his face. Clarissa never left Tyneham again except to visit her sister once or twice, and he kept the son away from her as much as he could. As I said, she was a lonely fool.'

'And the child was all she had.' Sir Esmond was speaking more to himself.

'No idea about the child. Nobody ever saw it. A girl, I think, especially since Tyneham would not want any doubt over the succession if the son should predecease him.'

'Well, she is a beauty, though Rothley dark, not Tyneham fair.'

'Have you fallen for a beautiful . . . by-blow, my boy?'

'Yes, but not because she is beautiful.'

'Ah, we now hear about her "sweet nature" and "delightful singing voice". Mawkish, I call that.' Lady Cottingham looked severely at her nephew.

'I have no idea if Miss Tyneham can sing a note, and her nature is far from sweet.'

The old lady raised an eyebrow.

'Then you interest me more.'

'She is selfish to the point where I do not think she

understands the concept that others have feelings. She delights in entrapping young men with her beauty and making them dance to her tune, whilst she torments them by flirting with others; she has nearly got herself and her long-suffering Hadlow cousins thrown out of Almack's, and has recently tried to blackmail an army officer into running off with her with threats of doing away with herself.'

'Good God, and you want to marry this girl? Why?'

'It is hard to explain, even to myself, and I promise you I have tried. You see, she is, like her mother, very lonely, and very afraid.'

'Doesn't sound afraid to me. Sounds a hoyden.'

'She acts the hoyden but sometimes I have caught the look in her eyes and . . . Think of it, ma'am. She grew up in seclusion as her mother's only company, her mother's sole outlet for affection. From what I hear, Lady Tyneham would not have her shown any boundaries to behaviour, as if to counter the imprisonment they shared. But the child did see that her mother was weak, and that the man she believed to be her father was uncaring. So I think she decided that the only person she had to look after her was herself, and that men should pay for what happened to her mother, to her. She is afraid of being incarcerated at Tyneham, but afraid of being a man's chattel also. She has never learnt to make friends with other young women, trusts nobody, and yet she stands there all alone, daring the world, challenging it. She is terribly afraid, and rather brave.'

'She could still be a heartless minx.'

'Yes. I know. But she is worth saving.'

'The thing about saving someone is that they need to want to be saved, otherwise they drag you down and you drown with them. Does she?'

'I do not think she even thinks anyone could want to save her. She believes it is her against the world, just her. I hope, I believe, that if she was supported and loved, not in the foolish "let her have her way in all things" way, but by being shown that she is not on her own, that there is someone always on her side, then I think she would be not cold and calculating and, yes, cruel. She would be passionate, vital, perhaps always a little challenging, and not a wife who sits there, meek as a nun's hen, and hems shirts, but a wonderful wife.'

'An ability to stitch neatly is a good thing in a wife,' Lady Cottingham murmured.

'Quite possibly, but not the sum of my aspirations, ma'am. I have viewed the "modern misses", as you call them, for the better part of a decade without any one of them inspiring me to contemplate giving up my bachelor existence. Many, if not all, have been better behaved, and full of maidenly virtues, but my heart has settled upon a remarkable minx, whom I want to protect, and nurture, and love.'

'Well, I can't stop you. If you want to risk making a fool of yourself, it is up to you.'

'Actually, it is more up to her. She might just accept me if no other offers are forthcoming.'

Lady Cottingham shook her head.

'She will either make your life a misery or make you the happiest man in England, and I don't think you would like to know which I think more likely.'

Sir Esmond sighed.

'Common sense, and you have always been a fount of that, ma'am, tells me the same, and yet . . . I may regret it if I do, but I am damned near certain, forgiving your presence, that if I let her go, I will regret it every day of my life.'

'Then you had best return to London before she sets the Polite World by the ears, and I wish you luck of her. If you can call that approval, then you have it.'

'Thank you, ma'am. The degree of ambivalence is . . . honest.'

'You know me well enough to know I don't believe in being mealy-mouthed.'

'Do you object to her because of her parentage?'

'Twenty years ago, I might have done so. Now? Well, one mellows with age.' Sir Esmond did not think that he had noticed much mellowness about his aunt, but said nothing. 'She has good enough blood on both sides, even though it was not legally bound. At least she has no smell of the shop about her. Never could abide cits, and that's a fact. Oh, and if you do manage to tame this termagant, bring her to see me, before I end up in the family vault.'

'You can be sure I will, ma'am, but I am confident that time is a long way off.'

'Hmmm.'

CHAPTER TWENTY

Unaware of Susan's planned elopement, Sophy foresaw her life becoming easier, with the arrival of a letter from her father, announcing that he would be arriving in Hill Street two days hence, 'to see how well my youngest daughter looks as an affianced woman'. He would be a moral support, but knowledge of her father told Sophy that Papa was not the man to take responsibility for running the family in a social context, or, more accurately, that he would only smile vaguely, tell everyone to enjoy themselves, and bury himself in his club once he found some crony in residence.

Despite this, Sophy felt positively light-hearted. She had missed her father, and, yes, her mind was increasingly full of Lord Rothley. When she took Harriet and Susan to Almack's that evening, several watchful ladies noticed her looking in far better spirits and looks, and put it down to the relief that Harriet was safely established. It was generally agreed that a severe burden had been placed upon her when Lady Chelmarsh had been forced to retire to the country.

Susan was being, if not pleasant, then less inclined to rebel than usual. When asked why by her suspicious cousin, she smiled and said that she would hate to be kept at home when the military review took place, especially since she had the scarlet jacket all ready to wear for the occasion. She was contented enough to dance with the few partners who presented themselves, disguising her ire at the realisation that her admirers were steadily diminishing in number. She was very slightly surprised that Sir Esmond Fawley solicited her hand for a waltz, because she had never considered him one of her beaux. Perhaps, she thought, he was doing so to make life easier for her cousin Sophy. She almost refused him, just to spite her, but an empty dance card was a thing of shame so . . .

When Susan departed with Sir Esmond for the first set forming after supper, Lord Rothley appeared at Sophy's elbow.

'Behold, you are briefly a free woman. Would you care to dance with me, or shall we sit this one out?'

'I notice, my lord, that you do not give me the option of not being in your company.' The tone was severe, but Sophy's lips twitched.

'No, I rather thought that to be a clever move.' He

smiled, that slightly wolfish smile that made her tingle, and his eyes danced. He had seen her, seen her looking with a bloom she had lacked for many weeks, and it made him suddenly cast caution to the wind.

'In that case, I would prefer the second option, sir, since conversation is more constricted when the dance keeps parting one from one's companion.'

She let him offer her his arm and they made a leisurely progress to where a gilded sofa remained unoccupied, probably, declared Sophy as she sat down upon it, because it was so very uncomfortable.

'That is to ensure that nobody settles upon it for the entire evening and robs others of the chance to enjoy a tête-à-tête, or to rest bruised toes.'

'How silly of me, of course.' Sophy laughed, softly.

He thought how very taking she was when she did so.

'And since you have not danced this evening, and cannot have bruised toes, we may use it for a tête-à-tête.'

'May we?' She coloured very slightly.

'Yes, I think we might.' He looked her in the eye, and she felt her heart miss a beat.

'My father is arriving in two days, from Suffolk, my lord.' She was not sure how to react to the look upon his face, nor the tone of his voice, and attempted to divert the subject. 'That gives me both pleasure and relief.'

'He does? Good, then it will save me posting into East Anglia.' Lord Rothley had no intention of being diverted at all. Her eyes widened for a fraction of a second. 'You have no objections, I hope, to me asking his permission to pay my addresses to you?'

Her thoughts whirled. She ought to say it was too soon, that they ought to know one another better, and yet, for all that she had forced herself to believe the worst of this man, she knew in her heart that there was no doubt. After a few moments she had herself under control.

'No objections, my lord.' Her cheeks coloured a little more deeply.

'No, you are too honest to dissimulate and deny truth. It is one of the many things I love about you.' There was a warmth to his words that, for no logical reason, brought tears to her eyes.

'Are you so sure? After the way I treated you?'

'Absolutely. You see, I happen to think that you, the inner you, has always trusted me.'

'Yes,' she whispered, 'it has been most confusing.'

'It had never occurred to me, before we met, that my name could be my undoing, and it was, so very nearly. My father has had so very much to answer for, as my poor mother would have vouched, but if, through him, I lost you . . .' He shook his head.

'But you have not lost me, my lord.' She gave a small smile. 'Technically, of course, you have not had possession of me to lose.'

'I do not yet have your hand, but, is it presumptuous of me to ask, do I have your heart, Sophy?'

'Yes, oh yes, you do.'

He touched her hand, fleetingly.

'I am sorry. This was not the right place or time, but I was so impatient to know. Forgive me that. I shall not be found beating upon the door as soon as your father sets foot in his house, but the next day, I shall request an interview with him, and then I shall speak with you privately, and ask for the hand that accompanies the heart, ask for all of you, to be my wife.' His voice, barely above a whisper, trembled as he gave a little laugh. 'And that is surely the length of time this sofa permits.'

He rose, taking her hand once more, bent over it and kissed it, then left her before the urge to kiss more than the fingers overwhelmed him. He could have danced a jig in the middle of the dance floor. She had said yes, informally, but yes.

For her part, Sophy sat very still for a minute, marshalling her thoughts, which had been scattered like the seeds of a dandelion in a summer breeze.

Sir Esmond Fawley looked down at the beautiful face of Miss Tyneham, with her perfect features, framed by raven hair, and her very blue, and very wary, eyes.

'You appear very thoughtful this evening, Miss Tyneham.'

'I am wondering, Sir Esmond, why you want to dance with someone of whom you disapprove, and why I agreed to let you lead me into this set.'

'I cannot provide the answer to the latter, but as to the former, "disapprove" is not accurate. I shall not explain further, but I do have a question for you.'

'For me, Sir Esmond?' Her finely arched brows drew into a small frown.

'Yes. Why, exactly, do you hate all men, Miss Tyneham?' He made it sound quite a casual enquiry, but she gasped, and it was a moment before she responded.

'You have met my brother, Tyneham. Surely that suffices as an answer, sir.'

'No. Hating him is something easy to understand, and if most people merely dislike him, you have the disadvantage of having been in closer proximity to him for longer. However, to expand this hatred to cover the entire male sex appears – a trifle excessive.'

'I do not "hate" all men. I simply see them for what they really are – selfish, heartless and arrogant.'

'And so choose to counter that by exhibiting those same traits? I see.'

'How dare you.' Her hand, clasped in his far larger one, tensed.

'Ah, now you are going to say that in my case you do hate me. Yes, I did rather fall into that one.' Sir Esmond smiled, a little ruefully.

'I am not going to say anything at all, sir,' she countered, proving herself wrong in the process. She coloured, which was odd for Susan Tyneham.

'Then I shall take the opportunity to say something. Devoting yourself to avenging your mama is not going to give you a life you will look back upon with pleasure in the years to come. Nor is alienating those family members who might otherwise have shown you kindness.'

'You mean pity. I would rather be hated than pitied, as my mama was pitied.' Susan's lip curled.

'Would not being liked, being loved, be better than both?' The question was put gently enough.

'Those things are transient, or feigned. My mama told me how my father wooed her, and once he had won her, all sign of love or liking disappeared. I will not be fooled as she was.'

'And could it not be that she was an unfortunate case and not the norm? Look about you, and ask yourself if all the married ladies you see here tonight look ignored, disliked, unloved.'

The frown grew deeper. She looked at him, more closely than she had ever before, and acknowledged a truth. Sir Esmond Fawley, the mere baronet who showed no fawning devotion to her, no sign of being in thrall to her, was dangerous. He was dangerous because he seemed so unthreatening – too . . . genuine, too nice. What he said had to be wrong, for if he was not – no, she could not believe she was so wrong.

'I think you are trying to persuade me, sir, for the sake of my cousin.'

'I am trying to persuade you for your own sake, if you would but believe it.'

'I do not.' The voice was firm, but Sir Esmond thought, hoped, that there was just the smallest hint of doubt.

When she was claimed by another at the end of the

dance, and appeared almost ferociously bright and flirtatious, he sighed, and shook his head. He must be a fool.

Sophy's recollections of the rest of the evening were vague. She had laughed at Harriet's almost stupefied happiness, but now understood it. All she could think about was her father being solicited for her hand by Lord Rothley. She returned to Hill Street still within her reverie, oblivious to Susan's unusual quietness in the carriage, and when she lay in her bed, fell asleep with a smile upon her lips.

She awoke at no very advanced hour, and enjoyed the luxury of lying in her warm bed, with a cup of morning chocolate, daydreaming about her future, a thing which had never previously appealed. The concept of having the running of her own house, having experienced it even briefly, was exciting, and that was before the intoxicating thoughts of what marriage to Lord Rothley might be like took possession of her. The idea of another person being in tune with her, understanding her, sharing unspoken thoughts, private jokes, and on top of that thrilling her as even the touch of his hand thrilled her, was so novel as to leave her without any formulated plan for the practicalities of the day, even down to which morning gown she would wear. Her maid, unused to her mistress being so vague, wondered if she felt quite well, whereupon, as she revealed to her closest confidante below stairs, Lady Sophronia sighed, and said 'perfectly well' in a dreamy voice.

'I think it is the strain what has got to her poor ladyship. It is thankful I'll be when his lordship arrives, and no mistake.'

In fact, before Lord Chelmarsh reached London, a missive arrived from his spouse. Bembridge lingered in expectation, and, as he had hoped, Lady Sophronia asked him to remain a moment. Sophy broke the seal with a degree of trepidation followed by a sigh of relief.

'Oh Bembridge, we may rejoice. Lady Tattersett has been safely delivered of a son, and both mother and child flourish.'

Bembridge so far forgot himself as to clap his hands together, wring them, and beam at his mistress.

'Heaven be praised, my lady. Her young ladyship has always been held in highest regard here, if you do not mind me saying so.'

'Not at all, Bembridge. Will you get Cook to make one of her tipsy cakes for the staff dinner tonight, and you may all toast the new arrival and safe delivery with a glass of sherry for those that take wine.'

'Yes, my lady, very gladly. If I may, I would like to go below stairs straight away with this good news.'

'Of course, Bembridge. I will go and find Lady Harriet.'

She found her sister sat with a copy of *La Belle Assemblée*, and making a list of those items she thought she might need as her trousseau. She looked up as Sophy entered.

'Harry, Frances has had her baby, a baby boy, and she

is well, she is well, dear sister.' With which she stepped forward, hugged her youngest sister, and burst into tears of joy and relief.

Lord Chelmarsh arrived the next day, unaware that he had become a grandfather, since he had left Suffolk before the letter from his wife arrived. He received the news with suitable delight, and declared that his family was increasing by the week. He had but recently found himself entertaining the scion of a ducal house, desirous of marrying his youngest daughter, which came as a complete, if pleasant, surprise to him. Naturally, Lord Edward had not mentioned Susan Tyneham, or any of the unfortunate events in which she had been involved. His lady, having recently informed him of all the recent events in the Metropolis, had given him pause for thought about how his eldest daughter had been left to control the uncontrollable for far too long. Setting the breeding of bovines aside, he decided that the time had come for him to take a hand and ease her undoubted burden. He knew his Sophy, and he had little doubt she was taking everything very much to heart. Whilst he could see why his wife had felt it necessary to go to Frances in her hour, or rather, weeks, of need, he rather fancied Sophy's need was not inconsiderable, and he was not an uncaring father.

He had expected to find her a little fraught, but instead was met by a daughter whose glowing looks could not be entirely put down to sisterly joy. He looked speculatively at Sophy but said nothing until after he had congratulated Harriet, made her quite pink with pleasure by saying how much he liked his prospective son-in-law, and then both girls laugh by saying he had already suggested he might like to consider starting a dairy herd on his home farm. Susan he found surprisingly meek, and far from the rebel he was expecting, but then thought about the matter and decided that seeing her better-behaved cousin find a husband must have shown her that conformity was the way to success after all.

When he found himself alone at last with his eldest child, he smiled gently at her, invited her to seat herself upon the stool at his feet, much as she had done as a child, and to tell him everything.

'Everything, Papa? Oh, there has been so very much, and most would not interest you at all.'

'Your happiness, Sophy, interests me exceedingly, so tell me about . . . fate.'

She smiled, and lowered her eyes for a moment, before raising them again to his. He saw the glow in them, and much of what she said became unnecessary.

'Fate has led me a merry dance, sir, but in the end has smiled upon me, upon us both. I have fallen in love, Papa, with Lord Rothley, who is *not* a . . . a loose screw like his father, not at all. And Papa, he has fallen in love with me.'

'That shows good taste, for a start.'

Sophy set about telling her father all about the emotional ups and downs of falling in love with a man she believed true, but whom she thought her mother and the world knew to be a rake, how she had been confused and held him off, how he had borne her blowing hot and cold with him, how well they understood each other notwithstanding the problematic name of Rothley. As she drew to a close, she smiled more broadly at her parent.

'I told him that you were coming to London, Papa, and he has said that he will wait upon you tomorrow, to ask your permission to pay his addresses. You will say yes, dearest Papa?'

'I would not be doing my paternal duty if I said yes without establishing the gentleman's credentials and ability to support a wife,' declared Lord Chelmarsh, sententiously, then relented. 'How could I not do so, Sophy, when you are so sure? Mind you, people make strange decisions when moonstruck.'

'Moonstruck? Oh no, do I seem so?' She giggled. 'Perhaps I am, Papa, for the world seems so much nicer a place since Lord Rothley made it clear that . . . that he wants to marry me.'

Her father took her hands, and squeezed them.

'You just wait until your mama finds out.'

'Oh, my goodness me! But she told me so very very firmly that we were to have as little to do with Lord Rothley as possible. I had, in a way, forgotten, once I knew about . . .'

'About?'

'About Susan, Papa. Tyneham told me.'

'Hmmm, I don't think much of young Tyneham,

but then I never liked his father either,' admitted Lord Chelmarsh. 'Personally, I think your mother would have been better to take you into her confidence, since you were left *in loco parentis*. I think that she will not react unfavourably when she returns. She has the security that Harriet is making a good match, and I would think she will be delighted to announce her eldest daughter is also joining the ranks of the espoused. She can safely announce that all her daughters are "well established", which I thought applied to shrubs, but . . .'

Sophy was laughing, laughing because the bubble of happiness within her could not be contained. He smiled. It seemed all they had to do was await the morrow, and Lord Rothley's visit.

Lord Rothley took extra time over his appearance the next morning. He had not slept especially well, though this was more anticipation than nervousness. He could happily have banged upon the Chelmarsh residence door at eight in the morning, but this would have been precipitate. He therefore remained at his lodgings, pacing about like a caged tiger, until a little short of eleven, and then went round to Hill Street.

Bembridge greeted him in what he felt was an avuncular fashion, Lady Sophronia having artlessly informed the butler that Lord Rothley was expected to call during the morning to speak with his lordship. Bembridge was perfectly able to put two and two together and make the answer four.

'If you will just wait in here, my lord, I will inform his lordship of your arrival.'

Lord Rothley was shown into a small saloon. A couple of minutes later, the door opened and Sophy entered, dressed for outdoors.

'Oh, I am so sorry, I should have said. I am taking Harriet and Susan to the Military Review in Hyde Park, and to get a good position for the carriage we need to leave now. When you have seen Papa, I will not be here.'

She sounded like a child about to be denied a promised treat. He took her gloved hand, pushed the glove back, and placed a small kiss on the inside of her wrist.

'Then I will return at a suitable time. I think I can keep my composure for a few more hours. What time is the review likely to end?'

'About three o'clock, I believe, and however patient you may be sir, I am not.' Sophy dimpled. 'I never had an offer of marriage before, and it is very exciting.'

He nearly said that if just the act of being asked was exciting he dared not envisage her response to actually getting married, being married, but he merely declared, 'Then I shall be here by half past that hour.'

She looked at him, her eyes very soft and full of tenderness, which made him want to kiss her very much.

'I hope you and Papa have a comfortable exchange. He is a very nice Papa, I assure you.'

He was still holding her hand, and he drew her gently towards him and brushed her lips with his own.

'Until this afternoon,' he murmured, a trifle thickly.

Sophy stepped back, one hand to her bosom, and nodded. She had no words. Then she turned and left, just as Bembridge opened the door. The butler stepped back and held it wide for her to pass, blushing, and gave what might just have been a sigh.

'Lord Chelmarsh will see you now, my lord, if you would be so good as to follow me.'

The natural nervousness of the suitor, even one expecting a positive response, made Lord Rothley feel unusually self-conscious. Lord Chelmarsh did not, however, greet him in the manner of one's housemaster after a discovered prank. Instead, he came forward, his hand extended, and an understanding smile on his face.

'Good morning, Rothley. Do take a seat, my dear fellow.' Lord Rothley sat, but not at ease. 'I will not pretend that I have no idea why you are here. Sophy has already instructed me on what I must say.' His smile lengthened. 'I am very fond of my eldest daughter.'

'So am I, sir.'

'Yes. Indeed, I surmised that must be so.'

'Your daughter is of age, of course, but I would like your approval of my paying her my addresses. I also felt you should know that my father has the title and an allowance, but that my grandfather ensured that the estates came to my stewardship. You need have no fear that Sophy will be in straitened circumstances.'

'That is very honest of you. I shall be equally honest. If I had the slightest idea that you were like your father, I would not be sitting here as I am, not only giving "approval" as you call it, but welcoming you into the family. Sophy is . . . One should not have favourites, but I will say that I have had an especially soft spot for my eldest child. She has rare qualities which have apparently been overlooked until now, since you are the first gentleman ever to apply to me for her hand.'

'I will value her, sir. Saying I will do everything I can to make her happy, love her, protect her, sounds rather trite. I suppose any man would say the same in my position. It does not make those things less true, though.' Lord Rothley looked rather serious.

His prospective father-in-law rose and pulled the bell.

'I think we are in danger of becoming too serious on what is a joyful occasion. I rarely come to Town, but I recall some very good claret in the cellar. This seems a suitable reason for broaching a bottle.' Bembridge knocked and entered. 'Ah, Bembridge, we would like claret, the really good claret. I am sure you know just where to find it.'

'I do, my lord.' Bembridge looked as pleased as if he had been invited to join them in a glass.

'Now, Rothley,' Lord Chelmarsh made himself comfortable, 'on your estates in Worcestershire, do you have many dairy cattle?'

CHAPTER TWENTY-ONE

Sophy climbed into Lady Chelmarsh's barouche in such a daze that Harriet had to ask her twice whether she wished to face forward or towards the rear.

'Oh, I am sorry, Harry. I do not mind, honestly I do not.'

'Are you quite well, Sophy?' Harriet noted her sister's flushed appearance. She had not seen Lord Rothley enter the house.

'Perfectly so. Now, where was it that Lord Edward advised us to place ourselves for the best view?'

Sophy tried to sound normal and calm, but in truth she had no interest at all in watching the brightly uniformed soldiery, and her mind was imagining what was going on between her father and the man to whom she was about to become betrothed. Half past three seemed so distant. She wondered, and nearly laughed out loud at her girlishness, what she should wear for such an important occasion as receiving an offer of marriage. She felt that Lord Rothley would laugh too, if he knew, and say it mattered not as long as she said yes, and that he was biased, and thought her beautiful in anything.

She paid little attention to Susan, who was sitting with her hands neatly folded over her reticule, which was, had anyone noticed, suspiciously full. She was wearing the scarlet spencer over a demure white muslin gown, and her bonnet had a scarlet ribbon tied about it. The picture she presented was enchantingly beautiful. Harriet did ask why she had brought a cloak with her, but she responded that she was not entirely convinced that the hazy clouds might not thicken and bring on a shower and the temperature drop.

'I would so hate to be seen with goosebumps.' It was a very Susan reaction.

Harriet had paid no interest to possible meteorological problems. She was going to see her Edward in all his glory upon his charger and in front of his men, and was so proud she thought she might burst with it. As she said to her sister, he was a hero, for he had seen action, been wounded. That the injury had been slight was down to good fortune.

'I keep thinking how lucky I am, Sophy.' Her voice trembled.

'You are lucky, but do not dwell upon what might have been in the worst of situations. Look forward.'

Harriet's smile returned.

Susan said nothing, and if Sophy had been attending, she would have wondered why she sat without any sign of disdain for her cousin accepting a man she found unworthy, in that he had not done as she had wanted.

The barouche entered Hyde Park and made its way to the area from which the crowds of onlookers were to see the display of men and horses. The first troops were marching on, and the deployment of column into line that the ladies observed was made with the apparently effortless precision which had helped win so many battles against Napoleon's marshals. A ripple of scarlet formed into long red ranks some time before the cavalry, with their jingling bits and ornate headdress, took up position. It was a hot day, and Sophy wondered if any of the men might succumb, standing as they did in the open without even the slightest shade. Notwithstanding Susan bringing her cloak, the ladies in the barouche had parasols, lest the sun's rays harm their delicate pale skin.

Lord Edward's recommendation that they should secure a place early was shown to be very wise. The flat area in the north-east corner of Hyde Park had long been used as a parade ground for these military spectacles, and its perimeter soon filled. Latecomers would be reduced to leaving their carriages and standing nearer to get an uninterrupted view. Harriet, with a very recently acquired interest in all things military, explained how King George II had reviewed troops there only two days before his death.

'Edward says that today's review is comparatively small, but some have been of thousands of men.' Susan could not help but snigger, and received a cold look. 'You find this amusing, cousin?'

'Not at all, if "Edward" said it.' Susan sniggered again.

Sophy winced, and gave Susan a repressive glare.

'Is it so hard to be amicable for just a few hours?'

'I do not know, cousin. We shall have to find out.' Susan smiled, but it was brittle.

Over the next half hour Susan seemed unable to restrain herself from mocking Harriet's choice of husband, by means of comments about the troops arrayed before them. Sophy had the feeling that Susan was actually setting out to annoy. Shortly after the Duke of York, who was conducting the review, had arrived and was commencing his inspection of the cavalry, Susan gave a muffled cry.

'Ow! Oooh, my foot! I have cramp in my left foot.'

'Try rubbing it,' advised Sophy.

Susan did so, but seemed no better.

'Please, may I get down and just walk up and down for a few minutes? Nobody will notice me.'

'Yes, but stay close to the carriage, cousin.' Sophy directed the groom to let down the step and hand the grimacing Susan down to the grass. She thanked him, weakly, declined his offer of an arm, and began to move the foot, gingerly setting it to the ground and hobbling to and fro to the rear of the barouche.

Harriet watched with bated breath as His Royal Highness approached the squadron of which Lord Edward's troop formed part, and gripped Sophy's hand in excitement, wondering if her betrothed might have the honour of being addressed by royalty. Her older sister was not as overawed, but took great pleasure in watching Harriet's wide-eyed anticipation. Neither was thinking about Susan, which was just what that young lady wanted.

Having hopped a little theatrically, up and down, she waited until no longer observed, and for the Hadlow sisters to be focussed upon the spectacle. She then, with a fleetness of foot which was quite remarkable for one so recently 'lame', scurried towards the rear of the coach lines, throwing her cloak about her shoulders and the hood over her head, to the possible detriment of the straw bonnet. Opposite the end of Mount Street she espied Lord Pinkney, consulting his pocket watch, and scowling in a very unromantic manner for a man about to elope to Gretna Green. He stood beside a chaise and pair.

'I had nearly given up on you,' he declared, gruffly, as she reached him, 'and why the cloak? It makes you stand out.'

'It may do so, sir, but nobody would know who is standing out, and my clothing is distinctive.' He offered his hand, and assisted her, rather ungraciously, into the chaise. 'And as for being late, timing was everything. I had to wait until Harriet's infatuation with her precious Edward would distract both my cousins for long enough that we might make our escape.' She sounded both excited and in control, which, like her previous behaviour, piqued Pinkney a little. A damsel really ought to sound nervous and fluttery in such a situation. He gave the postillion the word, and the chaise sprang forward.

'At last,' breathed Susan, 'this time I shall not be thwarted.' She sounded, thought Lord Pinkney, triumphant rather than excited.

Perhaps it was the combination of Harriet's enthusiasm and her own focus upon what the afternoon would bring, but whatever the cause, it was more than a quarter of an hour later when Sophy suddenly exclaimed, and looked about her.

'Susan!' She looked to the grooms. 'Have you seen Miss Tyneham?'

They shook their heads, having been making the most of what was as much an entertainment to them as their employers. Sophy's happy bubble burst, and was replaced by dread. Susan had been so biddable these last few days, and only her rudeness in the carriage had been on a par with her 'normal' behaviour. It made no sense until one realised it was the calm before a storm.

'Harriet, I must search the vicinity just in case Susan has simply twisted her ankle or . . .' Sophy thought this so unlikely she could not continue. She sighed. 'I will take Nichols and if we do not find any trace of her, I want you to return home as soon as the parade is over. If you remain for the present then if Susan should change her mind . . .' She squeezed Harriet's hand, and climbed down from the barouche. She then began what she frankly believed to be a fruitless search, with the dutiful Nichols in her wake. She could not, without raising suspicions, accost everyone, asking if they had seen a lady of Susan's distinctive appearance, but she did ask the coachmen of a couple of vacant carriages. The last said that he had seen a young lady answering that description, but that she must have been ailing, because she pulled a cloak about her as if cold. Sophy made an answer which seemed to agree with that view, and her panic increased. They left Hyde Park, and she knew that all she could do was get back to Hill Street as soon as possible. They crossed the road to head along Mount Street, and it was then that she thought to ask the crossing sweeper if he had seen a cloaked young lady in the last half hour.

'A lady, 'ooded and cloaked, comes out the Park and gets into a chaise with a swell gent, a tidy bit ago, ma'am.'

Sophy gave the man sixpence for this information, which left him speechless, and in need of spending at least tuppence of it in the nearest hostelry, and walked home as fast as she could. When she entered the house, Bembridge beamed at her, but her expression froze his smile.

'When did Lord Rothley leave, Bembridge?'

'His lordship left but a few minutes ago, my lady. You barely missed him.'

'Then send one of the servants to his lodgings, which are in Half Moon Street. Oh dear! I have no idea which number. However, I am sure someone in the street would be able to provide his direction. As long as he has not gone to his club! This is an emergency, Bembridge, so make sure you send someone swift-footed and who has seen him today and would recognise him if he catches up with him, as I hope.'

'Certainly, my lady, but what is he to tell him when he finds his lordship?'

'He is to request him to return as a matter of great urgency. Now, where is my father?'

'His lordship is in the library, my lady.'

'Bring Lord Rothley there when he arrives, please, Bembridge.' Sophy lifted her hem and half ran up the stairs. Lord Chelmarsh was contemplating an epistle to his wife, and looked up.

'Sophy, my dear, I—'

'Papa, Susan has run away again, with a man.'

'With whom?'

'I do not know. The only man she—Pinkney! Oh yes, he would, the rogue. Papa. I am so very sorry. We were watching the review and Susan said she had cramp in her foot and got down from the carriage to walk up and down a little, and then the Duke of York was reviewing Lord Edward's troop and . . .' Her words tumbled out as she described what had occurred as accurately as she could. 'When I noticed Susan was missing it was too late. She was seen climbing into a chaise by a crossing sweeper.'

'I shall have to follow them,' Lord Chelmarsh declared, heavily.

'No, wait, Papa. I have sent after Lord Rothley.'

'I may understand your faith in the gentleman, but he is not yet connected to this family and she is not his responsibility, Sophy.'

'No, but he has offered, many times, to do anything to help, not just because of . . . me, but because he feels a responsibility, since his father showed no care at all. Tyneham has been no help at all, a hindrance in fact, and would be so now, but Lord Rothley is just the gentleman we need in this situation. Besides, if you go off at the rush, everyone will guess the reason. Nobody else will associate Lord Rothley with Susan.'

At that moment Lord Rothley entered the room, waving away Bembridge without bothering to be announced.

'What has happened? Sophy, you are all right?' He was breathing a little fast.

'My lord, thank goodness you were traced swiftly! I . . . we, need your help. Susan has run away, eloped, with Lord Pinkney, as far as we can tell.'

'But did she not go with you to the review?'

'Yes, but upon a pretext left the carriage and then slipped away. She joined a gentleman with a chaise in Park Lane.'

'The devil she did! The little wretch! How many horses?'

'Horses, my lord?'

'Yes, to the chaise.'

'Oh! Oh, I do not know. I did not ask the sweeper that.' She put her hand to her cheek, distractedly.

'No matter. I doubt very much Pinkney could afford a post-chaise and four all the way to the Border. If he did set out in one, it would be for the first stages only and then he would transfer to a pair. I have my curricle in Town, and a tidy pair who can give me a good twelve miles an hour for the first stage, and that will be better than any hired animals.' He paused.

'Can you be sure they are heading north?'

'I can be sure of nothing, nothing.' Sophy sat down and buried her face in her hands.

Rothley stepped forward, regardless of Lord Chelmarsh's presence, and crouched before her, taking her hands gently but firmly from her face.

'Look at me. It is not your fault. The Border is the likeliest answer, and following them will not be hard. I will set off immediately but must be a good hour behind them by the time all is ready. I will catch them, and I will bring her back.'

'But it will surely be too late, too late to disguise her error.'

'That may be beyond any of us, my dear.' Lord Chelmarsh shook his head, as Bembridge knocked at the door, and upon entering, apologised, but revealed that Sir Esmond Fawley was at the door.

'He appears to have met Lady Harriet, my lord. Her ladyship is in some distress, I believe. I realise this is perhaps not the time, but—'

'Get him in here.' Lord Rothley looked up and interrupted without compunction. 'Lord Chelmarsh, Fawley is the one man who may be able to salvage my errant sister's honour. However, I must depart immediately. Sophy, dearest, this afternoon must be delayed, but I will be back.' Lord Rothley kissed her hands, gave her a look which spoke volumes, and strode out of the room, almost colliding with Sir Esmond.

'Ask Sophy for details, Fawley. Hope you catch me later.'

309

Sir Esmond raised his brows from their glowering frown, but Rothley was gone. He nodded at Lord Chelmarsh, but then looked at Sophy.

'She has done it again, hasn't she.' It was a statement, and he sounded grim.

'Yes, she has. We think this time she has run off with Lord Pinkney. Lord Rothley is setting off after them, but thinks it is you who can save Susan's reputation.'

'I would as soon race Rothley to be first to break Pinkney's neck.' Sir Esmond ground his teeth.

'I am sure that was not what Rothley intended. He did not wait to reveal his plan, however.' Lord Chelmarsh was slightly surprised to find two gentlemen keen to chase after his niece.

'He said he would catch them, and bring Susan back, so it must be her future that lies in your hands, Sir Esmond. If Tyneham hears of this he will cast her off without a moment's thought.' Sophy's brow was furrowed.

'Then that,' Sir Esmond brightened suddenly, 'is what I must do immediately.'

'You want to tell Tyneham?' Lord Chelmarsh looked confused. 'What possible use is that?'

'I want to wring his neck almost as much as Pinkney's, but, yes, I will content myself with that, and getting him to accompany me to Doctors' Commons.'

'Ah, I see your purpose,' Lord Chelmarsh was enlightened, but Sophy was not, and said as much.

'If Tyneham washes his hands of her, all to the good, but he is still her guardian. He will come with me and we will obtain a special licence, if he values his good name and his skin.'

'You mean you want to marry my cousin Susan?' Sophy could not keep the surprise from her voice.

'Yes, mad as that may sound. And from what Rothley said, however cryptically, I think he means I am to follow him north and probably join with him after he has brought their flight to an end. My estate is not far from St Neots. I will take her there, if she will agree. Now I must leave you and hope Tyneham is a creature of habit.'

'Wait. Sir Esmond, take me with you.'

'Lady Sophy, I will be travelling fast and—'

'If I am there it will lend a semblance of decency. There will be room for my maid also, surely. You will permit me to go with Sir Esmond, Papa?'

'Yes, but do not tell your mother I said so.'

Sir Esmond thought swiftly.

'Then be ready within the hour, ma'am, and bring such things as you may need overnight. Forgive my brusqueness, but I must find Tyneham.'

Sir Esmond left in as much of a rush as Lord Rothley. Father and daughter stared at one another for a moment.

'I must pack, Papa, and reassure Harriet, and, oh my goodness, what a day this is.'

'Yes. And by the by, my dear, I like Rothley.'

'So do I, Papa, so do I.'

Sophy had no time to dwell on the niggling worry in her mind of what would happen when Lord Rothley caught up with Lord Pinkney. She rushed up to her bedchamber, rang for her maid to assemble clean linens, a nightgown and requisites, and exchanged her spencer for a serviceable pelisse. She then went to Susan's room. Her hairbrush and comb were missing from the dressing table, so Sophy knew that she must have those stuffed in her reticule, but she took a nightgown, some stockings, a shawl and then two gowns from the linen press, and put them in the same valise that Susan had herself packed less than ten days earlier.

With her bags ready, she saw them taken down into the vestibule, and went to Harriet, who was in tears upon her bed.

'Harry, there is no call for you to weep.'

'But what will the Duchess say, when we are all disgraced?'

'You goose. She will not forbid the banns, you know. She has met you, she knows what sort of girl you are, and, in the end, you are a Hadlow, not a Tyneham, and as such, in the fullness of time, Susan's behaviour will be no more than a memory. Think of me, marrying into a family where my father-in-law is an elderly reprobate living in Europe.'

Harriet looked up at that, blinking away her tears.

'Has Lord Rothley proposed? Oh Sophy, I am so pleased for you.'

'Well, he has Papa's approval, and was going to speak to me this afternoon, but has instead gone haring after Susan, which brings me to the next thing. You must dry your eyes and be calm and speak to Cook and Bembridge, which will be good experience for you running your own establishment, because Sir Esmond is driving me in pursuit of . . .' she smiled, lopsidedly, 'everybody. I have things for myself and for Susan. I think that if it will be too far to return tonight, Sir Esmond is suggesting we stay at his house in Huntingdonshire. So I do not expect to be home for a day or so, and with luck, when I do, Susan will no longer be "a problem" because she will be married.'

'Married?'

'Yes, to Sir Esmond.'

'Oh, poor man,' exclaimed Harriet, involuntarily, and then covered her mouth with her hand.

'Possibly. Now kiss me, dry your eyes, and wish me luck.'

Harriet did as she was told, and was able to wait with her sister and father as they listened for Sir Esmond's arrival. Sophy hoped that Sir Esmond had been successful in finding Lord Tyneham. Had he done so she had little doubt that the viscount would follow his instructions. Sir Esmond was not a man who would brook refusal, as she thought Susan would swiftly discover.

Sir Esmond was a man on a mission, and even the irritating information from Tyneham's valet that he was gone to Bond Street to have his pocket watch regulated, did not give him pause. At Allam and Clements he drew a blank, but considered it more likely Tyneham, being rich and inclined to show it, would be further up the street at Perigal's, who had the Royal Warrant. He caught him about to step into the premises.

'Tyneham.'

Lord Tyneham turned, frowning. It was not a casual appellation.

'Yes? Oh, it is you, Fawley.'

'You are to come with me.' It was a command, not in any way a request.

'What on earth for? I am busy.'

'Your tardy timepiece can wait. We are going to Doctors' Commons.'

'We are?' Tyneham was so surprised he did not even bridle as Sir Esmond took his arm in a firm hold and hailed a cab. Only when within did the viscount query this near abduction. 'Doctors' Commons. Why there?'

'A special licence, what else? I need to marry your sister.'

There was a moment of silence as Lord Tyneham absorbed this information, then his cheeks went pink.

'You need to marry my sister, sir? Why, you black-hearted—'

'Don't be a bigger idiot than you look, Tyneham. I do not mean for *that* reason. She has run off with Pinkney, the foolish chit, and I am going to save her from herself, and from him too, if Rothley has not done so already.'

'Rothley? What has . . .' Tyneham was even more confused but latched onto the fact that Susan had run off, again. 'The baggage has eloped with Pinkney. Well, I wash my hands of her, and if he thinks he will get a penny from—'

'He won't be marrying her. I will.'

'You must be mad.' Tyneham was perfectly serious.

'Quite probably. Now, my intention is to take Miss Tyneham to my own home, and we will be married from there. Lady Sophy will be there as chaperone.'

'Much good she has done thus far!' snorted Tyneham.

'You may shortly become my brother-in-law but that does not mean I will not plant you a facer if you say any more against the Hadlow ladies, who have had much to put up with,' growled Sir Esmond, glancing out of the window to see how far they had gone.

'Then why are you so keen to wed the girl?'

'Because I am mad, as you say.' With which, Sir Esmond folded his arms, and withdrew into silence until the vehicle drew to a halt, whereupon he almost dragged Lord Tyneham from within, told the jarvey to wait, and hurried his charge into Doctors' Commons. They emerged a short while afterwards and Sir Esmond directed the jarvey to one of the larger posting houses where he knew the teams were decent quality beasts.

'But I need to get back to Bond Street. My watch, Fawley.'

'You can hire this fellow after I pay him.'

'But . . .'

'Oh, and I am not mercenary, or short of funds, but you will make a proper settlement on your sister, to keep the gossips from talking.'

'She is only my half-sister, so I need only give her ha—'

'Do not continue, Tyneham. I know her parentage, and before you say more it makes no difference to me, other than perhaps I am quite glad that she is not more closely related to you. You will treat her as your only sister, and devolve upon her all that you were bandying about in the clubs. Susan has had a wayward start, but from now on I want no scandal to follow my wife, so you will keep to the lie your father maintained.' Sir Esmond looked and sounded severe, and Lord Tyneham thought better of arguing the point. As Sir Esmond said, Susan would be his wife, his responsibility. At least she would not be dragging the Tyneham name through the mire henceforth.

Sophy was pacing up and down in the study, whilst Lord Chelmarsh wondered out loud how he might keep his wife from a spasm when she heard of events, when Sir Esmond knocked upon the front door once more. She gave a great sigh of relief when she heard Bembridge's voice, and that of Sir Esmond.

Sophy rose, and went to the door, opening it to see the pair of them in the hallway.

'I am ready, Sir Esmond.'

'I am impressed, Lady Sophy. I had thought that—'

'Do not say it, sir, or we will start our journey at odds, and we have hours in each other's company.'

Lord Chelmarsh came forward, shook Sir Esmond's hand, kissed his daughter's cheek, and wished them a safe journey and swift horses.

CHAPTER TWENTY-TWO

S IR ESMOND HAD HIRED A POST-CHAISE AND FOUR, and whilst the weight of three persons as opposed to one would slow them a little, he had no doubt that they would reach the point at which Lord Rothley would have stopped the fleeing couple well before the dinner hour.

'They had an hour's advantage, Sir Esmond, over Lord Rothley.' Sophy was not sure now if she was more concerned over the fate of her cousin or that of Lord Rothley.

'Yes, but he had a curricle and his own pair to Barnet, at least, and perhaps a little further if he nursed them a trifle. A jobbing pair will make no more than nine miles an hour at the best, and I would give odds Rothley will be a good three miles an hour faster than that. By my estimate he should catch them a little before Baldock.'

'Sir Esmond, what sort of a man is Lord Pinkney? I mean, will he put up resistance if confronted?'

'If he is so desperate for funds that he would abscond with a girl, then I imagine he would.'

'Does . . . does Lord Rothley stand in much danger?' Sophy tried not to let her fear bubble up.

Sir Esmond frowned. It was not something he would have considered if he had been in the vanguard of pursuit, and he doubted Rothley would do so either.

'I cannot quantify it, ma'am, but I would be very surprised if Pinkney would risk being arraigned for murder, even to obtain a supply of funds.'

The word sent a chill down Sophy's spine. Would fate rob her of happiness just when it had placed it at her very fingertips? She prayed, most fervently.

Once the road north left London, Sir Esmond had the postillions increase the pace to a canter, and where the road was open and straight, 'spring 'em'. The chaise, with three persons a little cramped within, was not comfortable at such speed, and the maid felt decidedly queasy. When Barnet was reached, she was very glad of the brief respite while the team was changed. Sir Esmond ascertained that Lord Rothley had not changed there, but the ostler said that a smart curricle and pair had passed through at pace, a little under an hour since.

'I think Rothley may try and keep his cattle going until Hatfield, if he trusts them. Besides, they keep good teams at The Eight Bells. I know this road well, and I recall mentioning the fact to him once. If he has a good memory, he will try there.'

'How long do you think it will take us to catch them all up?'

'If he overtakes them by Baldock then we will be there no more than half an hour after.'

Half an hour. Might that be half an hour too late? She clasped her hands together tightly. After a while, she forced herself to make conversation.

'How did Tyneham take the news of Susan's elopement, and did he require much persuasion to go with you for the special licence?'

'Oh, he reacted as one would expect, especially once he knew that I was aware of his sister's circumstances. What he said was unforgivable, but since it is not considered polite to throttle one's intended's closest relative, at least closest in the eyes of the world, and I needed him with me, I held back. He tried to suggest that her actions obviated any need for him to provide her with Settlements at all. Now, I have no need of the money, but for her sake, I would see her given her due. I made that clear to Tyneham, and he was . . . persuaded by my vehemence.'

'I would love to have seen his face.'

'It was not a pleasant colour, ma'am. At one point I thought he might suffer an apoplexy.'

Sophy paused a moment.

'Sir Esmond,' she was not sure how much she dare say with the maid present, but was worried, and so continued, 'you are not doing this out of some misplaced sense of chivalry, are you?'

'No, I promise you that. I could not explain why, even if the circumstances,' he glanced for a fleeting moment at the maid, who was still concentrating on trying to overcome her nausea, 'permitted, but it is not "misplaced chivalry". Your cousin has, I hope and believe, suffered from the confines of her childhood.' He tried to speak a little cryptically. 'The examples of both genders were infelicitous, and she had nobody with whom to share. All she learnt was that she could make people do what she wanted, and since love was "weak" it was dangerous. She has not experienced friendship, the urge to be generous, let alone the deeper feelings.'

'And yet you think she might discover them.'

'I do, and I had better be right, for both our sakes.'

These sobering thoughts led to silence for a while as the chaise bowled along the Great North Road.

Susan had expected to enjoy this journey, however, as the miles passed she found her pleasure diminishing rapidly. Lord Pinkney, having bemoaned her tardiness, had not appreciated her querying why there was only a pair, and not four horses pulling their equipage.

'Have you any idea how much a post-chaise and four would cost to the Border, miss? Clearly you do not, and I will be quite open and state that until such time as Tyneham gives me a draft upon his bank, even two horses are not easy to furnish. Thank goodness I can at least save upon our expenses at inns.'

'You mean we shall not eat large suppers?' enquired Susan.

Pinkney stared at her for a moment. She successfully gave the impression of a heartless woman of the world, but beneath the veneer, the girl beside him was actually remarkably innocent.

'I mean, my dear, that we only have the hiring of one chamber.'

'But we are not yet married, sir.' She sounded quite appalled.

He laughed. 'In view of the fact that we are eloping, madam, that is immaterial. Within a few days you will be my wife, and I have no intention of paying for a charade of decency over such an exploit as you, indeed, were the first to propose.'

'I . . . I think I did not quite understand, my lord.'

'Well, you can understand now.' He looked sideways at her slightly pale cheek, and his manner softened. 'Come, do not let us be at odds. You will find me an easy-going husband, I promise you, not always hanging about your skirts. My demands upon you will not be excessive, and I do not even feel as yet the great imperative of the need for an heir to the wealth,' he laughed in a rather hollow manner, 'and honour of the Earl of Pinkney, so I will not pester you. Besides, I have no turn for wide-eyed and ignorant damsels. Perhaps, in time, you will learn to please me, but if you do not,' he shrugged, 'it will matter little.'

Susan sat very still, as though moving would cast her into the depths of a chasm. On the one hand, the man beside her, whom she did not, she realised with a jolt, really know at all, had every intention of her sharing his bed before they were legally conjoined. She had absolutely no idea as to what this entailed, but she had bad feelings about it. At the same time, he was telling her that, whatever happened in such circumstances, would not thereafter happen very often because she was insufficiently interesting. She did not want his attentions, but yet it piqued her to think that she might not wrap him about her little finger at will.

She did not know that her face betrayed her thoughts, nor that Pinkney observed them.

'There is no going back you know, my dear. Once we are married, I shall take you to Tyllings, my house in Cheshire. I have at least kept the ancestral pile, if not much of the lands. When the dibs have been in tune, I have occasionally spent money upon it, so the roof does not leak, at least in the part I use.'

'Shall we entertain much, my lord?'

'Entertain?' Pinkney let out a crack of laughter, imagining the company he preferred in the rural depths of Cheshire, and the disapproval with which he was regarded by his country neighbours. 'I have no doubt a few ladies will come to view you and offer you their sympathy, but I have neither the funds not inclination for that sort of thing.'

'So we shall spend the Season in London?'

'I shall visit Town as often as possible, but you will find plenty of places to spend your pin money in Chester, and however impoverished, a countess is a countess, so you will be treated with deference if you wish to attend the assemblies. You should not look shocked, madam, for neither of us make a pretence of affection in this contract. You gain release from Tyneham, and, I think, a modicum of revenge; I get enough money to keep afloat until the next upturn in my fortunes, and even survive a few more losses, and will possess a very pretty little wife whom I shall endeavour to teach ways which appeal to me.' He smiled, and Susan repressed a shiver. 'Actually, the more I look at you the more I think it may be entertaining, and so different from having to pay every time. The muslin company can be devilish expensive, so when times are thin, I do at least have you for free.'

The delusion around which Susan had built her plans crumbled to nothing. She felt very alone, and small, and afraid. A small voice in her head suggested Sir Esmond might have been in the right. Lord Pinkney saw the fear, and it gave him a frisson. His hand closed over hers.

'Have I frightened you, my child? I have perhaps painted a picture too dark for you. Let me lighten it somewhat.' He leant closer, and his other hand took her chin, firmly, and raised it. 'I have never had complaints, you know,' he purred, and kissed her, quite expertly, but with as little passion as she had received Lord Edward's kiss at the Chelmarsh ball. She had been kissed before, from grooms to a duke's son, but all had been nervously fervent, aspirational kisses. This simply used her. She felt disgusted, and pulled back sharply. Lord Pinkney merely laughed.

When they next changed horses, at Stevenage, Susan wondered if she might hide herself, but his lordship was awake to that possibility and took the reticule that lay upon the seat between them, the only barrier she possessed.

'I think not. You see, without money you can do nothing. I have so very much experience of that predicament. Tradesmen and innkeepers can be remarkably rude, you know, and what would you do, in a town you have never entered before, without even the money for dinner and a bed for the night? No, you have made your bed, Sukie, and will lie with me in it.'

Nobody had ever called her Sukie. How dared he decide what to call her as if she were a skivvy.

'My name is Susan, sir, not that as yet you have my permission to use it.' She tried to sound imperious, but his eyes mocked her, and his response was chilling.

'You have given me the right to call you what I please. You did so from the moment you stepped into this chaise.'

Susan said nothing. She had no words, and even if she had possessed them, her throat seemed so tight shut he might as well have been strangling her. She wondered if her Uncle Chelmarsh might be in pursuit. What had at the outset been something she wished to avoid, she now desired wholeheartedly. The voice of reality in her head told her that if she had been as successful in her escape as she believed, nobody would have any idea where she was, and would spend fruitless hours looking for her in London. There was also the thought that she had become so obnoxious that perhaps her relatives would simply shake their heads and let her disappear, whilst concocting some excuse for Society. She remembered, with stunning clarity, what Sir Esmond had said to her in the ballroom, and that she had not made a friend of either of her cousins nor anyone else in London. And if her uncle did find her, then her fate would be only marginally better than being with this monster of a man. She would be without honour, however well the affair was wrapped in clean linen, and would be sent . . . somewhere. Her brother would have every excuse not to have her at Tyneham. She thought he might own small estates in Dorset and Devon. Perhaps she would be incarcerated on one of those.

For the first time in her life, she looked at herself from an outside perspective, and what she saw did not please her. The world had pushed her into this corner, but she could see that to the world she was not the victim, but the orchestrator of her own downfall. That was also what Sir Esmond had warned her. As the chaise passed through Baldock, she was weeping silently.

Lord Rothley's pursuit demanded a degree of concentration that precluded dwelling upon just how he would deal with his wayward sister when he found her, or indeed exactly what he would like to do to Lord Pinkney. He was a good whip, but the road was busy and even at a canter he had to keep his wits about him. His own horses were good to reach as far as Hatfield, and the pair he obtained from The Eight Bells were both a good match and in excellent condition. He hoped they would suffice him until he caught up with the eloping couple. He had ascertained that they were indeed travelling in a chaise and pair, so he had no doubt that he would overtake them in good time. It was a simple matter of time and distance, not a matter of chance. However, as Lord Pinkney would have assured him, chance was very much part of life, and in this instance appeared in the form of a cast horseshoe a little over halfway between Stevenage and Baldock, and just when he was expecting to catch sight of his quarry every time he turned a bend. He had, of necessity, to drop his pace to a walk, and it was a very frustrated viscount who obtained a fresh pair of horses at The White Horse. No chaise and pair had changed recently there, but as the ostler said, they might have done so at The George.

The stretch of road to Biggleswade was a good straight run, and with fresh horses, Lord Rothley dropped his hands and let them gallop a good three miles before an approaching mail coach made him lessen his pace. He still had no sign of a vehicle which might contain the runaways, but as he slowed through Biggleswade he saw a chaise and pair turn under the arch of The Sun, and pulled up across the entrance, instructing his groom to hold the horses there unless some other traveller required entry.

He strode into the yard, as an ostler yelled at him to move his vehicle. He ignored this, since he had just seen

Pinkney's profile as he stepped down from the chaise to stretch cramped limbs and take a tankard of ale.

'Good afternoon, Pinkney. Do not rush, because you are travelling no further.'

Pinkney turned, surprise vying with irritation upon his face.

'What are you doing here?'

'I would have thought that blindingly obvious. I am come to restore Miss Tyneham to her relations,' Lord Rothley explained, calmly.

'Mighty public-spirited of you, but unnecessary, since her closest relation is shortly to be me.'

'Now there you are in error, but then you are so frequently wrong.'

Mr Cass, the proprietor, at this moment came forward, polite but wary. There was something in the demeanour of the two unknown gentlemen which hinted that their encounter was not friendly, and an altercation in the very entrance of his premises was not good for trade.

'If your honours would care to step into a private parlour . . .'

'No, need, I am not staying,' declared Lord Pinkney, summoning a second ostler with an imperious finger.

'But I am.' Susan, dragged from her misery by the recognised voice, stepped down from the chaise, and bestowed a bright smile upon his lordship. 'And refreshment would be welcome.'

Mr Cass, appreciative of the lady's good looks, and responding instinctively to her air of assurance, indicated a room to his right, and she swept past to take possession of it. Lord Rothley smiled.

'That is clear enough, do you not think? The only problem is that it would not be polite to knock you down in front of a lady.'

'Please, gentlemen, I am sure any differences . . .' Mr Cass looked worried.

'You think you could knock me down, Rothley?' Lord Pinkney felt quite confident, since, whilst their height was not dissimilar, he was of a heavier frame and must have an advantage in weight.

'Convinced of it.' Lord Rothley smiled, slowly, insultingly.

'Presumably because of a mistaken belief that virtue always wins? I can assure you it does not.'

Mr Cass gave in. These two men were clearly squaring for a fight, and given the choice between his back yard and a parlour where they might be seen or heard and where the furniture was at risk, he suggested that any insurmountable differences be resolved within the former. As he saw it, a bloody nose here or there would not create a fuss outside his walls.

'Remain here, Miss Tyneham,' commanded Lord Rothley as he followed Mr Cass, 'and enjoy your tea.'

This, of course, fell upon deaf ears, since the thought of two men fighting over her, even engaging in fisticuffs, was too exciting to ignore.

* * *

The cobbled courtyard was some thirty-five feet wide and fifty feet long with an aged pear tree in one far corner, and a bench beneath the window of what, from the noise within, must be the kitchen. Lord Rothley shrugged himself out of his drab driving coat, laying it along the bench and following it with his coat and hat. He then began to roll up his sleeves. His opponent placed his coat over the arm of Mr Cass, and did likewise. Susan stepped from the doorway and stood against the wall, unsure whether she would find the spectacle exciting or revolting.

The two men squared up to each other, and there was a degree of jostling before Pinkney put in the first hit, which caught Rothley in the ribs and made him stagger back, half tripping on the uneven cobbles, and bored in to build upon his advantage, Pinkney's guard dropped and he only just managed to duck in time for a blow that would have landed squarely to glance off his jaw. If Pinkney had the advantage of weight, Rothley was the more nimble, and Mr Cass found himself, very reprehensibly, enjoying what was a very evenly matched bout. However, time worked for Lord Rothley, as his opponent began to labour, and he found an opportunity to throw him in a cross-buttock which sent him sprawling on the hard cobbles. Pinkney rose grimacing, but still game. Mr Cass thought the result a foregone conclusion from this point, and was proved right. Unsettled by the fall, Pinkney's blows were increasingly wild, and Rothley was able to pick his target. A sharp blow to the face dropped Pinkney once again to the ground, where he remained a good minute, dazed.

'Enough, gentlemen. Accept defeat and victory as the fight has dealt it, and shake hands.'

Breathing hard, and wiping the blood from his face, Lord Pinkney staggered to his feet and took his coat from Mr Cass's arm. It was the thought of an instant, but he was angry, his face hurt, and life was just so unfair. One pocket of his coat was weighted slightly by the presence of a small pistol, one which he generally carried when travelling, in case of highwaymen. He withdrew the pistol from the pocket, cocking it as he did so. Mr Cass fell back in alarm as he turned. Lord Rothley was rubbing his knuckles, and looked up at the sound.

Lord Rothley stood very still. There was nothing he could do.

'You really should not have interfered, Rothley. After all, taking the girl back to London will not re-establish her good name, and you have no interest in her yourself,' mumbled Lord Pinkney, his thickening lip and bleeding nose affecting his speech. 'Heroism is so overrated, and I have had a miserable day.' He sniffed and winced. 'I think putting a bullet through you will make me feel so much better.'

CHAPTER TWENTY-THREE

'YOU KNOW, I RATHER THINK YOUR DAY WILL BECOME more miserable,' drawled a voice from the doorway.

Pinkney remained with arm raised, but his eyes darted to the right.

'Yes, terribly disappointing, isn't it, to find two gentlemen prepared to fight for a lady's honour, but so it is. There are those who would say that to shoot a man already carrying an injury is bad form, but then, since you are quite prepared to murder a man who is entirely unarmed, I feel in this instance . . .' Sir Esmond Fawley took careful aim across the crook of his arm, and fired, clipping Pinkney very precisely above the right elbow. The sound was amplified by the enclosed space.

Pinkney staggered, but his finger jerked convulsively at the trigger and the little silver mounted pistol fired even as it began tumbling from his hand. Susan screamed.

'Pinkney pinked. How appropriate.' Sir Esmond smiled, but then saw Rothley reach his left hand up to the tip of his right shoulder. 'Caught you, did he? I apologise for arriving somewhat tardily, Rothley, but better late than never, as they say. I think I may also have the solution to Miss Tyneham's . . . problem.'

Susan had started forward to proffer his lordship her handkerchief, which was rather small to be effectual. Lady Sophy, who had appeared briefly in the doorway as the shots rang out, had withdrawn as soon as she saw that Lord Rothley had not fallen, and was demanding clean napery from an inquisitive chambermaid, bustling the girl indoors lest she hear what was likely to emerge.

'Problem? But Lord Rothley has rescued me and so perhaps . . .' She looked up at her wounded rescuer with genuine admiration adding to self-interest.

'Be a good fellow and fetch some brandy, will you?' Sir Esmond looked to the innkeeper. He wanted Mr Cass out of the way, before airing the truth. As the man bowed and withdrew he turned back to his friend and murmured, 'This, Rothley, may be where you make a clean breast of matters, don't you think?' There was dry amusement in Sir Esmond's voice.

'You do not wish to offer for me?' Susan looked affronted.

'You are the last woman in the world for whom I would offer, even if it were possible for me to do so.' Lord Rothley's shoulder hurt, and he no longer found his sister's assumption that every man she encountered wanted to marry her amusing.

'Possible?' She was now confused.

'It is impossible because I am going to offer for your cousin Sophy.'

'Sophy?' Susan squeaked, as if he had suggested marrying her maid.

'She is worth ten of you, miss.'

'So you came to rescue me to make Sophy feel better,' she complained, pouting.

'In part. You see . . .' Lord Rothley floundered, and looked to Sir Esmond.

'You see it was also a fraternal duty, Miss Tyneham.'

'Frater . . .' She frowned at one gentleman and then the other, and very slowly the import of what he said hit her. She coloured. 'Does everyone know?' she whispered. 'Have they been laughing behind my back all Season?'

'I doubt very much if any of your contemporaries is cognisant of it, Miss Tyneham, only those of your aunt's, let us say, "vintage". Scandals are forgotten very easily until something drags up the memory,' Sir Esmond saw the shock in her eyes.

'Then I am doubly ruined, am I not?' Susan murmured in a small voice.

'Not necessarily, ma'am. You will note, I hope, that I am not here out of any familial tie.' Sir Esmond smiled, a little wryly, for she was staring at him uncomprehendingly. 'Pinkney, if he values what blood remains in his veins, will say nothing of this unfortunate interlude, and in the vehicle in which I sped here I was accompanied by your cousin.'

'Lady Sophy is here?' It was Rothley's turn to look surprised.

'Yes. I would have preferred to travel faster, and alone.'

'So Sophy will take me straight back to London and there will be no scandal?' Susan sounded relieved.

'There does not have to be a scandal, Miss Tyneham, above the minor ones you have created all Season, but it is too late to return to London.' There was a hint of firmness to Sir Esmond's voice. Susan was ignoring the fact that Lord Rothley was wounded and that her cousin had spent a tiring few hours being driven at speed to catch her up.

'Too late for London?' She sighed, misunderstanding him. 'You mean I will go back to Tyneham, I suppose. Of course, who would want to m—'

'Those gentlemen with parents with good memories, and those who look for modesty, manners and decorum in a wife would not consider you for a moment. My parents are, however, deceased, and I do not possess "nice" notions of a wife. I repeat, ma'am, I did not come here out of familial duty.' Sir Esmond paused for a moment, and then continued. 'You are continuing to Croxton Priory, my home, which is not far from here, and where you will stay overnight with your cousin and her maid. Once everyone is rested you have but two choices: either you return to the capital, and a degree of gossip and perhaps exclusion, or you get married, to me, if you accept my offer. You may say it is not much of a choice, but you have left yourself no others.'

'You really would marry her. Are you sure, my friend?'
Lord Rothley sounded as if he thought it a bad bargain.
Susan had by now stopped dabbing at the red stain on the
outer aspect of Lord Rothley's shoulder and stared at Sir
Esmond.

'I know. I must be quite mad, Rothley, but yes, I would.'

'But you have never paid court to me, and you are
not . . .' Susan began, and faltered.

'Not what? Not elevated enough, rich enough, or
dashing enough for you to have had me upon your list
of possible conquests? I acknowledge this.' Sir Esmond
looked rueful.

'Not in love with me, sir.' Some of the other things had
been true, but Susan hated to admit any mistakes and was
not going to start now, or at least not right now.

'In love with the persona you present to the world?
Not exactly,' Sir Esmond stepped close enough to take
the hand still gripping the handkerchief. 'However, I am
perhaps the only man not just willing but eager to marry
such a glorious baggage as you.'

'Baggage! How dare you.' Susan's shock was replaced
by affront. She glared up at Sir Esmond, her eyes flashing
and one of her little hands forming into a fist. He took that
hand, enclosing the clenched fingers in his own, firmly but
gently. His eyes stripped away her facade.

'You are a baggage, madam, and that is the truth of it.
You have lived a life where nobody has ever said you nay,
and have thus become unmanageable. Well, you see, for
some inexplicable reason, I think that when you discover

that isolation is not security, you will be a wife worth having, a wife in a million, Susan.' His voice dropped. 'But I will not put you upon a lonely pedestal, and serve you like some sad acolyte. I will be at your side, on your side. You will learn that you do not need to lash out to keep all the world at bay to protect yourself from it, for I will be there, always, and you will not be isolated any more. You must know, though, that I will not permit you to flounce and play off your tricks on other men. I will not permit you to act like a spoilt brat any longer, for you are not a child, but I will watch a real woman emerge from the ill-disciplined girl. Such a woman.' His other arm went about her, and he pulled her into his arms, bent his head, and kissed her, not softly, not adoringly, but with an element of passion that she had never experienced. It took her breath away both figuratively and literally. It declared, even more than the words, that he would not let her rule him, and, much to her own surprise, the thought thrilled her. This was not, somehow, subjugation to whim. He wanted her, her specifically, not just as *a* woman, but *the* woman in his life. Pinkney's embrace had appalled; Sir Esmond's invigorated.

'You need not make your choice this minute.' Sir Esmond felt he had to be fair.

'But it is a simple one, sir.' Susan leant back a little in his hold and looked up into his face. It was, she finally admitted to herself, rather a handsome one. 'I can return to London and accept whatever gloomy fate my brother assigns me, with the world on his side, or I can marry you. The former can only bring me misery. Do you, really, think the latter will bring me, indeed bring either of us, joy?'

'That you have said "us" and thought not solely of yourself means that I say it has a very good chance. I cannot promise, but then it depends how hard you – we – try.'

'Then my answer is yes, Sir Esmond.' She looked at him very seriously, and he smiled and drew her close once more.

Lord Rothley, not wishing to be in the way, had stepped back and ostentatiously turned his attention to his wound, which, without the application of the handkerchief, was dripping blood down his arm. He did not hear Sophy approach. She had found several napkins and emerged from the inn to see her cousin in the arms of Sir Esmond, which evidently neither shocked nor surprised her. Lord Pinkney was sat upon the ground, bleeding, and Lord Rothley, looking almost as pale, was bleeding whilst standing up. She ignored Lord Pinkney.

'Let me, my lord.' Sophy came forward as he looked up. Her colour drained to his, but she smiled, waveringly, and took the folded linen to press as a pad to the wound.

He held out his good hand, despite the red stain upon it, and she took it and gripped it.

'I suppose this is where I ought to say "It is but a scratch", although I rather think I should omit the "but". Whilst it hurts like the devil, I shall not die of it, however, for it is merely through the sinews and no vital part.' He pulled a wry face.

She let go of his hand, and touched his cheek, smiling tremulously.

'You poor man,' she murmured, and at this endearment his free arm slid about her waist. She gave no sign of objecting to this, and so he leant and kissed her, softly.

She gave a little sighing moan into his kiss, and he felt her respond to him.

'Being shot may be painful,' remarked Lord Pinkney largely to himself, and irrationally disgusted by the sight of two embracing couples, 'but this is enough to make a man physically ill.' He sighed. He only wished he felt well enough to stand. 'Loth as I am to interrupt, would anyone be prepared to assist me to rise and make my way to the inn, where I might call upon the offices of a surgeon? Whilst you might prefer me dead, it might lead to an awful lot of difficult questions so . . .'

Sir Esmond, disengaging from Miss Tyneham with some reluctance, took the few strides to tower over him and extended a hand, which was taken with a grunted thanks.

'I think living with a bullet hole will actually be easier than—' Pinkney halted as Sir Esmond's expression darkened. 'Only my opinion, of course. No, I can manage now alone, thank you.' He winced. 'Neat shot, Fawley. Must have taken great control.'

'It did. It was so tempting to aim for your heart.'

'Don't possess one.' Pinkney managed a twisted smile, and glanced at Susan, regarding him severely. 'And, Miss Tyneham, I offer my apologies. I appear to have inadvertently thrust you into the arms of a man who will make a better woman of you, whether you like it or not.'

'Then you deserve my thanks, rather than my curses, sir.' She made him a curtsey, but her eyes were upon Sir Esmond. She had spent so long twisting men about her little finger, and deep down, despising them and being bored by it. Here was a man who would not be twisted, but would, on the contrary, guide her to a union which would be mutual. It was slightly scaring, and yet exciting. 'And I think, for the most part, I shall like it.'

Sir Esmond's eyes glinted. Lord Pinkney walked, only a little unsteadily, into the inn. Susan looked up at the man who claimed her, for it felt no less. He was, as he had said, not a man whom she had ignored as a potential husband because he was unappealing but because he was a mere baronet, and she had been aiming far higher. His voice might drawl lazily, but he had been quick enough to embrace her, and beneath the drooping lids his eyes seemed to possess her already.

'Shall you make me like the transformation, sir?' Her low voice could not help but be seductive, but she was playing no game.

'I fear you will like neither it nor me on occasion, my beloved baggage, for it will take some effort on both our parts, but overall . . . I may refuse to let you do certain inappropriate things, Susan, but I shall never "make you" love me, nor shall I beg for you to do so. That has to come from you, and from your own choice. I will, however, hope that you will come to love me as I love you.'

'I . . . I do not think I would mind if you did, make me

love you, I mean. Not if you did so with . . . kisses such as . . .' Susan Tyneham did something she had rarely done in her entire life. She blushed scarlet, and lowered her gaze. When she raised it again he was still looking at her.

'I will scribe a note to Hill Street to set minds at ease, and that can be taken aboard the next London-bound mail.' He held out his hand, not in supplication but command, and she placed her small hand within his large grasp. He turned to see Rothley and Lady Sophronia, their heads still whisper-close. 'My home at Croxton Priory is but a few miles from St Neots and under an hour from here. The ladies will be tired, and you are not fit to travel all the way back to London tonight. I am not entirely certain of the proprieties in this case, Rothley, but we have Lady Sophy's maid and you and I can always repair to the local inn once you have seen a surgeon.'

'True enough.'

Sophy shook her head.

'If we are to travel further, Sir Esmond, Lord Rothley should not move again once the surgeon has attended him. I am sure the proprieties can be observed, and if not . . . then in these extenuating circumstances, we lie,' she declared, firmly. 'You will travel in the chaise, my lord.'

'But that means I shall be with Sir Esmond, cousin,' piped up Susan.

'Yes, I know. It is unavoidable, though.'

'Not if I stay in the curricle,' volunteered Lord Rothley, and received a look from his beloved which indicated that this might be over her dead body.

'My cousin is in your care, Sir Esmond.'

'Of course, ma'am. I will give directions to the postboys. You do not object to me driving your curricle, I take it, Rothley?'

Susan sat quietly in the curricle as it bowled along at a rather less uncomfortable pace than it had travelled the miles from London. She had much to consider. Without a further change of horses they reached Croxton within an hour.

'Oh, do look at the house!' Susan sat suddenly very erect. 'It is not what I had expected. I had thought it would be some musty Tudor thing made out of bricks and bits of old stone. It is actually rather splendid. '

Sir Esmond smiled at her guileless implication that she had fully expected to be disappointed. The curricle had turned a bend and before them was a neat, ashlar-faced house with a semi-circular portico and large sash windows. It was not, perhaps, as large as Tyneham Court, but it looked friendly, and inviting, and the facade was little more than fifty years old, having been altered by Sir Esmond's grandfather. The horses slowed and came to a halt. Sir Esmond jumped down and came round to help Susan alight, but did not simply take her hand. Instead, he swung her down into his arms.

'Welcome to your new home,' he whispered.

The front door was opened, and, as he set her down, she gave him her hand, most graciously. She then ruined the regal effect by asking, with childish directness, how many rooms there were. He laughed, and said he had not counted, but would help her do so if required.

Sophy had spent the journey worrying about Lord Rothley's shoulder, but was trying valiantly not to sound as if fussing. When they passed the lodge gates of Croxton Priory and followed the curricle up the avenue of limes that led to the house, she heaved a huge sigh of relief, and squeezed his lordship's hand.

'You will soon be comfortable, my lord.'

He nodded, but said nothing.

Within the house, Susan was led into a small saloon, where the Holland covers were being hastily removed.

'What happens now, sir?' Susan enquired, suddenly serious.

'First of all, I arrange for food, since Lady Sophy and I have barely had more than half a cup of scalding-hot coffee and a cake since we left London, and we see to Rothley's wound.'

'That was not quite what I meant, Sir Esmond.'

The maid left the room, and he stepped close and took her hands.

'I know.' He smiled down at her. 'You will be delighted to know that Tyneham has washed his hands of you, my dear, but did come with me to obtain a Special Licence. Not for you a grand wedding and a multitude of guests, but we will send in the notice that you were married in a quiet family ceremony, here in Huntingdonshire.'

'Married. Really married?' Her eyes questioned, and his heart leapt because, for all her brassy manner, Susan looked a little nervous. He found it heartening that beneath the appearance of brazen womanhood, she was in so many ways just a girl fighting her way in a world she did not comprehend.

'Yes, really married. Had you not considered what it would mean to be married to Pinkney?'

'I thought I had explained it was a marriage of convenience and since he had my money he would not be interested in . . . me.' She coloured. 'However, upon the journey I did gather that he did not regard matters in that light.' She frowned.

'Was that the sort of marriage you wanted, Susan?'

'With him, yes. He was a means to an end, as I thought I was to him, but it would not have been nice.'

'What I offer is not a marriage of convenience, you understand that.'

'Yes, I do.' Her frown remained. 'But I still do not understand how you can want to marry me, when you find so much not to like.'

'Because I think that it is outweighed by the things I do find admirable about you. You have courage and you have great spirit. What I sincerely hope to find is that you have a heart, because you have kept it safe by keeping it buried. Love is not always weakness, Susan. Making oneself vulnerable does not mean having to be wounded. It can mean sharing in all the best that life has to offer.' He lifted one of her hands and kissed her fingers. 'Now, let me play host.'

He turned, to see Lady Sophy and Lord Rothley enter.

'Would you have me call the local surgeon?'

'It would be of limited use, I think. The wound is through the muscle and most likely clean.'

'Yet still the surgeon should be called. We can say it was highwaymen upon the road.' Lady Sophy was already removing Lord Rothley's coat, which had been tenderly draped over his shoulders for the journey. 'Do you have bandages and lint and basilicum powder, Sir Esmond?' Her voice was crisp.

'I do not know, but we can ask my housekeeper.'

'I would clean and bind the wound, and then the surgeon can decide whether it needs to be stitched. A professional opinion is important.'

'Yes, ma'am.' Sir Esmond grinned at Lord Rothley. 'You have no choice in this matter, Rothley.'

'No, I can see that I do not.'

'Basilicum powder, Sir Esmond.'

'My apologies. I will go and find out about it, personally, and will arrange for the ladies' baggage to be placed in the south bedchambers.' He looked at Susan. 'Will you come with me, and let me show you about the place?'

She nodded, and he led her out.

Lord Rothley's shirt was quite heavily stained about the wound, although the pad had done much to staunch the flow, and it no longer dripped. He watched Sophy's face as she surveyed it.

'It is not serious, you know,' he commented, more

interested in her than the injury.

'No, but any wound must be treated with caution in case of infection.' She knelt beside his chair and began to cut away the sleeve of the shirt with a small pair of scissors from an etui in her reticule.

'But with you to nurse me, I would be in the best of hands,' he whispered, close to her ear.

She tried to ignore the warm feeling his nearness gave her.

'I think from the bleeding, some minor vessel was severed, but a glancing wound such as this should, as you say, be clean, my lord. I am so glad he did not shoot you so that the ball became embedded.'

Lord Rothley, watching her profile at close quarters, smiled.

'So am I, my love.'

She turned at the epithet, her seriousness dissipated by a shy smile.

'It seems so strange that a gentleman should address me as that. I never anticipated . . .'

'You do not object to it, I hope. After all, you showed no objections to my kissing you, and I would hate to think you had taken a leaf from my shocking sister's book and become a tease, madam.'

He was smiling still, and the laughter lurked in his eyes.

'I do not object. I—' She halted as a maid entered with a bowl of water and clean cloths, bobbed a curtsey, begged her ladyship's pardon, and said that the 'basil's powder' was being searched for, and should be with her shortly.

'You were saying?' he asked, as the servant left.

'I feel as if everything has happened very suddenly, and yet gradually at the same time, which is madness. Only three days ago I did not even know if you had forgiven me.' She dipped the cloth in the boiled water, and began to clean the wound. He flinched.

'There was nothing to forgive, Sophy. It was a misunderstanding, and easily made.'

'But I let myself be convinced by it, did not listen to my heart.'

'But that heart never lost faith, did it?'

'No,' she whispered.

The tin of basilicum powder was brought in and placed on the small table beside them. She picked it up and opened it, and dusted the wound carefully with some of the contents.

'You know, I always dreamt that the man I loved would be tall, taller than me, I mean, but I have found a man I can look up to whilst also looking him straight in the eye, even when not in odd positions such as this one.'

'That does save getting a stiff neck, Sophy, my darling, and also makes it far, far easier to do this.'

He leant slightly and covered her mouth with his. She quivered, and gave herself up to the intoxication. His injured shoulder was forgotten until she drew back to catch her breath, and realised that she was still holding the tin of basilicum powder in her hand.

'I am not a very good nurse, I fear, for I am so easily distracted from my duties.'

'But you will be an excellent wife. This, by the way, you may take as your proposal of marriage. It is somewhat unconventional, and several hours later than I promised, but circumstances, you know . . .'

She dusted the wound again with the powder and took a soft pad of lint.

'Most unconventional, my lord, but I accept, nonetheless.'

'Your father and I had a most enjoyable interview, by the way. He did warn me how "managing" you would be, and—'

'"Managing"? Oh, what a . . . complete faradiddle,' Sophy expostulated.

'Who has taken charge of everything since Biggleswade?'

'This is different. You are wounded.'

'Not in the head. I can still think.'

'Yes, but . . . Do you really think me like that?'

'No, and nor does he, but we agree how worthy of love you are. By the way, I am very glad he does not regard my sire's reprehensible lifestyle as a barrier to my marrying his daughter. You know, I really am not profligate, or like him in any way.'

'Now there, sir, you are wrong, for you possess a wolfish smile, which I have seen upon occasion, and which I first glimpsed at our initial encounter, when Susan dropped her stockings.'

'She did what?' Lord Rothley laughed, seeing Sophy's expression as she realised what she had said, and then winced, regretting the movement.

'It was a parcel of silk stockings that she contrived to drop, that day in Bond Street, and I could see you knew just what she had done. I was not sure, from that smile, whether you were a gentleman or a dangerous rake, and if you laugh at me, you deserve to grimace.'

'I would rather laugh with you, Sophy,' he murmured, kissing just below her earlobe, 'and if wolfish, I promise to howl only for you.'

'Hmm, and not at all like your father, you said. Now, stop that while I bind your shoulder. I have never done anything so complicated with a bandage before and might make a complete hotchpotch of it. I do not want the surgeon tut-tutting over my handiwork.'

'You may take as many attempts as you wish if it means being so close.'

'I said you must stop.' She sounded severe, but her lips twitched.

'Pity.' He submitted to her ministrations in silence for a few minutes, taking delight, as he had said, in her proximity. She fashioned a sling for him.

'There. You look much improved.'

'I look disreputable. My shirt is in tatters and . . . Do I need a sling?'

'I am not sure, but it looks very heroic.'

'I was thinking more "theatrical".'

'Not at all. The surgeon will decide what is best in the case. I do wish he would arrive soon, so I may be easy, and he can give you something for the pain.'

'I do not need anything. I have you, and that dispels any pain.'

'Very pretty, my lord, but inaccurate.'

'Not totally. It certainly distracts me from it, so the best thing you can do is stay nice and close to me.'

This she did until the arrival of the local surgeon, who declared the wound clean, and declined to stitch it, saying that in his opinion it would heal better if left open but dressed. He recommended that his lordship rest for several days before returning to London, and keep the sling just so that he did not use the arm and move the muscles of the upper part.

'You were very fortunate, my lord. It is but a flesh wound. Two inches to the left and it would have shattered the bone.'

'Two inches to the right, and it would have missed me entirely.'

The surgeon laughed at this, though Lord Rothley afterwards told his intended that he had been completely serious.

'What a good job I asked for your father's approbation this morning. What man would wish to receive an offer for his daughter from a mangled wreck.'

'You look . . . brave. Besides, you rescued his niece from ruination, and his eldest daughter holds you in the highest possible esteem, my lord.' She became serious again. 'Papa is delighted. He said that he liked you, and I said I liked you too.'

This comment necessitated him indicating that the

liking was mutual, in a physical form. It was several minutes before Sophy had the breath to continue.

'You know he told me at the beginning of the Season that I should see what happened if I left matters to fate. If this is fate, I am mightily contented with it, and you may quote me upon that.'

'I shall.' He leant back, and held her at arm's length, admiringly. 'My Sophy.'

Sophy's smile broadened.

'You cannot know just how pleased I am to be at last escaping my cursed name.'

'That does not sound very polite, my love. Hadlow is—'

'No, you know full well what I mean. Once I have declared that 'I, Sophronia Annabelle, take thee . . .'

'Hugh Alexander,' he supplied, helpfully.

'Hugh Alexander. Ooh, I like those. The dreaded Sophronia need not be declared in public again. I can rejoice in being announced as Lady Rothley.'

'Who is not married to a rake.'

'Correct.'

'Lady Rothley sounds very good. I will rejoice in it also, and I promise never to call you Sophronia, even if you provoke me.'

'What more could I want?'

He pulled her close again.

'Oh, there is much more, my darling, but let us content ourselves with that for today.'

Sophia Holloway read Modern History at Oxford and also writes the Bradecote and Catchpoll medieval mysteries as Sarah Hawkswood.

@RegencySophia
sophiaholloway.co.uk